Whipped Fraternity

Robyn Anders

BooksForABuck.com

2013

Published by BooksForABuck.com

Chapter One

"**Ready, Nik?**"

I nodded. My wonderful husband James had tied me up especially tight the previous evening after a round with his quirt that left my rear tingly and sexy.

After eight hours firmly secured in my pallet on the side of his bed, my body was pins and needles—sensitized to the point where I would feel everything in exquisite and painful detail.

Not that I'd complain—I didn't ever complain. In ten years of marriage, my husband had taught me a lot, and the first lesson was to thank him for whatever he chose to give me.

"Morning sweetie," I told him when he removed my gag and lifted me onto his bed. "May I remove—"

I reached for my blindfold anticipating his response, but he grabbed my hands and handcuffed my wrists behind me.

"I like to watch your big cock while I eat it," I assured him. Like all men, he enjoyed being told how big he was. I hadn't been very experienced when he'd selected me from the girls enrolled in his 'Math for Humanities' class. I still thought calling it 'big' was a bit of an exaggeration—not that I'd ever tell him that.

"Not today, Nik."

My name was Nichole d'Angre, but he always called me Nik. I called him 'sir,' or 'master.'

"No blow job?" A lot of times, he was too tired for sex in the evening. I couldn't remember his ever not demanding his morning release, though.

"You can start me. But leave the blindfold on."

His cock was as swollen as I could remember it being and I stuffed it into my mouth. It was easier when he left my hands free, so I could rest my weight on my elbows and grip him with my fingers. James went out of his way to make sure I never got complacent, though. He'd cuffed me dozens of times and I'd learned to satisfy him without my hands.

"Take it deep, Nik," he told me, exactly as if he hadn't given me the same order thousands of times before. "Until you choke."

I tilted my head back, fighting the gag reflex as I sucked his cock deeper into my mouth and down my throat.

I couldn't breathe with it in that deep, and I'd panicked the first few times he'd held it there until black spots spun across my eyes from suffocation. I still felt the fear but James had taught me to control that fear rather than let it control me.

His legs trembled against my breasts as I made the purring sound he likes.

He moaned and grabbed my head, shoving his dick even deeper down my throat.

He'd been eating mustard again—I tasted it in his pre-cum—almost gagging me. I didn't think he even liked mustard but he ate it anyway just to give me the full sensation his taste.

My heart swelled when I considered how much he must really care for me, how he'd altered his life to make sure I was perfectly trained. He'd spent so much of his precious time helping me become exactly the woman he wanted. Lots of faculty wives complained that their husbands neglected them, ended up married to their work rather than to any woman. Lots also complained that their husbands were pencil-necked nerds. Nobody would accuse James of either of those sins.

I breathed again as he pulled out. This was when he normally gave me my morning facial.

Today, though, he rolled away. "Lick my butt, Nik."

I shrugged. He normally wanted his rim job at night. In the morning, it was blowjob, breakfast, and then go.

I confess I was a little disappointed when I felt his hips moving as I slid my tongue into his crack. Was he masturbating when he could fill my mouth or ass? Hell, it was my birthday—in honor of that occasion, I'd dared hope he might even spend in my vagina.

Complaining, though, was never wise. James gave me what I needed, regardless of what I thought I wanted.

I pushed my tongue deeper into his butt-hole. Even after all the years we'd been together, I still felt a little nasty when I tongued his bottom, as if a part of me worried someone could walk in and catch me while I was doing it.

Finally he rolled over and splashed my face with his semen.

I smiled, opened my mouth, and tried to catch it while he tried to make me miss and to cover my face and tits with his hot spunk. It was a game we played and I relaxed. Things were back to normal.

As I did every morning after I'd satisfied him, I got out of bed and knelt on my pallet. Occasionally he'd leave me there for the day, but generally he'd free me and let me make his breakfast. Once in a while, he'd allow me to masturbate or even pleasure me himself.

Today, though, he reached down and grasped my shoulders, squeezing them until I squeaked in pain.

"I told you just to start me. I didn't want to come on you."

Once, I would have argued he was being unfair. He'd told me to lick his butt and I'd followed his orders. Painful training had taught me not to complain. "It's my privilege to help you come every morning," I reminded him.

"That was before. Now you're thirty years old."

"It's not every day a girl turns thirty." I wondered again if he'd planned something special to celebrate. Had my over-enthusiastic tongue-work in his asshole kept me from getting my pussy filled with his cock?

"How about you jump back in bed?" I suggested. "I'll whip up some pancakes with the fresh strawberries I bought yesterday. Then, if you've got the time, you can fuck me any way you want."

He grabbed my handcuffs where they still restrained my arms behind my back, jerking them upward.

I had to drop my forehead to the ground, but I'd learned how to hit the pallet and didn't hurt myself. James liked me to grovel for him and it was fun for both of us as long as I didn't carelessly injure myself.

He didn't make me grovel for long, though. A jingle and a quick snick and my hands were free.

"May I remove my blindfold, master?" I asked. Once, years before, I'd taken it off without asking. It had been a mistake he'd taught me not to repeat.

"Sure. Take it off."

I slipped the black blindfold off my eyes and froze. A girl, undoubtedly one of his co-eds, lay in bed next to him. She looked pissed and wore a tiny silk robe so short it left her shaven pussy exposed. One of her oversized breasts hung out at the top.

Little co-ed wasn't the only person pissed. I'd known that James wasn't faithful. He'd explained to me that he was a man, had a man's hunger for variety. But he always left those floozies at school. At home, it was just the two of us. With me so perfectly trained, what use could he have for more.

"What the hell—"

James held out a hand. "Nik."

I ignored the warning in his voice—the first time I'd ever done that since I could remember. "I'm not going to—"

He grabbed my arm, twisted it, and forced my ball gag into my mouth, tying it behind my head with practiced efficiency. "Listen to me, Nik. You're thirty years old. In a man, that's nothing. For a woman, it's over the hill. It's time for me to move on."

I nodded, then gestured for the gag.

"Are you going to be reasonable?"

I nodded again.

He removed it, then caught one of my nipples between his thumb and finger and twisted. "Behave or I'll have to punish you."

"Yes, sir."

"You can go ahead and make breakfast for Amber and me. I'm certain she'll forgive you for making me come on you when I'd promised to squirt all over her double-D's. After all, we'll have plenty of time for me to spray her now that you're moving out."

"But—but I'm your wife. I live here."

He shook his lion-like head. "We *were* married, Nik. The divorce is final this morning. Right about now, in fact. Surely you remember signing the papers."

I looked at him. James was tall, blond, and muscular. He reminded me of the Norse god, Thor, only with an expensive haircut. I'd met him when I'd been eighteen and a freshman at Cambridge State University in Mississippi. He'd been a sexy young professor who'd cut me out of the gaggle of girls hanging around after his lectures, took my virginity, trained me to please him, and made sure my whole life consisted of pleasing him. I'd even dropped out of college before completing my degree so I could make his home perfect. And now, just because I'd turned thirty, he was dumping me.

I wanted to scream, to throw myself at a co-ed who looked about as young as I'd been when James had first singled me out. "How could we be divorced without me knowing?"

"You signed the paperwork months ago. You never bothered to read it."

Of course I hadn't. He'd trained me not to read anything. He didn't like it when I didn't instantly give him what he demanded.

"But what about alimony."

He laughed. "You're off the hook. I didn't ask for any."

"Doesn't the wife normally get the house?"

"My house? Hardly. It's always been in my name. Now, serve us the breakfast you offered. I've got a lot of training for Amber before I head for my classes."

Ten minutes before, I'd thought I was the happiest of women. Now, I was a thirty-year-old has-been, relegated to serving breakfast in bed to my husband and his new sex-toy.

"Don't even think about taking any jewelry," Amber said. "And I can't believe you made him blow on your face like that. That spunk was for me. He had his big cock in my ass until you tricked him into turning."

While James still held me, she used her fingernails to scrape his semen off my face and licked it off her hands. "This is all mine now."

I didn't want to cry in front of her, but tears spilled from beneath my lashes, running into the scratches she'd made on my face.

"We're ready for breakfast any time." James made it sound like he was doing me a huge favor letting me serve him despite my advanced age.

He shoved me toward the bedroom door. "Oh, and feel free to make enough so that you can have leftovers."

"I—"

He moved incredibly quickly, grabbing my long black hair and yanking on it. "What did you say?"

"I will, master. Thank you."

"That's better. Who knows? If you stay in the area, maybe I'll make time to give you a little extra training from now and then. It would be a shame to waste all the energy I spent on you, and most of the other men in this town are complete wusses. Which is why I end up training most of their wives. Plus I put a couple hundred dollars in your bank account. I'm sure you'll be fine."

I knew what to say. "Thank you, master."

"I don't see my breakfast."

"Right away, master."

* * * *

It took me fifteen minutes to put together a couple stacks of pancakes with strawberries and maple syrup, bacon, and hot coffee.

The first batch wasn't perfect and, for a rebellious moment, I considered giving it to Amber and keeping good ones for myself. James wouldn't notice—he only noticed what affected him. Worse than punishment, though, would be the knowledge I'd failed him. I set the undercooked batch aside for myself and put the others on china plates and trays.

I carried the trays into the bedroom and had to fight the temptation to throw the pancakes at Amber. James had always told me I wasn't the rebellious type, that I was a perfect woman. Hell, I always meant it when I thanked James for each bruise and stripe he'd given me with his riding quirt. Today, the urge to fight back was practically overpowering and that surprised me. Even before I'd met James, I'd tried to satisfy those around me. My mother had told me that a good southern woman exists to please others, and I'd taken those words to heart.

But James had crossed a line. He knew when I'd be coming with breakfast. He had to have heard me coming down the hall with my trays. Instead of waiting until I couldn't watch, he'd set Amber on her hands and knees on the bed and was taking her from behind, one of his big hands holding her long blond hair like a leash while he pulled his dick deeper into her butt with every stroke.

"Thank you, Nik. Put the trays by the table." He spoke without a break in his rhythm.

"Yes, sir." My rebelliousness evaporated at his kind words. "May I go and clean up, now." His semen was drying on my skin and in my hair.

"Straighten up the kitchen. I'll supervise your cleaning, later."

"Yes, sir."

Back in the kitchen, I plopped the slightly doughy pancakes into the bowl on the floor, knelt in front of it, put my hands behind my back, and ate, facedown. The bowl was marked 'Fido.'

It wasn't until James walked in on me that I thought to wonder whether I'd have to eat like this once I moved out. On my own, I could eat at a table, with flatware. I ate that way when we went to faculty parties, of course, but I hadn't done so in private since I'd moved into James's home.

"Good girl." James ran his quirt down my spine. "Did you lick up every bite?"

"Yes, master."

"Then it's time to clean up."

I nodded and stood. I knew I had food all over my face. I also knew I was dirty from having my face in James's butt and from his spewing me. But my food bowl was clean and James always inspected me before he left to be certain he didn't leave a mess behind.

"You and Amber in the shower," he commanded. "Clean each other off."

Amber and I were naked except for our dog collars.

James had presented me with my collar after we'd had sex for the first time, and I'd never taken it off since that day. Wearing it to faculty wives' meetings could be embarrassing, especially as he'd had it fitted with tags that identified me as his property. But I'd worn it proudly because it told the world that I was a part of James's life.

When she'd been on the bed with him earlier, Amber's neck had been bare. Now a leather dog collar, complete with small steel spikes, was padlocked so tightly that it left red marks on her skin... just as mine did to me.

Her tags sparkled in the morning sunlight. She looked proud of the collar—as indeed she should. James had sex with a lot of women but Amber was the first, since we'd married, that he'd claimed in such a visible way.

Unlike Amber and myself, James wasn't naked. His Chinese-print robe showed off his great build, and the erection underneath it. My mouth watered at the sight—just as he'd trained me to respond.

"Sir." I gestured toward his dick. "May I—"

He traced the riding crop across the collar, then let its tip feather my crack and lightly probe my vaginal lips.

"Get up and clean up. Amber and I have a run ahead of us."

I swallowed as I stood. James didn't allow me to argue, but clearly he was making a mistake. I'd be failing him if I let him continue. "I'm obviously better than Amber is, even if I am thirty. Couldn't you let me stay and—"

His crop whistled as it cut through the air, then smacked into my ass. "Shower. Clean Amber off. I'll be inspecting her and will punish you if she isn't completely clean."

I'd cleaned James, often enough. He liked me to lather myself, then rub my soapy body over his, playing special attention to his ass and cock. I'd never thought about how I'd do it with a woman. I never imagined I'd have to.

"Why don't *you* wash me, sweetie?" Amber simpered.

Crack. James brought his quirt down on her buttocks. "Call me sir. And follow instructions. If I wanted to wash you, I would have given that order."

James, I thought, would have his hands full training this one.

Not wanting the lesson of the quirt again, I hurried into the shower and soaped my body. I'd needed to get the food and semen out of my face and hair, anyway.

Amber entered the shower like a mouse entering a house full of cats. She jerked back from me when I stepped forward to rub my soapy body over her, and James struck her again, this time raising a small welt on one of her oversized breasts.

"See how obedient Nik is," he observed. "You'll have to learn how to anticipate my desires the way she does. Don't worry, though. You're young. You've got time. "

I rubbed Amber with my body, then slid my soapy hands between her legs to clean off her pussy and asshole. If I didn't clean her completely, James would make me finish the job with my tongue—it was an honor to clean *him* that way but I didn't want to stick my tongue up Amber's butt. "How old are you?" I whispered.

"A lot younger than you," she sneered.

James groaned as I spread Amber's lips wide to let the shower pour clear water into her pussy. "You do that so well," he said, "I'm almost tempted to set up a pallet for you in the kitchen and let you stay as our body servant."

"Please, sir," I breathed. If only he didn't kick me out, surely he'd soon see how much better trained I was, how Amber was hopeless. Surely he'd love me again.

He laughed. "No. I'm afraid I can't afford for my friends to think I'd have any woman over thirty in my life, even as a kitchen servant. Especially as you were once my special property."

"Sir," I protested.

"Be ready to leave when we return. I'll search you, of course."

* * * *

I'd never realized how little I owned. James liked me naked around the house, so I had only a few outfits to wear when I went shopping and to faculty parties. I put on my nicest casual clothes, a pair of khaki slacks and a top that tied around the midriff but didn't show all of my tits. I'd only worn it once, as James had never pulled it out of his closet after the first time. James would never admit he'd made a mistake, even in as simple a thing about buying an outfit that didn't display my body the way he liked to, so he hadn't returned it or thrown it away. Compared to my other choices, it was the safest outfit I owned.

It was the first time I'd picked my own clothes in ten years.

I didn't own any panties, and James only bought shelf-style bras with no covering for the nipples. Generally, my nipples showed through everything I wore, but this top's fabric was thick enough that they weren't real obvious. I'd need to find work and I didn't want to look like my only skill was sex, even though I feared that was the case.

After packing a couple of party dresses and my cutoff shorts, and a few cropped t-shirts into a shopping bag I knelt by the door to wait James's return.

Amber had a couple new stripes on her thighs, and her neck was raw from the collar when James unlocked the door, returning from their run. She heeled nicely, though, so I had to reluctantly admit the woman was learning. It had taken me several days of training to learn to stay at his heel and to instantly crouch whenever he came to a stop.

James had bought her a running outfit identical to what I'd always worn for our runs--shorts cut to expose most of her butt-cheeks, and a t-shirt cropped so high that the bottom half of her huge breasts were always visible.

James unhooked Amber's leash, tossed it into the bowl he'd always used for storing *my* leash, then jerked his thumb my way. "Kneel the way Nik is kneeling, Amber."

The co-ed immediately dropped to her knees and crawled over to me, only then raising her hands off the ground.

"Good job, Amber. You're ready to go, Nik?"

"Yes, sir. If you'd tell me the name of the bank where you opened my account—"

"Of course." He took a Sharpie from a stand in the entryway and wrote something on the underside of my breast. "That's the account information at First Bank of Cambridge. You'll have to let the bank manager read the number," he informed me. "I'm afraid it's out of your vision."

"Yes, sir." I studied him. The air conditioning had been running all night, and the day must be getting hotter because he dripped with sweat from his run. My pussy moistened at the sight of my sexy husband—or ex-husband, and in response to his firm grasp on my breast.

"I can tongue you dry before I leave, sir." I was terrified about being out on my own, desperate to prove that I was indispensible.

He shook his head. "Amber will handle that. Good luck, Nik. You're a good girl. If you don't find anything in a couple of weeks, give me a call."

My heart pounded. "You mean—"

"I might be able to sell you to one of the faculty bachelors who're too chicken to hunt themselves up more than an occasional co-ed. Or that gay one in the closet needs cover. He'd probably pay a lot to have a well-trained cunt."

I knew the guys he was talking about. Calling them dweebs was an insult to dweebs the world over. Still, he'd been thinking about me, worrying about my future. "Thank you, sir."

He poked through my shopping bag and pulled out my favorite dress--one he'd given me a month before but that I'd never had a chance to wear. "I'd think this would fit on Amber. Don't you agree, Nik?"

My eyes misted. I loved that dress. "Yes, sir. Of course."

"Excellent. Then we'll keep it. You may have the rest of this. In fact, there's no need for you to repay me their value. Consider it all my gift."

"Thank you, sir."

He dialed the combination on his safe and tossed my passport and birth certificate into the shopping bag, then finally added my food bowl. "I'll buy a new bowl for Amber so you can have this one, Nik. I saw one at the pet store last month labeled Spike. Amber seems more of a Spike type, don't you agree?"

I nodded. He'd claimed my papers the day we'd married and I'd only seen them since when he'd taken me along on one of his international junkets. Getting them back made it impossible for me to deny my situation.

"I'm sure I'll see you around, Nik." He pinched my nipple to command my attention. I know you won't claim recognition unless I make eye contact."

"Of course I won't, sir."

"Fine." He dropped his shorts and I wondered if he'd take me one last time. "Amber. Strip down and crawl over here. I'm sweaty and I don't have time for a shower before my first class."

Amber lapped at his balls while James grabbed her long blond hair. Both ignored me.

I got back on my knees and waited until he looked my way. "Is that all, sir?"

"Oh. Right. Come here, Nik." He pulled off his shirt and turned around so Amber could lick the sweat off his back and armpits.

Was he going to kiss me goodbye? I tried to remember the last time he'd kissed me on the lips but couldn't. It was funny to think that I hadn't even noticed when kissing had left our relationship? Not that he'd ever been big on kissing my lips. Generally our kisses had involved my lips on whatever part of his body he designated.

Instead of a kiss, he took a key and unfastened my collar. "You aren't my property any more, Nik. You don't get to wear my collar."

I straightened my blouse so my breasts were covered. Without the collar, though, I felt more naked than I had in my life.

I was alone in the world.

Chapter Two

The bank manager took his time reading the account number off the underside of my tit where James had written it.

Unlike James, there was nothing divine about the manager. He wallowed in fat, had a ring of hair like a halo around his bald crown, and showed sweat stains in the armpits of his 1980s-styled suit.

When James touched me, my body responded with pleasure. When the bank manager touched me, I wanted to scrub myself raw.

"Okay, got it." He dropped my breast, then entered something in the computer.

"How much—"

"That's funny. I thought I had it this time. Must have got the number wrong again."

I'd straightened my top when he'd walked away, but he untied the midriff bow and jerked my blouse up over my face, grabbing my breast by the nipple and yanked it up high to get a second look at the number. "Gotta take another—hey I thought that was a nine but it was an eight."

I suspected he was lying just so he could squeeze my tits more but I didn't dare accuse him. James didn't like it when I talked back to any men.

"Can you check my balance, sir?" I asked.

He tightened his grip on my nipple and licked his lips. "You have another number written on your cunt, by any chance."

"No, sir."

"Too bad."

"Sorry, sir."

He released his grip on my nipple, stroking his fingers down my midriff to my hip-hugging slacks.

His face had turned an ugly purple color and he gasped for breath, but he finally walked over to his computer. "Hope I got the account number right this time."

I'd reached my limit. This guy wasn't James. He had no claim over me, beyond James's orders to let him read the number. "If you didn't, perhaps you should look for another job."

"Oh, you've got a little spunk in you."

Spunk was one of the names James used for his semen, so it took me a moment to realize what the manager was saying—that I had spirit. Did I? Spirit wasn't anything James had encouraged and I'd modeled myself on being what James wanted.

"Just let me know the balance."

"Can't blame a man for trying, can you?"

I shook my head. I didn't blame him for trying at all. At least a thousand times, James had explained to me that any man would screw any woman he found attractive. That was why James had kept me at home... because other men would force themselves on me if he wasn't there to protect me and that, as his property, I was for his exclusive use.

Now, I was out in that world and James no longer wanted to make any claims on my body. Would I have to lay down for the bank manager, for any man who demanded me?

My training told me to say yes. James had never let me say no. On those rare occasions when he'd had other men in the house, he'd ordered me to serve their needs and I'd complied.

But I wasn't the bank manager's property. I didn't have to obey his orders.

"I think you saw enough of them."

"Lady, I don't think anyone could ever see enough of those puppies."

"Can we get to the balance?"

James had promised me a couple of hundred dollars so I was pleasantly surprised he'd deposited a three hundred.

"He must really love me," I murmured to myself.

The manager gave me a sharp look. "Want to make a deposit?"

"Withdrawal," I said. "I need it all."

He tapped on the keyboard, then leered at me. "I'll give you an extra fifty if you'll suck me off."

I studied him. I was used to James--a man with a god-like body. The manager's thin gold wedding band had nearly, but not completely, vanished into pudgy fingers.

I *could* blow him. It wouldn't cost me anything and would make him happy. And an extra fifty bucks would come in very handy. To my surprise, I just didn't want to. "Sorry."

He pounded a fat fist down on his keyboard. "I can go as high as a hundred.

Considering I hadn't worked since the summer before my freshman year in college, I might have to become a prostitute. But I wasn't ready for that. To me, sex was something between me and my owner. "It's not the money."

"If you didn't want to fuck me, why the tit thing?"

"My husband, I mean ex-husband, wrote the numbers where I couldn't read them."

"Ever hear of a mirror, girl?"

Tears filled my eyes—again. "He ordered me to show the number to the manager. That would be you."

He shook his head. "Seems to me that if he's your ex-husband, he shouldn't be giving you orders any more.

That was easy for him to say. He was a man. He'd probably always been stronger than the women he dated, the woman he'd married. He'd probably brought home the paycheck that left his woman completely dependent on him. He'd probably never noticed that he gave the orders and the women in his life meekly obeyed. One thing for sure—if a woman had been giving the orders, he'd be cleaner, have a better outfit, and would get those pounds off.

Not that I could imagine a woman giving orders to a man.

"He's still my own—" I cut off my words. James had taken my collar. He was no longer willing to claim ownership, which meant, I couldn't claim him, either.

"Well?" the manager demanded. "If you're divorced, why—"

"You don't understand."

"I guess I don't." He grabbed a business card from a holder on his desk, walked over to me, and stuffed it down my top, copping a slow feel as he did. "You get in trouble, you find your money gone, give me a call. I might see clear to give you two-hundred for a blowjob. Fifty, maybe a hundred just for a handjob. Take you what, two minutes. That's three thousand dollars an hour."

"If I could just get my money."

He handed me a printout to take to a teller. "Remember to call me if you need help. I like helping pretty women."

* * * *

The teller told me about a motel that offered furnished weekly rentals. Since it was within walking distance, I headed there, and plunked down a hundred dollars for my first week's rent.

My stomach growled, but I reminded it that I'd just had a batch of pancakes a few hours earlier. I needed to make my money last.

One necessity was a phone. Anyone looking to hire me would need a number where they could contact me. I blew another hundred making the cash payment for a mobile and some minutes. Then I headed to the public library.

Several of my sorority sisters still lived in town. I found their numbers in the phone book and started calling.

Amy had recently been divorced by her husband and was sympathetic but had financial issues of her own. Lauren asked for James's number and hung up on me when I told her he wasn't interested in anyone who'd reached thirty. Katy told me to get another husband but to keep away from hers. And Betty told me she'd invite me to join her professional woman organization once I'd found a job.

After two hours of calling, I'd made no progress.

"Can I help you with anything." A rich baritone startled me.

I realized I was dripping tears onto the library table and snuffled, then looked up.

The librarian was about my age, with dark hair, brown eyes that looked at me like a puppy, and a big smile on his face.

"Uh, I'm divorced so I need a job. I don't really know how to start."

"Great. The library has lots of job hunting resources. Do you have a degree?"

"I dropped out of college at the end of sophomore year."

"Some college is good. What was your major?"

"Art History."

His face dropped. "I'm afraid I haven't seen any openings for that field in town."

"I've pretty much forgotten what I learned over the last ten years anyway."

"Okay. But you've been doing something since you left college, right? What skills have you gained?"

My skills included eating from a dog bowl with my hands behind my back, making a man come in dozens of ways using my hands, tits, feet or any of the three holes in my body, and heeling on command. I already knew what I could do with those skills—give hand jobs to horny bank managers.

"I've pretty much been a housewife. No skills at all."

"Don't say that." He glanced at his watch and I knew he was looking for a chance to get away. Which made sense. He was younger than James—why would he want to spend more time with a washed-up thirty-year-old when the town grew a new crop of co-eds every year—every one of them hungry for a man more mature than the typical eighteen-year-old male?

"The library is closing in ten minutes," he said.

"Oh. Sorry, sir. I can come back tomorrow to look at--"

"It's not sir, it's Brandon. Brandon Tiel."

"I'm Nicole d'Angre."

"Can I call you Nicole?"

"I guess." I wasn't used to being called anything but 'Nik,' or 'slut.'

"Great. I've got an idea. We can't stay here but we can grab a bite at the diner across the street." He grinned at me. "I've got a copy of the *Cambridge Telegram* classified, and the library's Wi-Fi reaches that far. I can show you how to register with Monster and some of the other job boards."

I considered. Clearly I needed help. Equally clearly, I needed to eat.

Brandon would probably demand a blowjob or buttfuck in exchange for his help, but that sounded like a fair exchange. Besides, Brandon didn't gross me out like the bank manager had. As a male, he deserved to have his way with an unclaimed woman, and that was exactly what I was.

* * * *

"Y'all can sit anywhere," the cashier chimed when Brandon and I stepped into the Cambridge State University Diner. "Your waitress will be with you in a sec."

I waited. Brandon didn't have a leash, and I wasn't wearing my collar, but I'd instinctively heeled—at his side but slightly behind when we'd crossed the street.

"You have a preference?" he asked.

James had never asked me that, or anything. James always knew the answer. Even when his answer was wrong, he was smart enough, powerful enough, and decisive enough that he could generally make it the right answer. For me, that had been part of the appeal.

"Anywhere you'd like, sir."

"Do you want to look out the window?"

"If you'd like, sir."

"Brandon, remember?"

"Of course, si—Brandon."

He grabbed a chair, so I walked around to the other side of the table, only to find him standing there, still holding it.

"Did I do something wrong?" he asked.

I shook my head. "Of course not, mast—Brandon." He was the male. How could he do anything wrong? "Why do you ask?"

"Uh, nothing." He walked around behind me. "May I seat you?"

I flushed. He'd been holding the chair for *me*. James had never done that—the one time I'd asked, he'd explained a male holding a chair for a mere female made as much sense as letting a horse ride on a man. But I had dated before I'd met James and some of the guys I'd gone out with had been old-fashioned. Ten years of marriage had apparently erased those old memories. Just for a second, I wondered what else I might have forgotten.

Brandon stepped behind me, apparently intent on being a gentleman.

"That isn't necessary," I explained

"It would be my pleasure."

Sure, I'd dated guys who held my chair. All of them had been quick to feel up my butt when they'd seated me and I expected the same from Brandon. I was surprised when he pushed the chair forward as I sat down, then walked back to his side. Surprised until I remembered that I was thirty, not seventeen. There was a reason I was unclaimed... Brandon didn't need me to serve his needs, any of hundreds of younger women in town would take care of them.

A waitress, obviously a co-ed from the university, wiggled her hips at Brandon. "Whacha havin'."

"Nicole?"

"Yes, master?"

He shook his head. "What would you like to eat?"

"Oh." After my senior year of High School, some girlfriends and I had headed down to Rehoboth for a week at the beach. I remembered one time a wave had caught me, turned me on my head, and spun me around so quickly I'd lost all sense of direction.

I felt like that now, only more so. How was I supposed to know what I wanted? James had always ordered for me, arranged the menu, taken care of me. I hadn't put in my own order for over a decade.

"Maybe you could order for me."

Brandon shook his head. "But I don't know what you want."

"What are you going to have?"

He smiled at the waitress. "Is there a special tonight?"

"Pot roast."

"I'll have the special."

"I'll have that, too," I said.

"What to drink."

Brandon ordered iced tea.

"Just water for me," I said, happy I wouldn't have to lap it with my tongue the way James made me drink it, even out in public.

The waitress shrugged her shoulders, wiggled her perky breasts, and scurried away.

Brandon opened his computer bag, taking out his newspaper, which he passed to me, and a tablet computer. "Are you looking for something local, or—"

"Definitely local," I said. What if I moved away and James changed his mind? He'd be angry if he had to track me down in another city.

"That makes it a bit harder," he said. "Unfortunately, the college students are a bit of a drag on the job market. Have you thought about going back to school and completing your degree?"

"I don't have the money for that."

"Maybe we can find you a job with tuition benefits, then." He folded back the paper and turned to the classified section.

I unbuttoned another of the buttons on my top. I didn't think Brandon was gay, but something wasn't working right. He wasn't responding to me the way I'd always learned a man should respond. Sure, he wouldn't be interested in a long-term relationship with an over-the-hill woman like me considering he could have his pick of the co-eds, but surely he wouldn't be wasting his time with me if he didn't expect at least a blowjob. Yet he hadn't even felt me up. Even the bank manager had done that.

"Ah—" he turned bright red. "Not that I'm complaining, but it's a little distracting..."

I looked down. My nipples weren't even showing. How could a little cleavage be distracting? I'd spent most of the last ten years naked and I'd only distracted James when he'd wanted to be distracted.

I quickly buttoned my shirt to the neck—and figured the answer. James had stroked my breasts and shot his wad on my face because he liked me. But now I was thirty. Brandon hardly knew me—and apparently was even less attracted by my aging body than I'd imagined. I must have misunderstood his invitation to dinner. Perhaps he wanted someone to clean his toilet or something. I was good at that.

He breathed a sigh of relief as I hid my tits. "Okay, there's a bookkeeping job at the furniture store. Some college required, so you'd fit. How are you with financials?"

"Not."

"You said you were a housewife. I've read that running a household is like running a business."

"My hus—ex-husband might have run it like a business. I'd tell him what we needed and he'd tell me whether I could have it."

"Okay, we'll put that one on reserve. I'm sure we'll be able to find a lot of others."

By the time the food arrived, we'd rejected a lot of other. Finding something that matched my skills had turned out to be harder than Brandon had guessed. I wasn't surprised, though. The pallet on James's kitchen floor sounded better and better.

The waitress put our plates in front of us.

"Permission to use silverware, sir—Brandon?"

"What?"

I realized I'd just told him a lot more about myself than I'd intended. Unless James had trained them, most women didn't eat all of their meals out of dog bowls, with their hands held behind their backs. "I just—never mind."

"Have you been abused, Nicole? Should we call the police?"

I couldn't help it. I laughed. James hadn't abused me. Sure he'd trained me with his quirt and decided my wardrobe, my daily routine, my diet, and my sleeping arrangements. But he'd made sure I got plenty of exercise, ate a healthy diet, and even allowed me to finger myself to orgasm at least twice a month. In the twelve years we'd spent together, ten of them married, I couldn't remember a time when he'd actually punched me, hard anyway. He'd always been calm when he'd struck me. He'd never left me unfed for more than a couple of days, and that only when I'd been stubborn. He'd never even yelled at me. "I'm not abused, Brandon. I've been trained. There's a difference."

I felt certain an ordinary man would be intrigued, would want to know about the ways James had trained me to respond to his commands and his subtle cues, the way he'd gradually heightened my sensitivity until he could bring me close to orgasm by the light stroke of his quirt against my clit or his dick up my butt.

Brandon didn't ask any of those questions. Instead, he shook his head. "That seems weird to me."

I knew better than to disagree—out loud. Men might differ, but none wanted a woman to disagree with them.

Still, Brandon was wrong. Living without training, without basic guidance on how to please your man, having always to guess and then put up with the silent treatment when you guessed wrong—*that* sounded weird to me. If a guy wants something from his wife, why should he have to hint or whine for it? Why shouldn't he train her to give him what he wants—and let her know how happy her obedience made him?

I unwrapped the napkin from my silverware and waited.

In about forty seconds, I realized Brandon was waiting, too.

"What?" he asked.

James would check my food for me, make sure it was suitable, before allowing me to eat. His sensitive tongue could detect certain spices on my body and he'd often have my meal taken away if they contained them. But I wasn't with James any more. I wondered if Brandon might be disgusted with my taste if I ate the wrong thing. Then I wondered if I'd gone insane. Obviously Brandon wasn't interested in my taste. He probably saw me as a research project in job hunting.

Still, he was waiting for me to start… and I was hungry. I dug in.

For a couple of minutes, our conversation was limited to polite nonsense and requests for condiments. I'd only been able to force down one pancake that morning and I'd skipped lunch, so the silence didn't bother me.

Once we'd both satisfied our strongest pangs, though, Brandon asked me about my family.

My father had died when I'd been in high school, a victim of obesity, high blood pressure, and a stressful lifestyle. My mother had retired to a senior living center when James and I had married. After James ordered me to give my stepfather a handjob, my mother had cut all contact. Not that I told Brandon that detail.

"Your ex-husband didn't force you to cut your contacts?" Brandon demanded.

For just a second, I wondered if that was what the handjob had been about. James hadn't even liked my stepfather. But then I realized I was being silly.

I put down my fork. "Listen, Brandon. You've got the idea that I'm a victim, that James kept me from my friends and family. He loved family. He encouraged me to meet with my girlfriends and participate in activities with other faculty wives. He wasn't big on me associating with other men without him being there, but let's be honest—that is basic self-protection. I don't know about Yankee women, but here in the south, women are raised to say 'yes' from the moment they're born. It doesn't take the kind of training James gave me to leave a woman susceptible to any man who decides he wants her. And then there's rape."

I'd given him a second chance to ask about the training—another chance he passed up.

"So, do you see anything else that might be suitable for me?" I asked. "Other than the bookkeeping job, I mean."

He folded back the paper. "You won't want the job at the fraternity. Those guys are—"

"What job at the fraternity?"

"You don't want it, Nicole. You deserve something better."

If James had told me that, I would have immediately backed off. But Brandon wasn't James. Here in Cambridge, Mississippi, fraternities provided housing for students—and for the full-time staff who worked them. Getting room and board, in addition to a salary, sounded ideal. "I appreciate your concern, Brandon, and your feelings about what I deserve. But even if I deserving something, that doesn't mean I'll get it. If I'm not qualified for jobs I deserve, I'll have to take jobs I can get."

"They want someone to clean, and also to stand in as their adult supervisor. It only pays minimum wage, though."

"Plus room and board?"

"Yeah, but—"

"Give me that paper."

He looked up, shock on his face.

"Sir," I added, my body cringing as I waited for the sharp swish/crack of the quirt against my buttocks or breasts.

Brandon shook his head. "Please don't call me sir. It makes me feel like I'm your grandfather."

I suspected he was actually a year or so younger than me, unlike James who was a good eight years older.

Rather than beat me, he handed over the paper.

I entered the number in my phone. I'd never actually make a call while I was at dinner with a man, but I didn't think just entering a number counted.

We lingered over pie, Brandon savoring a cup of coffee while I inhaled that divine scent--James had forbidden me coffee since he said he could smell it in my juices.

Between sips, Brandon asked me more questions and tapped on his computer.

I'd spent countless nights like this—me naked and between James's legs, sucking on his cock or licking his bottom while he worked on his computer, researching for his latest paper or grading student papers. Between those old memories and being with a man as sexy as Brandon, that familiar knot at the very base of my gut tightened up and my vaginal lips swelled and moistened.

"I've got you entered in Monster." He snapped his computer shut. "Why don't you wait a few days before doing anything silly and see what happens with the computer job search."

I smiled at him, then slid my foot up his leg. "Thank you, si— Brandon. I'm sure you'll want a reward for all of your hard work."

He blinked, hard.

At first I thought his flush was one of embarrassment. Could I really have run into Mississippi's only twenty-eight year-old virgin male? But the clenched teeth gave him away. He was mad.

"Do you really think I've helped you as a sort of value exchange— my research skills to get into your pussy?"

Humiliation washed over me. "I'm sorry, sir. I certainly didn't mean to imply that you couldn't do better, that I consider my aging body to be some sort of equal payment for all the hard work you've done for—"

"Shut up."

In our ten years of marriage, James might have given me that command twice. My jaws snapped shut so hard, I worried I'd chipped a tooth.

"When I hear talk like that, it make me want to track down that scumbag husband of yours and beat him into a pulp. I can't believe he rejected you because of your age. I can't believe he systematically brutalized you, training you like you were a puppy in danger of soiling the carpet. You're a beautiful woman, Nicole. Any sensible man would give his left nut for a night with you. Don't sell yourself short."

I nodded.

"Aren't you going to say anything?"

I shook my head. Brandon wasn't James, but he'd told me to shut up. I wasn't going to say a word until he released me from it.

Finally, he got it. "I'm sorry I yelled. I'm not mad at you, Nicole. I'm mad at your jerk of a husband. He's the one who ground your self-esteem into the mud, made you think of yourself as someone whose only value comes from your vagina, as a whore."

I shook my head. I'd used my mouth, my ass, my breasts, my hands, much more than my vagina in pleasing James. My pussy, he'd reserved more for the quirt.

Brandon clenched his fists and stared at me as if trying to peer into my brain. After a good twenty seconds, he snapped his fingers. "You're waiting for me to give you permission to speak, aren't you?"

I nodded.

"Well, talk. You're driving me crazy."

"You're so completely wrong. James didn't abuse me. My self-esteem is fine, or it was until I turned thirty, anyway, and it's not James's fault I got older, I did that on my own. I don't think of myself as a whore. I had a chance to earn two hundred dollars today just to give a man a blowjob and I turned it down. So don't be slinging around that kind of accusation."

"I'm sorry."

"Well, I'm glad you let me know what you really think about me so I wouldn't waste my time entertaining fantasies you might be interested." I stood, then realized I'd left most of my money back in my motel room. I wasn't sure I had enough to pay my share of the bill. With James, I'd never worried about money. I'd kept current in the magazines and with Yahoo, though. I knew the guy wasn't expected to do all the paying any more, especially if he wasn't going to be getting a sexual reward at the end of the evening. Maybe I could talk to the manager about washing dishes or something. I reached for the bill to see how bad the damage was going to be.

Brandon was on his feet almost instantly, stripping the bill from my hand. "I invited you. Of course I'll pay."

"All right." I didn't mind doing dishes but I wasn't going to turn down a free meal.

He threw a twenty and a five on the table. "Now, can I walk you to your car?"

"Oh. I don't have a car."

Brandon's gaze looked like pity to me. That was absolutely not how I wanted anyone to see me.

Chapter Three

Brandon insisted on walking me to my motel.

In Mississippi, the summer was always hot, and temperatures barely dropped in the evening. We were both sweating by the time we reached my cheap motel and I hoped I'd left the air conditioner on. I also hoped Brandon would miss the damp spot in my pants. I'd been faithful to James since our first date, except when he'd ordered me to service another man, and I was surprised I reacted so strongly to Brandon. Apparently, though, my body knew what it wanted even as my mind beat me up about it.

"This isn't a safe place for a woman," he observed as I put my key in the door to my first floor room.

I'd heard that kind of come-on before. I'd been getting Brandon's signals confused all night, but I couldn't have missed that one.

"It probably isn't safe," I agreed. "Why don't you come in and protect me. I'll give you a blowjob and make sure you have a nice time. We can turn off the lights if you'd prefer not to look at me."

He'd held my arm lightly as we'd walked—it wasn't the same as heeling on leash, but it was close enough that I'd felt comfortable.

Now he dropped my arm like I'd caught fire. "You've got to stop that."

I looked and made sure I hadn't been crazy, but I wasn't. His boner pushed against his slacks like he hid a two-by-four between his legs. James had been a pleasant six inches but Brandon had to be eight—or more. He wouldn't respond to me that way if he was gay, would he?

I decided to find out. "If you're gay, I can pretend to be a boy. You can do my butt—I like it in there. Although I wouldn't think you could tell the difference if I pleasure you with my mouth."

"I'm not gay. And I'm not staying. I'm holding onto my control by my fingernails now, and I don't know how long before I snap."

I truly couldn't figure the problem. Despite my age, Brandon wanted me. I wanted him. He'd been nice to me and I could be nice to him. A lot of the time, James had played poker with his guy friends using blowjobs from their wives and mistresses as stakes. While he generally won, and I'd rarely had to deliver, he'd been adamant that a blowjob isn't being unfaithful. His logic made sense to me—sucking a guy off was just being nice and showing respect, like a handshake or a kiss on the cheek. Not a big deal.

Brandon didn't see it that way. "See you around, Nicole."

I waited until he'd vanished around the corner, went into my tiny motel room, and tore the sheets and blankets off the bed to make a little pallet on the floor—someplace I could feel at home.

In the past ten years, I hadn't gone to bed without at least a few spankings, so I told the wall all I'd done wrong, pretending I was talking to James, then I announced my punishment—five stripes on each buttock. Then I dug around in my shopping bag until I found a metal belt that worked perfectly as a whip.

Once my butt was stinging, exhaustion overcame me. I handcuffed myself to the bed, put on my blindfold, and fell asleep.

I didn't have to do that anymore, I knew: I could even sleep on the bed if I wanted. Lying on the hard pallet on the floor, my butt stinging and my hands chained, almost let me feel like I was back to normal, like I'd wake up and discover this was a nightmare, that James was waiting for his morning blowjob.

* * * *

The next morning, though, I woke alone in the shabby motel room.

I unlocked my cuffs, poured cereal and milk into my Fido bowl, set it on the floor, put my hands behind my back, and ate.

Waking up without giving James his morning blowjob made me feel empty. I'd gotten used to it the way some people got used to coffee in the morning. Still, James had insisted that I keep my body trim. I'd missed my morning run the previous day but I didn't want to get into bad habits. James wouldn't want me back, even as a kitchen servant, if I got fat. So, I dressed and started out.

The route James and I usually took crossed the campus. I suspected he'd be out running Amber and I didn't want to see that. So I took a different route but still ran through the shady trees and grassy squares of Cambridge State University.

As I ran past it, I checked out the fraternity house that had advertised for a live-in cleaning woman and chaperone.

The house was a bit of a wreck with loose shingles, a couple of missing pickets in the fence, and a baseball-sized hole through an upstairs window. A couple of students hung out on the front porch, drinking beer at eight in the morning. Classes wouldn't start for a week, but the fraternities opened early for returning students.

I wondered if the drinkers would make it through the semester if they started drinking that early in the morning, then realized they probably hadn't stopped from the previous evening.

Both whistled and shouted moderately tame suggestions they thought would shock me as I ran by, but I didn't stop. I wasn't going to a job interview dressed in a t-shirt cropped to the bottom of my tits and a pair of shorts that crawled up my butt and showed both cheeks.

When I got back to my room, I realized my mistake. I'd worn my only respectable slacks the previous evening and now they had a big stain from my arousal. I should have rinsed them out before going to bed.

I considered waiting, but I was afraid someone else would get the job, so I took a cool shower, put on one of my party dresses with a pair of sandals, and walked back to the frat house.

The dress, a tight white that would show every speck of dirt, was cut too low in front, all the way to my ass in back, and fit my rear like it had been vacuum-sealed. Considering the state of my slacks, this was the most respectable outfit I owned.

By the time I reached the fraternity, Mississippi's summer heat had gotten to me. Sweat moistened the sheer fabric and my nipples showed through like twin searchlights.

The two guys were still drinking out front, the stink of stale beer mixing with that of male sweat.

"I'm interested in interviewing for the cleaning woman job," I told one.

He stared at me for a moment, then leaned over the porch railing and vomited into the holly plants.

"Cleaning job," I reminded the other one.

He considering a holly bush himself but pulled himself together. "Chick looked just like you ran by an hour ago. Tits hanging out. Sure love to get me some of them."

"Right now, it looks like you need cleaning more than you need breasts."

"Can't need nothin' more than I need a bouncy set."

"Lucky for you school opens in a week. There'll be hundreds of freshman women who're both looking to put their high school boyfriends behind them and away from their parents for the first time." I remembered how I'd reacted to that freedom—too much freedom until James had taught me some discipline. "Now, can we talk about the cleaning—"

"Lots of girls, right." He let out a belch so stinky it made *me* want to find a holly bush. "Thing is, they want grad students, or seniors, or professors. Even other freshmen, so's they can hang around and explore things together. Nobody's got time for a sophomore."

I shook my head. "I think you're blaming the wrong thing. It's not your age, it's your attitude."

He turned and this time he did vomit.

The first boy still looked green, but he'd heaved his guts out and seemed finished with that part of his morning entertainment.

"You talk a lot," he said, "for a cleaning woman wanna-be. Like you'd know what it takes to get a bitch. I mean, like someone who looks like you ever had a hard time. With guys it's different. Sure, if you're a jock or a genius, you can get a girl. But ordinary guys like me'n Russell here never get noticed. Think about it. If you weren't looking for a job, would you notice us? I don't think so. You're old, but you're still pretty. You know what I mean. No offense, 'course."

I looked at him. His jeans had seen better days--but not recently. His t-shirt advertised a band I'd never heard of. From the poor quality of the graphic, I suspected nobody else had heard of them, either. Although his arms and neck were scrawny, and his chest appeared to have gone concave, he already had a gut on him.

"You're right," I said. "No co-ed is going to look at you twice unless you're really smart or at least sort of rich. You smart or rich?"

"Him?" Russell laughed. "We spent most of last year tutoring him to pass his classes, and he drives an old Ford Escort."

"Then you're going to have a hell of a time getting a girl interested long enough to learn you've got a great personality."

"Except Arny doesn't," Russell put in.

"Too true," my new best friend Arny admitted.

"You sure you're looking to be a cleaning lady," Russell demanded. "You look all dressed up for a party or something. Nice dress, by the way. I like it when bitches wear those tight dresses that would show panty lines if they weren't wearing a thong, and where their tits look like they'll pop out if you just take a deep breat--"

"I need a job," I said. "Maybe I you can introduce me to the president of your fraternity and I'll let you get back to your drinking."

I'd been shocked at first when I'd been able to talk to these kids like that. James had insisted that I call all men 'sir,' and that I defer to their wishes, except in sexual matters where I answered only to him. Twice, he'd let other men in the faculty put me over their knees, pull up my skirts, and spank my butt just because I hadn't treated them with as much respect as he thought I should. But James and the other professors in the department were grown men with Ph.D.'s, experience in the world, income, and physical strength. These kids were a long way from the kind of man James was—or the kind of man Brandon was.

I shook my head angrily. I wasn't going to let myself think about Brandon any more. That man confused and frustrated me. He'd turned me on more than anyone had in years—including my own ex-husband—and then he'd shot me down when I'd offered him a friendly blowjob. Hell, he hadn't just shot me down, he'd treated me with as much contempt as if I'd acted like a master myself and demanded he lick out *my* asshole.

"She wants me to introduce her to the president of the fraternity." Russell giggled, then ralphed up another couple of quarts of beer."

"And she says we can get back to our drinking," Arny agreed. "Except this is the end of it. Last bottle, gone."

"I'm fraternity president, Russell said. "Show me your tits and the job is yours."

* * * *

With no conscious involvement by my brain, I reached for the halter tie behind my neck and yanked on the bow. But James had taught me the power of presentation. Occasionally he'd gone for shock, ordering me to 'accidentally' let a breast slip out at a faculty party or to raise my arms and let my boobs pop out of a tube top at a dance. Generally, though, anticipation forms as much of the enjoyment as the display— which explained, James had told me, the eternal pleasure people take from the tease.

I held onto the ties, intending to slowly reveal, and that pause gave my brain time enough to catch up.

If James had ordered me to put my tits on display, I'd do it. I'd do it even if he'd ordered me to dance naked at a church revival meeting. But these guys weren't James. They were college sophomores, barely more than children. They hadn't earned the right to be my master.

Both Russell and Arny had pasty skin with slight greenish tinges, scrawny arms that drooped out of t-shirts that didn't disguise underdeveloped chests, and the slightly swollen bellies that came from eating too much fat, drinking too much beer, and not getting enough exercise. I didn't think either of their necks was thicker than my own. Sure they would be physically stronger than me—guys that age were filled with testosterone. But I didn't feel compelled to obey them the way I had James—or Brandon.

As a college professor, James was big on lecturing. Often, after he'd tied me up for the evening and put in my gag, he'd lectured me on why I was the one tied up on the ground while he leaned back on his comfortable bed, his semen running out my butt but his dick clean from my tongue. I'd paid close attention to his lectures, partly because he made sure I did, flicking me with his quirt when he thought my attention wandered, but largely because his theories explained my situation and helped me understand the world.

"Only part of dominance comes from force," he'd explained. "Most comes from acquiescence."

Maybe he was right. My gut told me that if I flashed these guys my tits now, I'd become a cum-bucket for the entire fraternity—and that I'd rarely see a paycheck.

"That's all the show you guys get." I re-tied my halter. "Besides, I'm old enough to be your, well, big sister or something."

"You can be Arny's big sister." Russell's face blushed red. "Far as I'm concerned, you're a perfect MILF. What an amazing rack. Are you sure you don't want the job? Just pull those suckers out and let's have a good look at them. That sounds like little enough to ask, considering we'll be paying you every week."

"Oh, I want the job. But you're going to give it to me without seeing my breasts."

He licked his lips. "Now why would I do that?"

The real reason he'd do it was because he wanted to see those breasts and would do just about anything for a chance, especially as he'd come so close. It had to be driving him crazy that I'd undone the halter and pulled the straps forward, uncovering enough of my breasts to at least hint at the nipples underneath. He'd feel certain if he could get so close, it wouldn't take much to cover the rest of the ground— with my pussy following not too much later. But I couldn't tell him that—I needed to give him a justification. At least, that's what James had always told me, back in the early days when he'd needed to persuade me to follow his orders. For the past ten years, I'd simply obeyed without question.

"For one thing," I said, "you don't want me to sue you for harassment. Do you have any idea what would happen if I told—"

He held up a hand. "Oh, no. Don't go there."

"Who would believe you," Arny sneered. "It's two against one. And we're reputable students while you're looking for a minimum wage job."

Russell giggled nervously. "Who would believe her? Try anyone who looked at her, checked out those jugs, and then looked at us."

Arny sighed. "So, we don't get to see those titties? Damn, she was so close."

"Shut up," Russell demanded. "That's the kind of talk that will get us in trouble."

"I can't say tits? What am I supposed to say? Boobies? Milk buckets?"

Russell shook his head. "He's incorrigible but he doesn't reflect the policy of the fraternity here."

I looked at Arny, then at Russell. "If he reflects badly on the fraternity, he should be punished." James had taught me a lot about punishment.

"Yeah, sure. We'll punish him, okay? Anyway, just tell us what you want."

"I want the job," I said. "Two dollars an hour over minimum wage for the first forty hours. If I have to work more, it'll be time and a half. I'll do basic cleaning and I'll sign the forms you need for an on-site supervisor. I'll take weekends off—"

Russell shook his head. "The Greek Council requires that we have our adult supervisor here on Friday and Saturday night. It's got to be part of the job."

I felt a rush of power from my control over these kids. No wonder James had enjoyed tying me up and ordering me around. I wasn't attracted to these two young men at all, but my pussy still tightened up and moistened as they deferred to me. The bulges pushing the fabric of their shorts out from their groins told me that they were aroused as well—and that further excited me.

I reminded myself not to turn around. These kids would be watching and would get the wrong idea if they saw a wet patch.

"Okay, I'll take two nights off during the week but it'll still be time and a half for those nights. Room and board is included, right?"

"Yeah, sure."

"You have to buy beer for us." Arny rubbed his own bulge. The poor guy was at the edge of orgasm just from looking at me. I wondered if he'd ever gotten any real action.

"Some of us…" he gasped for breath, "are, uh, under twenty-one."

"I'm not buying your beer."

"Yeah, forget that." Russell said. "And Arny, cut that out—it's disgusting."

It was disgusting. It was also sexy to see these two young men respond to me. It had been years since James had been able to achieve an erection without a fair amount of work on my part. With these guys, I barely had to look at them.

Arny snatched his hand away from his groin. "Man," he whispered, "you didn't have to call it to her attention. As far as the money goes, we only budgeted minimum wage, and we're running a deficit as it is."

"We only budgeted for fifteen brothers," Russell whispered back. "Check out that rack and tell me we won't be able to fill every room in the place, even the basement. Can you imagine having her shake you awake every morning?"

I smiled, pretending I wasn't listening.

Russell turned back to me. "You do understand that part of your responsibility will be seeing that the brothers get out of bed and off to class. We always have one who's shy or something and doesn't want to leave the frat house. Right, Arny."

"I wasn't that ba—"

"It took three brothers to drag him to his classes every day for an entire semester. He was bad."

"You may show me the facilities now," I announced.

A part of me waited for the 'ah-ha, gotcha.' Early in our relationship, James would play that game, pretending to negotiate with me, agreeing to do what I wanted in return for me doing what he wanted. Then he'd laugh, remind me a man doesn't have to honor his agreement with his property, and stripe my butt with his quirt until I begged him to forgive my presumption.

These boys weren't James, though. I didn't think they'd learned to hide their thoughts the way James had.

"Come-on in and take a look around," Arny said. "It's a bit of a mess, but you'd expect that since we hadn't hired our cleaner until now." He stood, swayed for a moment, then tossed his not-quite-empty quart beer bottle into an overflowing trash bucket. "Guess I've had enough beer for last night."

Russell looked longingly at his own beer, then dropped it when his gaze got tangled up in my breasts.

I was barely a C cup—there were plenty of co-eds with bigger tits, including the annoying Amber. With James's training and constant exercise, I'd kept my boobs firm and bouncy, though. Knowing these two guys had raging hard-ons for me brought the nipples to points that showed through the thin fabric of the party dress.

I almost laughed at the way Russell stared. Men were so funny the way they'd look at a woman's breasts instead of her face. I wondered if they thought they could convince breasts to pop out of dresses through will power.

"They're not going anywhere," I told him.

"Huh?"

I couldn't help myself. I wiggled my hips, which sent a jiggle through my breasts, then cupped each of them in one hand and squeezed so the nipples almost popped through the fabric. "My tits. You don't have to watch them like they're going to run away or something. They're attached. Sort of come with the job."

"Jeez, lady." Russell bit down on his jaw, trembling for control.

The tents protruding from both Russell and Arny's shorts swelled even more, proving that they might be a bit scrawny in the rest of their bodies but their dicks were all grown up.

The sight of those desperate hard-ons, doomed to be denied the touch of my hands, mouth, ass, breasts, and pussy, made me squeeze myself in earnest.

Russell turned red. "Shit, lady. What the hell—" His body jerked. "Fuck-me. I've got to head upstairs."

A wave of power swept over me and I channeled my husband. "You, Russell. You will not leave my presence until I give you permission."

I watched moisture spread across his shorts from where the tip of his boner pressed against his shorts.

"But that's not fair. Tell you what. Why don't you let Arny show you around? I've got to—"

"Oh, no. You're the president. You're the one who'll have to make decisions."

"But—"

I smiled. I was starting to see why James had enjoyed some of his little humiliation digs. Maybe not all of the training he'd given me was strictly for my own benefit. "But what, Russell?"

I wondered if he'd admit to me that he'd come in his pants just from watching my breasts--and I hadn't even taken them out of my dress. Back when I'd first been with James, before I'd learned better control over my body, James had called attention to it every time he'd gotten me wet. If we were in a crowd of men, he'd have me stand on something and turn around so they could all see the wet stains. Then, when we'd get home, he'd make me lick my dress clean.

I decided I didn't need to be quite so heavy-handed with Russell. Women, after all, are the subtler of the two sexes. Still, it was unfortunate that Russell had such poor control over his body. He really needed to get himself a trainer, someone who could bring him to the point of orgasm, then let him draw back, gradually increasing his staying power until he could pleasure a woman all night long and only climax when he chose, or when his trainer gave him permission.

"So, what's behind the front door?" I released my hold on my breasts and smiled at the two males.

"I, uh, sort of need to go to the bathroom."

"Pinch your cock between your fingers to hold it for a few minutes," I said. "I told you, I want you to show me around. If this place isn't suitable, I don't want to waste any more time here than I already have. I've got more places to check out today."

That part was a lie and James had trained me never to lie. He'd also taught me that it was all right for *him* to lie because he was the dominant.

Could I be the dominant here, or was I just acting?

"But—"

"You might as well do what she says." Arny's hands shook, but not, this time, from alcohol. He wanted to grab his dick and squeeze the semen out of it, wanted to splash it all over my breasts.

That, though, wasn't going to happen.

"Women like her," Arny continued, "always get what they want. The only question is, how much pain do guys like us have to go through before we give in. I vote that we give in right away."

"You're smarter than you look," I told him.

"I'm a genius. What's your name, anyway? Or should we just call you lady."

"My name is Nicole d'Angre. You may call me Mrs. d'Angre or you can call me ma'am."

"How about just Missus. Ma'am sounds old to me, like someone my mom's age."

I considered, then nodded. "Missus is fine."

"Great. Come on in, then. This here is the ballroom." Arny put a bit too much emphasis on the syllable 'ball.' "We use it for our orgies. Get it?"

"Oh, really?" I followed him inside and looked around.

A huge plasma TV hung from one wall. Although no one was watching, the TV was on and a large-busted woman was bent over a hitching rail outside a bar being humped from behind by a man with a horse-size schlong. Various Playboy pinups, mostly dating from the 1980s, before any of these boys had been born, were stuck to the walls with yellowing tape. A Ping-Pong table piled deep with empty beer bottles sat in the middle of the room. Over a couch, a row of dusty woman's underwear hung on a knotted twine clothesline.

Arny saw where I was looking. "Some of our conquests. Women who come in here, they know what's going to happen. They leave their panties for us as trophies."

"You don't say?" I stepped closer to it and considered the collection. The few pair that looked like they'd been added over the past decade appeared completely unworn, as if someone had hung them directly out of the shopping bag. "My guess," I said, "is that the orgy thing hasn't been working well for you guys lately."

Russell held both hands in front of his leaking bulge. "Look, missus. Everyone here knows we're screwed up. The fraternity is in a death spiral. We don't attract the bitches, so cool guys won't pledge. But since there aren't any cool guys here, bitches won't bother stopping by. Bottom line, we're the worst fraternity at Cambridge State University. If we'd just get some nerds, we'd be better off. At least some co-eds are smart enough to know that the nerds will end up making the big bucks after they graduate. Unfortunately, we can't even bring the nerds in."

"We almost got that guy from China last year," Arny pointed out.

"Yeah, and we almost saw Missus D'Angre's tits. Only we didn't. Last year, we got four new pledges. This year, we've had interest from three guys, and of those three, only one is committed. If the whole orgy thing were working better for us, we'd have guys lining up to pledge. Now, can I go and change my pants?"

"You shoot your spunk, you walk with it," I said. "What else have you got here?"

To my surprise, the dining room wasn't bad. Three long oak tables lined with padded chairs filled the center of the huge room. Along the walls, assorted highboys and built-in shelves held cheap china and serving dishes. The floors were spotless. While there was a high-quality print of Botticelli's Venus Rising from the Sea, the tacky nudes from the ballroom were conspicuously missing.

"Servers complained," Arny said by way of explanation. "They're hard enough to attract as it is. No pun intended."

I stared at his crotch. "Was there a pun there?"

"Missus, you're killing me."

James wouldn't train a male—he was too much of a homophobe to even consider it. But if Arny thought I'd given him anything approaching a hard time, he desperately needed a dose of the kind of training James had provided me.

I looked at the clean floors. "You guys actually eat here?"

"Uh, during the year we do," Russell admitted. "We hire a cook to come in for dinner, eat cereal for breakfast, and have sandwiches and things for lunch. Like Arny said, we pay a couple of work-study girls to help out with serving and bussing the tables. The girls never last long, though."

"I wonder if it's the atmosphere," I said. "I sure hope there's a back door for their access. If you make them walk through that disgusting ballroom, you're going to be looking at lawsuits even from pliant southern women. If you accidentally hire a Yankee, she'll probably castrate you first, and sue you later."

Both young men reflectively reached for their groins. There was something about the word *castrate* that makes men cringe.

"The girls clear the plates and the cook does the dishwashing," Russell said. "You'll have to clean the floors and shit."

"Shit? I hope you're speaking figuratively."

"Wha—oh, sorry." He laughed self-consciously. "There's actual scat on the floor only once in a long while. One or two of the guys think it's funny so they—"

"Let's try for never."

"We can always try."

It didn't sound to me like he'd be trying too hard. We'd see how that worked but I was getting some ideas.

"Okay, that's enough of the dining room. Are there any other common rooms?"

The library was surprisingly nice. Old books lined the shelves and the paintings, while amateurish and a bit overly concentrated on the female nude, were real paintings—probably created by long-ago fraternity brothers who'd studied art. Comfortable leather chairs and a few writing tables filled the rest of the space. It had probably been the library for the cotton-mill millionaire who'd founded the town and built the building that had eventually become this fraternity. The built-in bookcases had a solid opulence that would cost thousands to replicate.

The last room, Russell told me proudly, was the President's den.

"For meetings of the fraternity board, or for special occasions." Russell grinned. "I keep some real liquor here—not just beer. Plus, if I'm too drunk to make it upstairs with the bitch of the moment, I can always bring her in her and bang her. Or could, anyway, if there was a bitch of the moment. Cool, huh? Most of the guys have to hang their woman's panties on their doorknob to keep anyone from walking in on them."

"Really?"

A set of stairs led down from the kitchen into a finished basement. Vinyl wallpaper, designed to vaguely resemble the dark paneling popular when my parents had been young, peeled from moisture-stained walls.

"This is your room." Arny threw open a door barely wide enough to let me in. James definitely couldn't have fit inside.

I peered through the open door. A twenty-watt lightbulb cast a reddish light over a cheap cot. The mattress had yellow stains that looked like they'd been setting since Mississippi was stolen from the Chickasaw and Choctaw. A chipboard chest of drawers, missing one of the drawers and topped with a basin and water pitcher, was the only other furniture.

"We'll fix it up for you," Russell promised when he noticed my silence. "It won't be so bad."

"Most of the guys you'll share a bathroom with won't get up early enough to bother you," Arny added. "'Course last year that wasn't a problem because we didn't pledge enough brothers to fill any of the basement rooms. Ole' Debbie didn't have to share at all."

I shook my head. "I see. Let's take a look at the other rooms."

Russell led me to the second floor.

The upstairs rooms were filthy, but larger and better furnished.

"They're a bit dirty," Russell admitted as he opened the door to the last room.

"Dirty? This is a pig sty."

He grabbed a pair of jeans from a pile of laundry on the ground and pulled them over his hips, finally covering the wet spot on his shorts. "It's not that bad. We just--"

I kicked a pile of dirty laundry, raising a musty odor that smelled more like male spunk than sweat. Despite myself, my body reacted. For years, I'd associated James's semen with my pleasure.

"Face it," Arny said. "Missus is right. You're a pig. It'll take her an hour every day just to clean up after you. If we get the twenty guys we need if we're going to pay her what you promised, she'll have a never-ending job. Real job security." He licked his lips nervously as he studied me, obviously wondering how far he could push me. "If you don't mind me saying so, Missus," he said, "I'm sort of turned on by the idea of seeing you on your hands and knees scrubbing the floors. I hope you always wear low-cut tops like that dress so your tits hang out, and that you stick your butt—"

I held up my hand and stared at his crotch. "I already know that you're turned on. I understand that males your age don't have much control over your dicks, so if you get a stiffie from looking at me, I'm not going to get mad."

He grinned like he'd won. "Well, that's—"

"But you should have some control over your dirty mouths. When you talk to me, or talk about me, I want to hear nothing but respect. And that does not include words like tit or butt unless I tell you that you can use those words."

"What do you want me to call them?"

I grabbed his ear and twisted it. "Arny, I can't think of a single reason you'd ever need to mention my tits, my ass, or my cunt to another person in the world. But if the need ever does arise, you can come straight to me and I'll tell you how to describe them."

"Hey, that hurts."

"You're lucky I grabbed your ear. My other choice was to grab your balls. I'd have done that, but thought I might yank them off."

He muttered something to Russell, who grinned at him.

"What did you say?" I tightened my grip.

"Uh, nothing."

"Nothing, what?"

"Nothing, Missus."

"I think you're lying to me, Arny. Do you know what happens to boys who lie?"

"I don't suppose you blow them."

I dropped my hands from his ear. "You're not taking this seriously, Arny. Pull down your pants and bend over."

"Sorry, Missus."

"You'll be sorry in a few minutes. Now, obey."

I had him lean over what had been Russell's desk, found a ruler, and gave him ten slaps on each butt cheek.

With each strike, his dick got harder. He finally made a choking sound and came with the last slap.

"Jeez."

"If you think I'm going to clean that up, you're crazy. Pull up your pants, get a bucket, and wipe the desk down."

Arny looked at Russell, then back at me. For a moment, I wondered if I'd pushed too hard. I had a vague memory that I'd fought back when James had claimed me and begun my training. I hadn't thought about it in years, but there had been a time when I'd fought back, tried to match him strike for strike. That had been foolish, of course. James had been so strong I'd never landed a single punch, and James had always punished me severely for trying.

Arny wasn't James, but he was much stronger than I.

Still, if I was going to live her, I needed to establish an environment I could be comfortable with, and an environment that James wouldn't be ashamed to rescue me from. If I let all of them have me, he'd never take me back. So, I just couldn't have a herd of college-age boys smirking about me, treating like shit just because they were paying me and because I was female, grabbing me in the dark when they could pretend it was an accident, squirting their juices over me while I was sleeping.

I put my hands on my hips and stuck my tits at him. "You may think you're pretty old to get a spanking, Arny but you're wrong. If you don't behave, you're going to spend a lot of time bent over my desk."

"My desk?" Russell demanded. "No offense, but I'm not sure I want Arny and the other brothers creaming up my desk. I work here."

"You did work here. I'm afraid that room in the basement is completely unsatisfactory. I'll be taking this room."

"Can she do that?" Arny whispered.

"Who's going to stop her?" Russell whispered back.

"We pay her. Doesn't that make us her boss?"

"You're the one with your shorts around your ankles, red butt-cheeks, and sperm dripping down your legs. Does it feel like we're the boss?"

"The university is going to ask me to sign papers stating that I've taken responsibility for your behavior," I said. "That means that *I* am the boss. I'll make the rules, enforce the curfews, decide what goes on at your parties, and control how you treat your women."

"Gotcha." Arny turned around to face me, his shorts and underwear still around his ankles, his dick, oversized for a scrawny runt like him, pointing straight upward. "Lucky for us, we don't have any women to mis-treat. We never have bitches here: except the ones who help serve meals. And let me tell you, those chicks head out the second they've cleared the last plate."

Despite my resolve, my certainty that it would destroy my position with these young me, a part of me desperately wanted to get on my knees and take that cock between my lips, kissing, caressing, sucking it until I'd swallowed every drop of that precious juice running down his legs and still leaking from the tip of his penis.

I called on every bit of the will power James had drilled into me in my fight against the very reflexes he'd also drilled into me. I'd never dreamed, while I'd been under his training, that his punishment could actually make me stronger against a male. Now, though, I saw the possibilities. But it would happen only if I let it.

"That sounds like a pretty pathetic attitude." I made my voice a growl.

"Well," Russell said, "it happens to be the truth. Last year, we got exactly one co-ed from here, and that one girl from Cambridge High into the frat house. The girl from Cambridge High's parents dragged her off before she finished her second beer. The co-ed took one look at the place, then ripped off Mike's fraternity pin, tossed it on the floor, and ran out."

"I could have guessed that without you telling me. Answer me just one question. Is that the way you want it? Or would you rather have women wanting to check this place out, lining up to date any of you guys."

"While we're wishing," Russell said, "might as well put something in about winning the lottery. Once, this fraternity attracted the cool guys, guys bitches go for. Sure, we'd like to have more chicks around. Even the gay brothers like chicks. Girls smell better, they're nicer to look at, and, well, they're chicks."

I had a Julie Andrews moment—like that ancient movie *Sound of Music* where Julie Andrews decides she's been sent by God to rescue a bunch of children from the Nazis or something like that. Except, in that movie Julie Andrews had been the young thing horning in on the thirty-year-old Countess, like Amber had horned in on me.

Still, I knew I could help these guys. I'd paid attention to James's training. I knew what motivated women, and what made men appealing. If Arny and Russell were typical of the guys in the fraternity, I didn't have much to work with in terms of raw material. Fortunately, most college women didn't have high standards. I thought I had a chance to make a difference.

"First, Arny," I said, "pull up your pants. If I want to see your dick jerking around like a flag stuck coming down a flagpole, I'll tell you. Second, I happen to know something about women. If you want to be attractive to women, I can help you. But you'll have to follow my orders, even if they sometimes don't make sense to you. All of my orders."

Arny bent over, reaching for his shorts. "But—"

"It's up to you. I can just take the job, clean up after you, and make sure you follow the University regulations, and stop there. Or I can help you."

Arny struggled to get his sorts over his still raging dick. "How much extra is this going to cost us?"

I should have thought of that angle. "What do you think it's worth?"

Arny jerked his shorts over his dick and stared at my breasts, going back into a trance. Finally he shook himself like a dog. "I'll never have the money it'd be worth to get a chick like Amber McGill. But hey, boffing a girl like her, that's pure fantasy. She's almost as hot as, ah, you are, Missus."

That last remark saved him from fifty or so spankings. Amber had been a common name eighteen years earlier, but I wondered how many super-hot Ambers there might be at Cambridge State. Could the Amber McGill Arny wanted so desperately be the same Amber who'd been licking my husband's butt the previous morning? Considering that James would cut the hottest co-ed on campus out of the herd, it wouldn't be that big a coincidence.

"I can't work miracles," I said. "If Amber is the blonde slut with size D breasts and the tramp-stamp of a pair of geckos on the base of her spine, I'm afraid she's out of your league."

"Amber is not a slu—"

"Told you she's impossible," Russell said. "Besides, she's a senior and you're a sophomore. You could be a millionaire and she still wouldn't look at you."

"I didn't say impossible," I corrected. "It's a long stretch, though."

"You know her?" Arny leaned forward, his eyes, for once, on my face rather than on my tits. "You *know* Amber McGill? I've been dreaming about her ever since I walked into Calculus and saw her sitting there at the front of the class, leaning forward so she could hear better. She wore this pink sweater that showed just a hint of tummy, but scooped down-"

She'd been leaning forward so her prof could look down that top and see her double-D's was my guess, although she had to have some smarts to take calculus. I remembered studying my ass off just to pull out a marginal B in that class.

Russell rolled his eyes. "We heard about that damned sweater so often last year, we bought him one. You should have seen him hold it like a security blanket. I think he jerked off in it every night."

"Did not."

Arny flinched a little when I took his chin and turned it so he faced me. "Tell the truth. Did you masturbate into a sweater?"

"Of course I didn't. That would be juvin—"

"The truth. You know I'll have to punish you if you—"

"Not *every* night. I might have a few times..." he paused, "a week. Amber McGill is beautiful. Anyone would want her."

"Okay." I shook my head. "No more masturbating into sweaters that didn't even belong to the girl you want. That's your desperation talking and there's nothing a woman runs from faster than a desperate guy. If you follow orders, I can improve you guys to the point where you can get girlfriends. We'll have to set Amber as a stretch goal, though. She's, uh, dating a professor right now."

A couple of tears sparkled in Arny's eyelashes. "Damn."

"Hey." Russell slapped Arny on the shoulder. "You just got yourself a new nickname--Stretch. We'll tell the guys not to let anyone know it stands for the size of your dick. It'll be all over the campus in a week."

That might work. If a man brags about his own cock, women will run away. But if she hears whispers coming from someone else, she's likely to be intrigued. Considering he was well under six feet in height, Arny's boner had a definite heft to it.

Like a lightning bolt from a clear sky, I saw the possibilities. If I could get Amber away from James, win her for Arny—Stretch, James would *have* to come back to me, at least for another year. There was no way his pride could stand being connected with the *second* hottest co-ed on campus, so he wouldn't dare find a substitute for Amber until she'd graduated. A year would give me time to persuade him I was irreplaceable.

"Tell you what, Arn—I mean Stretch. I'll do everything I can to help you get that bitch."

Chapter Four

The rest of the returning fraternity brothers were due the following day, so I ordered Stretch and Russell to spend fifteen minutes each in their showers with the water on full cold, then had them report to me naked.

There was no way they could attract women if they smelled like vomit and self-abuse.

While they showered, I went to work on my new room.

Fortunately, the chest of drawers and wardrobe were empty, with all of Russell's clothes on the floor. I tossed the fetid rags into a laundry pile in the hallway outside my door, then yanked down thirty years worth of pinups from the wall.

I still had a couple minutes left, so I scrubbed my tub—something the previous generations of cleaners had neglected, then stripped down and inspected myself in the mirror.

I didn't look any older than I had a week before. My breasts weren't quite as perky as they'd been when James had singled me out as an innocent freshman, but they didn't droop, either, which wasn't bad for thirty-year-old C-cups.

A wicked memory swished into my brain and I walked out, naked to where Stretch's cum formed large globs on my desk. I'd have to punish him for not cleaning it up right away. In the meantime, I gave myself the pleasure of deeply inhaling that nasty but sexy smell of male semen.

I took a few breaths. If it had been James's semen, he would have required me to lick up every drop. But cold sperm didn't appeal to me and I needed to teach Stretch to clean up after himself. I left the spunk untouched, climbed into the tub, spread my legs around the faucet, and let warm water pound down over my pussy and clit.

I wasn't interested in dating the boys, but that didn't mean I hadn't noticed their raging dicks, been intrigued by the sheer volume of spunk they'd produced or impressed by the force with which Stretch had shot his wad over my desk.

It took me only seconds before the water and a little handwork brought me to the best orgasm I could remember. I felt hugely rebellious at coming without James's permission, without him watching to supervise. But that was fine--I might be over the hill but these college kids found me sexy. With luck and some hard work, I'd have him back, and he could impose his rules on me once more.

The only annoyance was, I found it hard to concentrate on James when that rush of orgasm overtook me. Brandon the librarian kept slipping back into my mind, which was completely unfair. Sure the librarian had a body that shouted non-stop sex, but he didn't seem much interested in delivering on that promise. I still smarted from his rejection when I'd summoned up the nerve to offer him no-obligation oral sex. What kind of man would turn down a free blowjob, anyway? I definitely didn't need more of that aggravation.

* * * *

I kept the boys waiting, spending my time cleaning my new room, making notes of what I'd need to buy to get rid of some of the pure maleness that clung to it like painted-on-testosterone, and simply letting the guys steam. If they were going to date, they had to get used to waiting.

Finally, I put back on my party dress. Since I wasn't wearing panties or a bra, that didn't take long.

The guys waited where I'd told them to, in what had once been the fraternity president's office but which I'd decided would serve as my own office.

When I saw their towels wrapped around their waists, I drew on twelve years of experience. "What the hell do you guys think you're doing? Can't you follow the simplest order in the world? How the shit am I supposed to make you date material if you can't even do that?"

"Huh?" Stretch scratched his nose. "We've been here, we've been waiting."

I grabbed both towels and yanked. "I said naked."

With James, a boner had taken time and effort—and generally a moderate amount of punishment—of me. I believed him when he explained my spankings were really for my benefit, but he got a lot of pleasure out of pounding his hand or his quirt over my butt as well.

Then again, James wasn't twenty. Both of these guys had orgasmed within the past two hours, but their dicks stood at full attention, like overactive soldiers.

"We were just standing here," Russell complained.

I poked him in his sunken chest. "Answer honestly. Did you masturbate in the shower? What about you, Stretch?"

Eyes on my breasts, both young men nodded.

I shook my head. "That's two orders you've chosen not to follow. I instructed you to wait here naked, yet you stood around with towels. I didn't give you permission to jerk off, but you did. Do you think women like guys with no control over themselves? Do you really think anyone's looking for a man who squirts nasty-juice every time he gets a look at a tit or a pussy? Do you know what happens to boys who fail to follow orders?"

"Come on, missus," Russell protested. "We just wore towels while we waited. I mean, what if anyone saw two guys naked together? We would have taken them off if you'd asked us to. And I don't see why it's your business what we do in the privacy of our showers.

I'd turned toward Stretch while talking but I whirled back on Russell, closing the distance between us until my covered breasts pushed against his too-soft stomach. "You're right. It is your business. It's your business if you want to keep being losers, if you want mother palm and her five daughters to be the only lovers you ever know, if you want to spend your college years surrounded by some of the most beautiful women in the world and know you can look but you can't touch. It's only *my* business if you want to get some of those women to like you, to beg you to take them out on dates, demand that you carry them to bed and pound your dicks deep inside of them."

"Oh, shit," Stretch said. "When you talk dirty—"

"I'm not talking dirty. I'm talking about you choosing to stay losers."

"That's not what I want," Stretch said. "I'm ready to follow instructions."

"Sorry. This isn't an *a la carte* menu. Either every man in the fraternity obeys all my orders or I'm out of here. There are other men on this campus, real men, who'd be willing to make some sacrifices for the chance to have Amber writhing under their bodies, feel their hard dicks inside her cunt, her mouth, her ass, between those beautiful double-D cups she slings around like watermelons just wanting to be grabbed and sucked. Can you imagine, Stretch, how good it would feel to bring yourself to the point of orgasm just sliding your cock between her tight tits while she tongues your butt, then pulling back and spraying all over her pretty pouty fa—"

"Oh, shit. I'm coming again." Stretch's entire body spasmed and I had to hop away to keep from getting spattered.

"I'm not saying we don't want you to teach us," Russell whined. "I just want to be reasonable here. We're not children."

"Leave that alone," I commanded Stretch when he reached for his towel, clearly intent on cleaning up the cum mess he'd made.

I didn't tell him I was impressed by his volume—this was not the time to yield anything to his ego. Still, I couldn't help noticing that he'd produced more spunk on his third orgasm in two hours than James managed on his first. If Stretch ever got Amber in his bed, she was going to discover a new experience in overflowing mouthfuls. I had to force myself not to grin at the thought.

"You want this reasonable, do you?" I asked Russell.

"Is that so much to ask?"

"I'll tell you what's reasonable. You're a sophomore so you spent your freshman year here. Think about the co-eds walking around. Think about their short little skirts, the way they crop their tops so high the bottoms of their nice firm tits hang out in plain sight."

"Come on," Russell said. "That doesn't have anything—"

"Now think about the way their asses wiggle when they walk. You know why they wiggle, don't you? Because their asses are attached to their pussies. When co-eds flip their hair, lick their lips, they're sending signals—the signal is, *you can fuck me*. But they don't send those signals to guys like you—they want the right guys.

"Those girls are hoping to get laid, praying that some cool guy will notice them, call them out of the crowd and pay attention to them, then take them off to his bed—if only for an hour or a night. They believe that they can prove themselves, with their hands, their pussies, their mouths, their tits or their asses. They'll do whatever they can, whatever it takes, to get themselves one of the winners, a cool guy to call their own."

"That's bullshit," Russell argued. "These are southern girls. They don't put out. Besides, if they were so desperate to get themselves a guy, why not look around. There are as many guys here as girls. So, how come we don't all have girlfriends?"

"Good question. Why do you think that is?"

"Because girls are stupid."

I laughed. "Keep telling yourself that, Russell. You can spend the rest of your college career assuring yourself that you're not getting laid just because girls are dumb. Here's my question, though. If *they're* so dumb, how come *you're* the one who suffers for it?"

"I don't know." Anguish tore at Stretch's voice. "It seems like there are a couple of dozen guys that all the chicks hang over. And those guys are all jerks. Girls should go for guys like us, guys who'll be nice to them. They should know they don't have a chance with those few guys. So, they end up not getting any and I don't get any. We could all be better off."

I shook my head. "You guys have it easy. If one of you gets laid by some dog, you'll get slapped on the back. But if a woman settles for a loser, she's ruined. All of her friends will look down on her. It's better to do without, or even to blow a cool when you know you're his third date of the night, than to settle for a loser. Women don't follow the same kind of logic you men do but we're not stupid. We don't give a shit about finding a man if that man isn't worth finding. We're going to compete for the winners. As far as we're concerned, losers like you aren't even in the game."

"But girls like jerks," Russell said.

"Suppose you had twenty beautiful women lining up to suck your dick. Wouldn't that make you a little arrogant? It doesn't hurt to be a jerk. In fact, being a jerk is one way to advertise that you're not desperate, that you have all the girls you can stand."

Russell shook his head. "Let me get this straight. If I heard you right, you're saying that being a jerk is a way to get a girl to like you. That doesn't make sense."

"I'm not saying you can be a complete jerk. But unless you act like you can take any particular girl or leave her, you're never going to get her. Face it, it's going to take extreme measures to turn your fraternity around. You may not understand my orders, and I have no intention of explaining them to you and letting you decide whether you want to follow them. Either you're going to trust me, do what I tell you, or I'm gone.

"Now, are you in, or should I find a fraternity that wants to improve their status, that's ready to be the chair girls want to sit on."

"Shit, lady."

"Call me ma'am or call me missus."

"Sorry, missus," Russell said. "I'll do what you say."

"Then bend over and grab your ankles."

He followed my instructions.

"You, too, Stretch."

"But I'll get semen on myself."

"You think I didn't notice you squirting like you're some kind of April Fools trick? Grab them."

I was going to have to invest in a quirt if I kept this job. In the meantime, though, the leather belt stuck through the greasy jeans Russell had left on the floor next to a not-too-clean t-shirt and even less clean underwear would do.

I jerked it through the loops and gave Russell twenty hard slaps on each cheek. Since I'd already given Stretch some, and since he hadn't argued with me, I settled for five on each.

Leaving the two grasping their ankles, I went to the desk, grabbed a pair of scissors, and cut the belt into thin straps.

"Lesson one," I announced. "You've got to learn to be both aware of your maleness and in control of it. No more ejaculations just because you're horny."

Russell straightened. "How the hell are we going to—"

"One more question and I'm gone. Now grab those ankles and hold on."

When he bent back over, I walked behind him, grabbed his stiff cock, and wrapped the leather straps around it, tying a couple of loops around his balls.

"Jeez, I'm—"

"You will speak when I give you permission." I gave his dick a squeeze. "If you come on my hands without my permission, you're really going to regret it, Russell."

"Sorry, ma'am." He gritted his teeth and held on.

A bit of cum leaked out the end of his dick but I decided to pretend I didn't see it. He was barely twenty, after all, and just starting to learn self-control.

Stretch wasn't so easy. "I'm only going to do this once." I wiped the semen that dripped down his legs up with my hands.

He shivered, his dick hardening again. Damn, after all the work it took to get James hard, these boys were like Christmas in September.

"If you could—"

"Don't even think about it, Stretch." I held out my spunk-covered hands. "Lick this off."

"That's *my* sperm. Gross."

"You want Amber to swallow it, don't you? Maybe you should have an idea of what you're asking for. Anyway, you gave me dirty hands and you're going to clean them."

"You'd better do it," Russell said. "I sure don't want to."

I let Stretch straighten his back to lick my hands clean, then made him bend over again while I strapped his dick.

"These harnesses will keep you aware of your cocks," I explained. The straps around your balls should help you control your release. Women like it when guys think they're sexy, but a man without control of himself is as useless as a capon in a henhouse.

"We can't go around like this," Russell said. "People would—"

I'd cut up Russell's belt, so I yanked Stretch's out of his jeans and gave Russell a couple of hard swats with it. "Women also don't like slow learners."

"Sorry, ma'am."

"We're going to have to buy you some new clothes. In the meantime, you can put on your jeans and t-shirts. Clean t-shirts.

"What's wrong with—"

Russell shushed Stretch, but not in time to spare him a belt striping. "Stale sweat is disgusting. Just because *you* can't smell it doesn't mean a woman can't. Now, come on."

We piled into Russell's pickup, with him driving and me sitting between them.

I kept a hand on each of their dicks as we headed toward the motel where I'd left my few things.

"I've got to stop in at the library." I tossed my motel key to Stretch. "Load my clothes and bowl in the truck, then join me there."

"Yes, missus." Stretch didn't seem in any hurry to get out of the truck, though. I wasn't a college graduate, but it didn't take a degree to know what he was about.

"Did you hear me when I said women don't like men who are desperate?"

"Yeah?"

"So, even if it drives you absolutely crazy, you've got to learn to walk away from it. I took his hard dick in my hand and twisted it. "Sure you want me to give you a hand job. But that isn't going to happen. And no girl is going to do it, either, unless she thinks you could walk away and get it from just about any other co-ed in the school if she doesn't put out."

"So I just pull away while you're stroking me?"

I nodded. "You've got it."

"Damn. This isn't going to be easy."

I couldn't remember when I'd ever laughed as often as since meeting these guys. "If it were easy, everyone would have Amber's tongue in their ass."

Instead of just James.

* * * *

Brandon looked up when I walked into the library. "Damn, you look good, Nicole. A little dressy for visiting the library, though, isn't it."

"I need some help."

"I've got your Monster profile started. If you'd like, I can put together a resume for you. I'll need some details on—"

"I took the job at the Pi Iota Sigma fraternity."

He shook his head. "That's crazy. They're the biggest losers in the school."

"That's what I need help with. There've got to be some yard sales. I'm looking for exercise equipment."

He nodded. "I can help with that."

Dominating the guys had been easy. Giving orders to a man who was only a year or two younger than me was harder. Especially because my pussy was sopping wet from stroking two cocks, from spanking two butts, and from the forbidden orgasm I'd given myself in the tub. I desperately needed Brandon to order me to get on my knees and take him in my mouth. That, however, wasn't happening.

"I may need some help loading stuff. Why don't you drive me and the guys can follow?"

"Guys?"

Russell and Stretch showed good timing walking into the library right then.

Already, the two looked better. The straps around their cocks made them more aware of their bodies and they didn't slouch the way they had, earlier. Their butts had to sting from their belting, so they jutted their hips forward just a little, giving each of them an admittedly false look of confidence. Confidence, though, can be faked. And false confidence can turn into the real thing.

"Brandon," I said. "This is Russell and Stretch. They're the president and treasurer of the Pi Iota Sigma fraternity."

Brandon looked jealous, which I took as a good sign. If my plan was going to work, I needed the handsome librarian to play his role. The guys were too young for James to consider them a threat. Sure, I intended to help Stretch steal Amber away from James, but James would take that as a sign of Amber's immaturity. If I could show him that I'd happily replaced him in my own life, that would twist him where it hurt. He'd beg me to come back.

Following Brandon's directions, we spent the next three hours driving around Cambridge. I located a couple weight sets, a bench, a heavy bag, and a couple of speed bags, and had Russell buy them.

It was six by the time I decided I'd found everything Cambridge had to offer.

"Back to the dollar store," I told Brandon.

"I really should get back to—"

"Brandon," I interrupted, "I need you to do something for me."

"Sure, Nicole. What's that?"

I'd spent a lot of time thinking about it but I'd finally figured Brandon out. "I know you're a sub, Brandon. That's okay if it's your thing but it isn't going to do the job for me. I'm going to need you to learn to give a convincing imitation of a dom. Do you understand?"

"I'm not a submissive. I just want—"

"Lying to yourself doesn't help your situation. Now, are you willing to try?"

"No offense, but I've already risked losing my job for you by taking off when I should have been working. Why should I participate in whatever kinky fantasies you're cooking up?"

"Two reasons." I dragged a fingernail all the way up his inseam, from his knee to his crotch.

His dick swelled amazingly under his too-baggy khakis.

"Wha—"

"First, since you're a sub, you want to make me happy and playing my game will make me happy. Second, once you agree, I'm going to let you come in my hands. Don't tell me you haven't regretted turning me down when I offered you a blowjob last night. Unfortunately for you, you're not going to get another offer that good. But you'll take the hand job and thank me for it."

"I don't get why *you* want this."

I considered telling him the truth. Brandon was a sub, after all. He probably wouldn't think he deserved more than to be a tool in my plan to win back my husband. Still, James had taught me not to explain things to a sub. You give the orders and she, or he, obeys. "You let me worry about why I want it and start worrying about how you're going to give it to me."

He pulled in front of the dollar store and Russell pulled his truck, now loaded with weights and exercise equipment, alongside.

I rolled down my window. "You two head inside and buy enough leather collars for every member of the fraternity, plus one more. Be out here in exactly five minutes."

"Yes, missus," Stretch said. He and Russell jogged into the store.

"Pull down your zipper and yank it out," I told Brandon.

"Here? In public? I could lose my jo—"

"I'll tell you when you can talk. Right now, I want to see your cock."

"But—"

"Good point. I'll need to see your butt, too. A lot if you're not more obedient. You've got four minutes before the guys are back."

"What if they're early?"

"Then they'll watch and I'll punish them later. Pull out that dick. Now!"

"Okay." He pulled down his zipper and drew it out.

James had a nice dick. Brandon's, though, was as long as Stretch's—a good eight inches—and substantially thicker.

It took all the will power I could summon not to get down on my knees and take that monster in my mouth, but I'd frighten Brandon away if I did. He didn't need the kind of service, the near-worship James had depended on. Instead, he needed to worship a woman. It wasn't natural for me, but I had to become that woman for him.

Instead of giving myself the pleasure of taking him into my mouth, of worshiping his huge dick with my tongue, of taking his load on my tits, my face, my hair, and my tongue, I squeezed down as hard as I could and jerked my hand up and down along that hard rod.

"You've been a good boy," I told him. "And you get a reward."

"Thank you, Nicole."

"Call me missus," I said.

"Uh, thank you, missus, uh...I'm com—"

I'd felt his body tremble before he came and pointed his dick at the windshield, letting his dick splash wads of spunk against the glass.

"That was—"

"That was completely unsatisfactory," I lied. "I told you to take four minutes and you lasted about two strokes. Now clean up this mess. And if I ever catch you wearing underwear again, I'll have to punish you."

"Yes, missus."

My young protégés headed out of the dollar store one and a half minutes later, exactly on schedule. Brandon had located a box of tissues and was wiping his spunk from the windshield. The car had filled with the rich scent of male cum, and my pussy was dripping. Again.

I grabbed a couple of the tissues from the, handed them to him, and pulled up my dress. "Wipe me off, Brandon."

"But the guys—"

"This time, I'm choosing you to wipe me this time. Perhaps next time it'll be one of them. Would you rather I skip your turn."

"No ma'am. Thank you, missus." He drew the tissues across my shaved lips, collecting my female dew.

I let him wipe a bit longer than really necessary, then snatched his hand away from me. "I said you could clean me, not fondle me. Now, go home. You may stop by the Pi Iota Sigma fraternity house tomorrow morning to get your new orders."

He nodded, his face a picture of frustration and joy. Well, I knew those feelings. When I got James back, I'd experience them again.

I lowered my window. "Hand me one of those collars, boys."

Stretch rummaged through the large grocery sack he carried. "Which one?"

"Do you have one with spikes?"

He pulled out a leather and chrome number. It was almost too much—nothing *I'd* want to wear. Then again, I wouldn't be wearing it.

"Lean over this way," I ordered Brandon.

He obeyed and I turned to face him, but he stopped before I wanted him to.

I jerked his head down—into a position that was both a bit more submissive and that also brought his mouth to where my breasts stretched the fabric of my party dress.

"Don't move." I managed to keep my voice steady, but doing so strained every ounce of my being.

I fastened the collar around his neck, leaving it loose enough that it wouldn't constrict his breathing, but tight enough that it wouldn't catch on things. "This collar marks you as my property, Brandon. If another woman wants you, you will seek my permission before you accept—or reject. You'll wear this collar at all times. You'll wear it to bed, in the shower, while you're working out, when you're at work."

"But—"

I looped my fist through the collar and twisted just enough that he'd feel the constriction around his throat. "There are no buts, Brandon. You will follow my orders."

"I just don't understand what kind of game you're playing here."

"It isn't your job to understand. It's your job to obey your orders."

"Yes, missus."

Chapter Five

"Get up. Time to go."

I kicked Russell and then Stretch.

"Huh?" Russell rubbed his eyes as he sprawled across the mattress on the floor of the room he and Stretch now shared. What time is it?"

I'd made them sleep naked, of course, except for their new collars and the straps I'd wrapped around their dicks.

Morning was a hard time for me. Looking at those two hard cocks got my knees shaking with an almost desperate need to grovel on the ground and take them in my mouth, letting their cum squirt over my face.

Instead, I kicked Russell in the ribs—again.

I missed James more in the morning than other times of day. We'd had our rituals, things that many people would consider disgusting or humiliating, but that had bonded us together. For more than ten years, he'd showered me with a face full of male spunk every morning, before he'd made me tongue-clean his ass. Those routines had given me a sense of belonging, a place in the world—at least a place in James's world. Amber had ripped that from me and I missed it.

Those two hard cocks reminded me of James.

If I yielded to temptation, though, I'd lose all of my power over the guys. And if that happened, I could kiss goodbye to my plan to win Amber for Stretch—and reclaim the place I deserved in James's bed and in his heart.

Instead of licking his balls, I kicked Russell a third time.

"Ouch. Damn, lady."

"Missus."

"Damn, missus. What time is it?" He glanced at the clock on the floor next to his mattress. "It's five in the morning. No wonder I'm still—"

"The two of you have five minutes to shave, shower, and put on deodorant, then report to me in my office."

"Didn't take long to turn into *her* office, did it?" Stretch grumbled.

"No coming in the showers," I added.

"Can we take off our collars and these dick holders at least?" Russell was whining and I laid a leather belt across his naked ass.

"No whining and no you can't take those off."

"She's going to get me Amber," Stretch whispered. "I wish you'd humor her."

I gave him a stripe as well. "You've already wasted a minute."

* * * *

"I've always hated running." After a mere two miles, Russell gasped for breath, pausing between every couple of words. "Running with you is certainly a more pleasant experience."

"A more pleasant experience, what?"

"A more pleasant experience, uh, missus."

I'd forgotten to have the boys buy leashes for their collars but I suspected leashes would scare away more women than they'd attract, anyway. To win Amber, aI was going to have to teach these guys to blend submissiveness with strength since few Mississippi co-eds were looking for men who wouldn't at least put up a fight before succumbing to their pussies. I wouldn't make them wear the leashes in public but I'd buy them anyway for use in the house. Nonverbal reinforcement could be so much more effective than threats.

"Are you trying to tell me something, Russell?"

"The tongue-tied idiot means," Stretch interrupted, that you're completely hot and that he's running the three-legged race by himself "

I was setting the pace for the guys, a moderate six-minute mile, so I hadn't noticed that the tip of Russell's dick, constrained by its straps, hung down below his shorts.

I reached between his legs and flicked that sensitive tip with my thumbnail. "Save your energy for running."

Just for fun, I upped the pace, thinking we'd do a five and a half minute mile and then work the weights. The boys had only turned twenty that summer: they should have been able to keep up with a thirty-year-old woman with no problem.

A quarter of a mile later, both Russell and Stretch were heaving their guts out on the side of the road.

Even without leashes, I wasn't helpless. I tugged Stretch's leather belt from around my waist, then made them pull down their shorts and grab their ankles. After a couple of minutes letting the anticipation build, I gave them each ten swats. Co-eds were looking for guys who could perform at distance, not for sprinters.

We barely made it home before Brandon appeared.

Although I hadn't run as hard as I normally did, I'd sweat in the early September heat. My cropped t-shirt clung to my breasts like shrink-wrap, and the silky fabric of my high-cut shorts outlined my camel toe. Brandon's dick was instantly at attention.

"Reporting as ordered, missus." Brandon made his voice ironic.

I'd never had any problems with being submissive, but I was a woman. I couldn't speak for the rest of the country, but in Mississippi, at least, women were expected to be submissive. Guys who simply needed orders, who got turned on by being dominated, seemed like freaks.

A part of me wanted to comfort Brandon, to tell him I understood his pain. But that would frighten him.

I tossed him a pair of shorts. "Strip down and put these on. I want you to help the guys with their weightlifting."

He fingered his button-down oxford shirt. "I'm not wearing a t-shirt under this."

"Did I tell you to wear a t-shirt? I'd make you do this naked, but I don't want your dick rubbing against weight benches I might use myself.

He took the shorts and headed for the frat house but I stopped him.

"Change here, where I can watch you."

"You already know what I've got."

I grabbed his collar and pulled.

He tumbled out of the car, landing on his knees. Not that I was strong enough to lift close to two hundred pounds of muscular male that way, but he hadn't wanted to be choked and he was, after all, a submissive.

"I don't have time for backtalk, Brandon. Strip."

I watched while he stripped. I'd seen him in his clothes, and I'd jerked him off in his car, but this was the first time I'd seen him naked.

He wasn't as tall as James, but he was even better built, with smooth olive skin and a bush of hair surrounding his swollen dick.

I'd thought James had broken me of the habit of wanting dick in my pussy. He'd used my mouth or ass for his dick, occasionally stuffing my vagina with a big dildo. Over the twelve years I'd been with him, I couldn't remember more than seven or eight times he'd put me on my hands and knees and taken me doggy-style. Still, Brandon's big dick gave me wicked ideas. When I won James back, I decided, I was definitely going to insist on a bit more pussy action. In fact, I'd ask James to lie on his back and let me pleasure myself on him. I could barely restrain myself from climbing on top of Brandon. Maybe I could have the boys lick on my tits while I…

I shook my head. The guys needed to think of me as an unattainable goal. The second they thought they could take me, they'd stop listening and start making demands.

I took out my frustration by yelling at Brandon. "Faster."

"Sorry, missus." He reached for the shorts.

"Let me take care of that first."

He froze. "Another hand job?"

"Are you giving me orders, Brandon? Because believe me, if you are, I'll make you regret it."

"Just anticipating."

"Control your anticipation because that isn't happening." I had a few straps left from Russell's belt and I wrapped those around Brandon's dick and balls.

If my hands trembled a little while I secured the ties, neither of us dared mention it. "Report here every morning before work to help the guys with their weightlifting routines. I'll check on the strap and determine if I need to tighten it. Any questions?"

"No, ma'am."

"Then put on your shorts and head out back."

"What about underwear?"

"You're out of the underwear business, Brandon. When I look at you, I want to see the outline of your dick through your pants fabric.

"But at work—"

"That co-ed library assistant can look as much as she wants. If she wants to touch it, have her come to me. I'll decide whether to give her permission."

"I'd really rather have yo—"

It hurt to see him like this, especially since I wanted him too. But I wasn't getting James back by having a sub-sub relationship with Brandon. Brandon needed me to dominate him to be happy and James needed to see how happy I could make a man.

"You know, Brandon, what you'd rather have doesn't really enter into the equation, does it? You get is what I tell you you can have."

"Oh. I guess I'd better go help the guys, then."

Russell and Stretch lay on the ground like overheated puppies, their tongues hanging out, sweat dripping from their chests, and their shorts pulled up high enough to show the red stripes where I'd spanked them.

"Can we eat now?" Stretch demanded.

"Watch me carefully," I said. "I'm going to demonstrate weightlifting technique. Brandon will supervise you and report on how you do. You really don't want him to give me a negative report."

I straddled the bench, lying down on my back, the lightly loaded bar on the supports over my chest.

The silk of my shorts and brushed cotton of my cropped 't' provided unfamiliar friction, considering that James had insisted I lift weights nude. Those sensations, coupled with three sets of male eyes looking at me, hoping that my breasts would slide free of their minimal confinement, and the knowledge they'd soon realize they could stare up my shorts and get a good look at my shaven pussy, made me wet.

I grasped the bar, lifted it from the support, lowered it to my chest, then extended my arms until they were barely bent. I lowered on a five-count, feeling the negative burn, then lifted again.

During that second lift, my breasts broke free of their pathetic covering.

All three males groaned.

Damn, that was hot. James had kept me naked, but he'd rarely bothered to look while I went through my workout routine. Occasionally he'd think it amusing to fuck my mouth while I lifted, or to sit on my face and have me clean his ass. But I couldn't remember the last time he'd simply appreciated what was still, despite my thirty years, a pretty good body.

I scolded myself for thinking negative thoughts about my once and future husband. After all, he'd insisted I take up weightlifting and encouraged me to turn my short jogs into eight and ten mile runs. Without his support, I wouldn't have this body in the first place.

I completed my twelve repetitions, then let Brandon wipe me down me as we replaced the bars.

"Three sets like that," I said. "Nice and slow. That'll help with your pecs and triceps. Co-eds notice things like that, believe me."

I waited until I'd finished talking before tugging down my shirt.

There wasn't anything I could do to hide where my pussy, excited by the three males staring at me, had left a wet spot on the bench. Instead, I decided to turn it into a lesson.

"Brandon and Russell, both of you have questioned my authority today. Because of that, Stretch gets to lap up that wet spot."

"Really?" He looked not at my breasts, for once, but where my juices stuck my shorts to my twat. "Cool."

"Use your tongue for licking, not talking. I'm going in to get the house ready for the arriving fraternity members. I want you three to put in a workout, then come in and take your showers."

"Missus, we already showered today," Russell said.

"Guess you don't get to lick my pussy juices tomorrow, either. You do what I say, without question."

"Yes, missus."

While they worked out, I took my own shower. Once again, it took me only seconds to bring myself to a guilty orgasm. I tried to think about James, the attention he'd showered on me as he'd trained me to reach my full potential. Mental pictures of Brandon kept interfering. Not that the man wasn't drop-dead gorgeous—now that I'd seen him naked I was even more aware of that. Still, he was a submissive. Put two submissives together and nothing gets done.

Chapter Six

I spent some time with the cook, cutting sweets and empty carbs from the fraternity menu. No wonder the guys were pudgy. They'd browbeat the cook into providing ice cream with every meal. That and the huge quantities of beer they consumed would undo all of my plans—and move James forever beyond my reach.

I knew I was crazy to do it, but I insisted on checking out all three of the guys after their own showers, making sure they'd cleaned everything and that they hadn't lost control and masturbated. Brandon looked so hot with his dick trussed up and his cut muscles straining that I barely resisted throwing myself at him.

Instead, I stroked his cock until he trembled and he tottered on the edge, then handed him a shopping list. "When you come back tomorrow morning," I told him, "bring these with you. It's obvious you can't dress yourself—you look like an old man in those baggy khakis.

His jaw strained but he nodded.

"I'll be checking your dick, so don't masturbate. If that co-ed you work with wants to suck you off, I'll consider it, but call me for permission."

"I need some relief."

I pinched one of his nipples. "What you need is what I say you need. Come back tomorrow at six-thirty. Wear running shorts, your collar and straps, and nothing else."

"Yes, missus."

It was all I could do not to rush back upstairs to my room and masturbate again. The man was seriously hot.

Early that afternoon, the remainder of the returning fraternity brothers wandered in.

My task was far worse than I'd imagined. Stretch and Russell weren't the worst—they weren't even average. Every single brother was overweight, nerdy, and sweaty.

I greeted the parents who were dropping off their sons, told them I'd set new curfews and that their sons would be under close adult supervision, and sent them home.

A couple of the dads suggested they try me out, but I laughed them off, drawing strength from my hope that I could win James back. I no longer felt that desperate need to be owned by someone just to be owned. And a fling with one of the dads would set a horrible example for the guys.

At five, I lined up the fifteen of them and ordered them to strip.

Chuck, one of the fattest of the bunch and the one I'd identified as most likely to cause me troubles, shook his head. "You're the cleaning lady. You don't give orders around here. And where are the pinups we had in our ballroom? Some of those were collectable."

From the very beginning of our relationship, James had made it clear that he was the master, I the submissive. My gut said that I had to do the same thing here, putting down any attempt at rebellion so harshly he'd never even consider fighting back again.

"That's where you're wrong, Chuck. I am the boss here. I do give the orders."

"Make m—"

The poor kid didn't even put up his guard. I drove my palm into his jaw, them followed up with a knee to his groin.

He went to the ground, holding his injured balls like they were sacred.

"Bring me a pair of scissors," I told Stretch.

Stretch ran to my office, then quickly walked back.

I took them, then snipped Chuck's shirt down the back, continuing with the cut when I reached his shorts.

His tighty-whities had semen stains in the front, but I ignored those, cutting his clothes off until he lay on the ground completely naked.

"You see, Chuck, I decide what goes on around here. I've decided that I'm going to transform your fraternity into something you can be proud of. I've decided that I'm going to turn you guys around so far that you'll have co-eds lining up outside your front door for a chance to pay to take you out on a date and have a chance of getting one of your dicks inside of her. The president and treasurer of your fraternity agree with my program. Now, do you want to quit, or do you want to become someone women want?"

Tears ran down his cheeks. "Get real. As far as the chicks around here are concerned, I'm the invisible man."

"Invisible boy is more like it," I said. "Roll over."

He didn't respond, so I kicked him in the ribs and told Russell and another kid, Davie, to do the job.

As I'd suspected, there was a reason for Chuck's reluctance. His dick barely stuck out through rolls of fat.

"I agree there isn't much there, Chuck. But here's the thing. Women care about that—who wouldn't prefer a big swollen cock if they could get it. But big dicks are like big tits. You can be a pretty girl, get as many dates as you can stand, and still barely carry more than a couple of mosquito bites on your chest. A guy without much in the cock department can learn to make his women happy in other ways. Besides, once we get some of this fat off of you, I guarantee you a couple more inches."

"No girl—"

"Don't tell me what girls will or won't do. I am a girl. I've been one all my life. I spent twelve years of my life with a guy whose dick barely reached six inches and every day I told him what a monster he had. I was happy. You don't need to be overly endowed like Stretch here to give a woman a perfectly satisfactory ride. What you've got to do is believe in yourself, believe in your dick, and learn the techniques that will make you a great lover."

Chuck managed just the hint of a smile. "How am I supposed to learn them? There isn't a co-ed in the school who'll look at me?"

I looked around, made sure all of the other guys had stripped down, then gestured for them to approach me.

Being surrounded by sixteen naked guys, most of them with their dicks straining, was intoxicating. "Face it, guys. You're mostly going to be trying for freshman co-eds. You've peed in the well a bit too much to attract any women who've seen you in the past. But any freshman girl worth having will arrive on campus already having boyfriends back home. It'll be mid-October, after their first trip back, that they realize it's time to move on. That's our timetable. We've got six weeks to turn you from fat stinky boys into men. Frankly, I'm crazy to take on the challenge. But I agreed to do it and I'm willing to hold up my end of the bargain. Any of you want out, let me know. But this is your last chance. Once you're in, there's no backing out."

"What do you think, Chuck," Russell asked. "Are you willing to do what missus says."

He looked up at that circle of naked boys, their dicks waving around like bobble-head toys, and grinned. "Shit, why not. I'm sure not getting any action with things the way they were."

I looked at each of them in turn. One by one, they nodded.

I wasn't surprised. Boys can be led by their dicks.

"All right. Drop down and give me twenty pushups."

I think Russell and Stretch could have managed—if their arms hadn't been burning from the workout they'd done that morning. Davie completed fifteen, and he was the best of the rest. Chuck only turned out four.

"Pathetic," I announced. "If a miracle happened and you persuaded a woman into your bed, you'd crush her under your weight. Muscle isn't just decorative, it's practical. Not to mention muscle burns more calories than fat. On your backs. Give me fifty crunches.

They formed a circle around me, all raging testosterone and puppy-like desires to be loved. I'd had that desire once myself, and it had led me to James. I wondered how many of these young men I could actually help, and how many were beyond what anyone could do.

Instead of doing stomach crunches, Chuck was doing head-bobs, dragging his head off the ground with his arms while barely moving his shoulders.

I barely restrained myself from applying the belt, but I judged this a mistake made in ignorance rather than willful rebellion. "Stop," I shouted. "Hasn't anyone ever showed you how to do a decent crunch?"

From the stunned looks I got, I realized that was a stupid question. None of these kids had been active in sports—which would have taught them the right way to exercise. Being mad at them for being fat slobs was like being mad at a pigeon for crapping. They just didn't know any better.

"I'm going to show you how to do this," I said. "I'm going to show you exactly once so you'd better pay close attention. Next time you screw up, you get the belt instead of a lecture. Now, on your feet. Circle around me so you can see.

I got on my back, lifted my legs as if an invisible chair were on the floor under me, put my fingertips behind my ears, and tightened my tummy muscles, lifting my shoulders from the ground.

On the second crunch, my croptop slid up, uncovering my breasts. My silk shorts were tight enough to outline my pussy. From the whispers, the guys had noticed. If they got the lesson, I didn't mind—I was a woman, after all. And what woman doesn't want admiration, even if it comes from guys she'd never, in a million years, consider screwing?

I went through a set of fifty crunches, showing them I wasn't asking them to do anything a thirty-year-old woman couldn't do, then I got to my feet and looked around.

Every dick in the room stood straight up.

On your backs, losers. Give me fifty.

This time, I was generous with the belt, slapping it into thighs and soft tummies when I saw slacking.

"That was pathetic," I announced when Barry, the only brother fatter than Chuck, wheezed to a stop. In the unlikely event that any of you gets a woman into your beds, she'll be looking for stamina. If you can't do fifty crunches without effort, how do you expect to satisfy a woman?

"Maybe," Chuck offered, "we could get the chicks to sit on our dicks and do all the work. That's about all I feel up to right now."

I shook my head. "Don't bet on it. Speaking of making a woman happy, you've got to have some stamina in the dick department as well. Everyone grab your dicks, squeeze hard, and move your hands—one stroke each, up and down each second. I'll count, you stroke."

I walked around the room, adjusting hands and making sure nobody was faking their grips before the count.

"One." A brief pause. "Two." Another pause.

By the time I reached four, Chuck shot his wad.

By the time I reached ten, only Stretch and Russell remained. The two of them lasted to twenty.

"Russell and Stretch know the drill," I announced to the cum-drenched group. Wipe it up with your hands and lick it off. I don't want any of you asking a woman to swallow anything too horrible to go into your own mouths.

It took a couple more swats with the belt before they complied. I got a lot of grumbling, and some gagging, but all of them successfully swallowed their wads.

"Shower off and report back here naked," I ordered. "That was a disgusting effort. Believe me, if you can't last twenty seconds when you're inside a woman's pussy, you're not getting a return invitation. Women like giving their lovers pleasure, but we're selfish enough to want a bit of enjoyment for ourselves. Now shower those messes off your chests, brush your teeth because I don't want to smell your spunk, and get back here in ten."

"You sure this is going to get me Amber?" Stretch whispered as the guys filed out.

I shook my head. "I'm sure it *isn't* going to get you Amber until both you and your entire fraternity perform a lot better."

"That's what I thought. Oh, want to know something?"

I sighed. "What?"

"Licking my semen wasn't so horrible when you let me do it off *your* hands."

"Keep thinking about Amber, Stretch. She may be a long shot for you, but you don't have a chance with me. I'm taken."

"Seems to me that your ex-husband dumped and divorced you. I don't see what claim that gives him."

"You don't understand."

"You're right. I don't understand because it doesn't make any sense at all."

"You've wasted five of your ten minutes. You'd better hurry."

I had to spank two of them. Not only hadn't anyone taught them to exercise, they didn't even know how to shower. Their butts stunk like, well, butts. I certainly wasn't going to give them their dick-leathers if it meant putting my nose anywhere near that stink.

After a second set of showers, I presented the guys with their collars and strapped their dicks.

"No masturbation without permission," I said. "I'm going to be timing your performance and we need to set a baseline. No sex without permission. There will be no high school girls in this fraternity house, even if they claim to be over eighteen. "Now, get to bed."

"Will you tuck me in?" Chuck asked.

I glared at him. "I'm not your mother and I'm not your lover. If you need anything, remember this, you're supposed to be a fraternity. And that means brotherhood. Look out for your brothers. You've developed a reputation as the biggest losers on campus. You achieved that feat, against a highly competitive field, I might add, through a cooperative effort. If you want to turn that reputation around, you're going to have to work together again."

"But we always have a party and get drunk when we come back to school," Barry whined. "Where's the beer."

"There's not going to be any more partying until you can party with women."

"I'd party with you."

"You'd party with Paris Hilton, too. But guess what—she isn't in the mood for losers like you. Neither am I."

Chuck snuffled, tears running down his face, gathering on his chin, and dripping to his fat stomach. "We always have fun when we party."

"You made your choices. Now it's chicks or bust." I decided to lighten the mood a little and rolled my hips, letting my tits jiggle a little for their benefits. "Maybe I should say, chicks and bust. Now go to bed—oh, and toss all of your clothes into the hall first."

"What for?"

"You hired me to clean, didn't you? Trust me to do my job."

* * * *

When my alarm went off at five the next morning, I rolled out of bed pissed at the world. When I'd been with James, I'd known what to expect. For the first time since I could remember, I didn't exactly miss his morning treats. Maybe licking his ass had to be more pleasant for him than it was for me. Still, it had been my world and I'd known how to deal with it.

By the time I was out of the shower, Brandon had arrived—a couple of coffees in hand, along with a big sack full of running shorts.

I grabbed the coffee, took a big hit, and then looked at Brandon.

He looked hot in running shorts and nothing else. I grinned at him and told him to drop them.

Without a word, he obeyed.

I cupped his balls and cock in my hand, looking downward so he couldn't see my grin. "Those leather strips are holding you up nicely, Brandon. Do you like the way they feel?"

"Truthfully? It's distracting from my job at the library. And in those tight pants you made me buy, anyone who looks can see the straps."

Anyone who looked right then could have seen his swollen dick, too. My mouth watered. I wanted to suck him off in the worst way, but Brandon would know he hadn't earned it.

"If they want it, I might give them permission to take it." I gave his beautiful cock a half-dozen quick strokes, letting the pressure build until he trembled under my hand, then dropped it, just when he was about to explode. "For now, though, I think you can hold it in a few more days. You agree, don't you?"

He didn't look like he agreed at all. "Yes, missus," was all he said.

"Since you're being a good boy, you deserve a treat." I climbed up on the desk in my new office, grabbed my coffee, and spread my legs.

"You may tongue me through my running shorts."

He looked pathetically grateful. "Thank you, missus."

"I didn't say you could talk." I spread my legs and hiked up my shorts until they rode up into my pussy. "Lick me, but don't you dare let your tongue touch my skin—shorts only."

He nodded, got to his knees beside the desk, and went to work.

Outside, I heard the sound of the guys getting up, groaning as Russell and Stretch prodded them into action. I tried to think about the way I'd made them form a circle the previous night and jerk themselves off. When that didn't work, I tried to think about James. Finally, though, I couldn't think of anything other than Brandon's tongue pressing the sheer fabric of my running shorts against my clit.

I came in less than three minutes. Only years of training gave me the control I needed not to scream as waves of sensation washed over me. I grabbed Brandon's head, pressed it deep into me, and let him continue licking until my orgasm subsided.

He had to know I'd come—my whole body had shuddered. Still, he kept licking until I pressed him away.

"You left a dripping mess," I told him. "Bend over and grab your ankles."

He looked startled, but I didn't miss the pleasure in his eyes. Of all the guys in Mississippi, how had I ended up attracted to a submissive?

"Don't you dare squirt," I grabbed his balls from behind, tugging them toward me, then laid ten stripes across his ass.

"I'll try to do better," he promised.

"You'd better. Now, we've got work to do. I'm going to divide the guys into two groups. One will stay here with you and work the weights. The other will go for a run with me. When we get back, we'll switch off."

"Yes, missus."

I was definitely going to have to check my calendar. Although he was all wrong for me, Brandon had already given me a better orgasm than I could ever remember James providing—not that James worried about *my* orgasms much. I couldn't just give him sex—a submissive like him wouldn't appreciate that. But I fully intended to figure out a way to let him come a time or two.

I'd seen the way the co-ed at the library looked at him. I knew she'd be willing to spread her legs, ass, or lips for him. If I were any good at all at being a dominant, I would have ordered him to walk up to her and demand that she get on her knees. Oddly, I didn't like the thought of him shooting his spunk into any other female.

Chapter Seven

In three weeks, I saw…progress.

Running without shirts gave the guys tans. Lifting weights tightened their muscles, giving them a bit of definition as well as some bulk. Eliminating the beer and replacing the starch and sweets-heavy diet with a healthier mix of protein, complex carbs, and fiber, peeled pounds from their waists.

Still, we were all nervous. We needed a good rush from the freshman class and the three-week mark was when the fraternities and sororities would take pledges. We *had* to get kids in for our rush party, and we *had* to persuade them to pledge or the fraternity would go broke and we'd never get girlfriends for my poor little protégés.

I'd attempted to create an air of mystery. The guys wore only black to their classes--from their black leather collars, to black t's that highlighted developing muscles, to tight black jeans, to black sneakers or army-style boots. I'd ordered them back to the house immediately after their classes, not confident that their inner nerds wouldn't come out if they had a chance to socialize.

It was working.

My boys reported being approached by freshmen wondering about the black uniforms. Stretch confided that eight separate co-eds had sidled up to him when they thought nobody else could hear and demanded an explanation for his nickname. Co-eds started waking up early and taking drives along the route of our morning runs. Sure they leaned out of their cars and shouted insults—but I could smell the estrogen going. Those young woman couldn't help responding to semi-naked men with increasingly cut bodies.

Then disaster. Russell reported whispers about strange things going on at the Pi Iota Sigma fraternity—rumors that the guys were looking better because they'd sold their soul to the devil—had a demon as house mother. When I wandered the campus, disguised in sunglasses and the slobby cheap clothes only a graduate student would choose, I found stylized graffiti of a woman with a whip, accompanied by the Greek letters, Pi Iota Sigma, scribbled on campus blackboards and spray-painted on dorm walls.

Then Brandon overheard a professor telling another that Professor D'Angre, my darling ex-husband, had discovered the fraternity was attracting sexual deviants, perverts, and fags. Mississippi wasn't what it had been a generation earlier, but there were still plenty of people who worried they'd somehow become infected if they shook hands with a homosexual, would go to hell if they weren't vigilant against demons, and might doom the entire planet if they didn't take a stand against perversion.

On Brandon's advice, I let the guys handle the rush party. For the event, I relaxed my rules about beer and told Brandon they could smoke a little marijuana if they wanted. He shook his head. "We're not going to mislead them. We took a vote on this and we all agreed. What they see is what they're going to get."

"Haven't you ever heard of marketing?"

"We've been marketing." We were in the ballroom, with one day to go before the party and I was worrying we'd have zero attendees.

I waved the copy of the *Cambridge Claxon* I'd grabbed during my run that morning. "Every other fraternity has a full page ad. We've got what? A small black box that says 'check out the darkness'."

"See." Russell puffed out his chest. "Marketing."

"Speaking of marketing," Stretch put in, "the guys took up a collection and bought something for you." He grabbed a box from a stack of what I'd assumed were party supplies.

The word *presents* didn't have universally pleasant connotations for me. Once, James had given me a set of manacles with inwardly pointing spikes as a special *gift*. Then there was my thirtieth birthday present—a cum bath followed by dismissal. I stared at the box like it held a clutch of rattlesnakes.

"If there's something nasty in there, you guys are going to suffer. You know that, don't you?"

Stretch's hands shook a little, but he didn't withdraw the box.

"Brandon helped us pick it," Russell said. "But we paid for it."

"Okay. Open it."

"You don't want to--"

"Stretch. If I wanted to open it, I wouldn't have ordered Russell to do it. Open it."

Russell pulled back the brown paper wrapping, lifted the lid off the box, and exposed—black leather.

"What the—"

He lifted out the first piece—a bustier with ties up the front. A black leather microskirt complemented the top, with spiked leather anklets and arm braces to complete the look. At the bottom, a black quirt was encased in black velvet.

"I'll look like that caricature I've seen all over campus."

"That was the idea." I hadn't even seen Brandon, but he grinned at me. "The guys recognized that they couldn't compete based on the gallons of beer, number of co-eds, or high-end accommodations. So, they decided to play to their strength."

I stroked the butter-soft leather. "What strength? The rumor that we're a satanic cult? You told me yourself that James is trying to destroy us."

"James is a math professor. He doesn't get marketing. You know the saying: the only bad attention is no attention."

"Tell that to Britney Spears."

"You're better looking than she is, and she doesn't have a black leather outfit. Try it on."

Just for an instant, old reflexes kicked in. Hundreds of times during the years I'd been with James, he'd ordered me to try something on. Generally it had been something painful, like the enormous dildo he'd made me stick up my butt or the spiked cuffs. Painful or not, I'd learned to leap to follow his orders. The guys got a boob-flash as I tugged up my crop 't' before I caught myself.

All three males were grinning, Brandon even more than the others. All three of their dicks strained at their shorts.

"Oh, no," I said. "No way are you guys getting away with that shit. On your hand and knees. Butts up, shorts down, heads down."

Just for fun, and to show them I appreciated my new toy, I pulled the quirt out of its holding spot, then went down the line of male butts and dolled out a dozen hard swats to each of the six exposed cheeks. Because Brandon had done the actual dirty work, playing on what he knew was my training, I added a couple whip-flicks to his scrotum.

He moaned deliciously and I had to grit my teeth to prevent myself from stroking those cute balls, taking them in my mouth while I brought his gorgeous cock to orgasm.

"Close your eyes—all of you," I ordered.

I walked to the other side, checking to see that they'd complied.

When James had ordered me to close my eyes, I could normally expect a golden shower and I was tempted to deliver one to the guys. I decided, though, that the cleanup wouldn't be worth the fun. Instead, I devised another punishment.

"I'm taking off my top now," I announced. "My breasts are exploding out of the constricting top. Now I'm taking each breast in one hand. They're heavy—so heavy I'd like a man to help me hold them, but there are no real men in this room, only pussy-men. So, I'll have to hold them myself, squeeze them to bring the nipples to sharp hard points. They're hot—and my arousal, an arousal that comes from squeezing them myself rather than from any of you, is darkening the tips."

I followed my words with action, bending near each guy in turn, letting my fingers and the slightest touch of the underside of my breasts lightly brush against their naked backs. When I got to Brandon, I decided he needed a little more.

"You can feel my nipples on your back, can't you, Brandon? They're hot from me stroking them." I laid a quirt stripe across his back, then traced it with the tip of my nipple.

He shuddered beneath me.

"Now I'm taking off my shorts. I'm not wearing underwear, of course, so I'm completely naked. If I allowed you to open your eyes, you'd see my shaved pussy all wet from what I've done to myself. Can you smell it? It's hot, isn't it? You'd love to plunge into it, kiss it, let me rub it over your entire body. But you know that isn't going to happen. I'm not going to let you look and I'm not going to let you touch."

I rubbed my twat, sliding my fingers along its moist length, toying with my clit until it trembled.

"Lick my fingers." I pressed them into Brandon's mouth. "You can taste my pussy juices, can't you? It makes you want to get on your knees and worship me with your tongue. Maybe I would have let you do that today. But because you toyed with me, that opportunity is lost. Too bad. I want a real male to lick me clean. Maybe I'll pick one of the kids coming to the rush party, let him lick me while you watch."

Brandon groaned. A beat of cum swelled at the tip of his dick and I flicked it off with my quirt. "You do not have my permission to climax, Brandon. I'll be very disappointed in you if you squirt my clean floor."

He gritted his teeth and held on.

Next to him, though, Russell wasn't as successful in retaining control. He shot what looked like a quart of milky-white spunk over the floor.

I flicked his dick with the whip. "Bad boy."

He only spasmed again, adding another couple of shots. "I haven't gone this long without coming since I turned fourteen," he said. "Pressure built up. I'm sorry."

"How do you think a co-ed would respond if you squirted that kind of load all over her legs before you went into her, Russell?" I checked the straps, squeezing his dick as I did so. "Weren't you listening when I told you that they're looking for a guy who can control his impulses? If you want them to come back for more, if you want them on their knees begging for your cum in their faces, if you want them telling their girlfriends that the guys from Pi Iota Sigma know how to satisfy a woman better than anyone else on campus, you've got to learn the basic rule—girls come first."

"Yes, ma'am." His words were a thick groan.

"I'm putting on my new top now," I announced. My pussy is still naked. The air feels cool as it evaporates the pussy-juices from my lips. Because I keep it shaved, except a little tuft of hair a real man could use as a handle, it would be easy for you to see it—if I allowed you to open your eyes.

I reached for the leather microskirt. "While I put on my skirt, I want you to think about what we should do with Russell's cum. I'm tempted to put crime scene tape around it, to warn any co-eds who make it to our party that we've got a student here who can't restrain himself, who's prone to premature ejaculation."

"Please don't do that," Russell pled. "Let me lick it up. I'll do better in the future."

I nodded. "Russell, stay down on your hands and knees and tongue-clean it. Stretch, you were a bad boy, but of these three, you were the best. Get up and open your eyes. You can help me with my straps.

The bustier strapped up the front, showing off the diamond navel ring I'd bought with my first paycheck to replace the cheap stainless steel one James used to hang a leash off of. Ties up both sides exposed expanses of my waist and the sides of my breasts.

Stretch knew enough not to pull up his shorts without my permission and I savored the way his dick strained against the leather straps I'd bound it with. His legs shivered with what I recognized as an almost overwhelming urge to press his sex against my leg, to gain himself some measure of release not from my pussy—he knew that was an unattainable goal—but from friction against any body part he could reach. I recognized that urge because I'd been there. James had relished teasing me, bringing me to the point of climax through his words, the touch of quirt against my breasts, anus, and twat. At faculty meetings, he'd have me sneak in early and hide under the table, then slide his toes between my lips and rub them against my clit.

I wondered if he'd ever felt the urge let me have that release. It would have cost him so little. Certainly I could barely restrain myself from taking Stretch's swollen cock in my hands and letting his semen shoot to the floor to join Russell's.

I pretended I simply didn't notice. "Tighter," I ordered. "My tits need to pop out the top."

"Yes, Missus."

Despite the late September heat, his hands felt like ice. Every drop of blood in his body must have descended into his dick because I'd never seen it so big."

"Russell." The tight top made me sound breathless. "You may open your eyes. Make sure you check carefully for anything you've missed. Stretch, help him look. If I find any spatter, you'll be the one sucking it up. And yes, the two of you can pull your pants up. No point spreading rumors that the Pi Iota Sigma fraternity is full of little dicks.

"Yes, missus."

"Brandon, come with me."

"Yes, ma'am."

I hooked a finger through the steel loop on his collar and led him upstairs to my room. I'd been so sure I was strong, that I could resist temptation—but James had been right about me after all. I was a woman with a taste for dick. James had spent years breaking me of my weakness, but clearly I'd failed him.

When we arrived at my room, I flicked the quirt across Brandon's naked back. "Strip off those shorts."

His dick hadn't relaxed a bit. If anything, he'd grown more excited. "How would you like me to give you a blowjob?" I traced the big vein in his cock with the tip of my riding crop.

"I'd like—"

I cut off his response with a flick of the quirt. "Wrong answer, slave-boy."

"I'd like to give you pleasure in any way I can."

How often had I echoed those words, or words just like them, to James?

"And you really think me sucking your dick, taking your hot sticky disgusting cum in my mouth, letting it rest on my tongue, dribble down my chin, spray in my hair and on my tits—you think that would give me pleasure?"

"Permission to speak freely, missus?"

"No." I shook my head. "I don't think I'd care to hear anything you've got to say. On the bed."

He looked at the pallet on the side of the bed, then back at me. "Which—"

"Listen to me and stop thinking so much."

My mouth watered as he crawled onto the bed, his balls dangling, his butt all tight and muscular. If only he weren't such a sub, I would love to lick out that ass. But that would scare the hell out of him.

"On your back, Brandon. What do you think? That I'm going to get *under* you? You've got to be on drugs."

He silently complied.

I sat down next to him. My pussy was so wet, I knew he had to smell it. James would have laughed at me, made me wipe myself with my fingers and lick it off. Brandon's nostrils flared and his cheeks trembled with the effort not to smile. The poor guy—imagine liking the stink of a woman's twat.

"Reach up over your head and grab my headboard."

He silently complied. The position stretched out his body, highlighted his cut abdomen, the hard plates of muscle that crossed his chest, the bulges of his thighs.

He'd been cut the day I'd met him at the library, but weeks of running shirtless in the sun had bronze his skin, deepened the muscle, and turned him into somebody who'd make any girl's vaginal muscles tighten.

I untied the straps from his dick, then used two of them to secure his wrists to the big brass headboard. The third tie went around his balls--tight. I didn't want him coming until I gave him permission.

I kept my own restraints on my pallet next to the bed and I used those to fasten his feet to the footboard.

"I'm going to use you like a giant dildo," I told him. Your job is to stay still and let me enjoy myself. If you wiggle, you'll be punished. If you talk, I'll gag you. If you understand and agree, nod your head.

He nodded quickly, almost frantically. In his own way, Brandon must want this as much as I did. If only his way was a bit more dominating. Then again, if everything went according to plan, I'd win James back. A real relationship with Brandon would only complicate matters. While James might occasionally loan me out to his friends, I didn't think he'd go for me having a servant-boy of my own.

"Before I use your dick, I'm going to get myself a bit more ready. Naturally I'm not going to let you tongue my pussy. So, I'll finger myself. Do you understand?"

He nodded again.

I wondered for a moment why I'd never considered the dominant lifestyle for myself. This was more than a little fun—and extremely exciting.

"You may," I told him, "lick my asshole while I'm masturbating. I'm afraid I took a shower a little while ago, so it won't be as dirty as you'd probably like."

He didn't look like he'd mind, so I hiked up that ridiculously short leather skirt, straddled him facing his big dick and lowered my butthole right over his mouth.

He stuck his tongue right in and licked.

Damn, that felt nice. From the dozens of times James had stuck his dick into my asshole, I'd known that the butt is intimately connected to the huge cluster of nerves that make up a woman's sex. What I hadn't realized is how sweet a man's tongue could feel as it licked and caressed every inch of my crack, then plunged into my asshole itself.

I almost forgot to masturbate, then I didn't need to masturbate. I ended up doing it for Brandon. A good submissive wants to please his mistress, but he can't be allowed to believe that he can make her come on his own.

Four quick strokes with my finger had me squirting girl juice and biting down on the handle of my quirt to keep from letting out a scream that would have every fraternity brother in the house running to my rescue or, more likely, wanting to pile on with whomever had finally gotten me in the sack.

"I'm a little messy now," I told Brandon when I could finally trust myself to speak. You may lick my thighs and the outside of my shaved vaginal lips. Do not dare put your shit-covered tongue inside me.

He nodded--which sent some pretty spectacular sensations through me, then followed orders. I knew his tongue wasn't shit-covered. A decade with James had made me intimately aware of how clean I was and exactly what a dirty ass smelled like. Still, I figured Brandon deserved a bit of extra humiliation.

My quim didn't stop quivering, but it calmed down to where I thought I could handle the next step so I pulled my butt away from Brandon's face.

He sighed as I moved away and I remembered the numberless times I'd done the same thing when James had taken his hairy butt away from my tongue, my lips, my caresses.

"I'm going to climb your pole now," I told him. "Do you have any requests, first? You may speak."

He licked his lips. "Can you get naked?"

I laid the quirt across his upper thighs. "What do you think, Brandon? That I'm doing this for your pleasure? If you were a real man, you'd make me get naked, you'd push me down to my knees and come on my face, then wash your sperm away with your hot piss. But you're a sub, which means you take what I give you. And I'm sure as hell not going to give you my naked body."

"Yes, mistress."

I felt just a surge of guilt. I wasn't any big bad dominatrix. I was a sub, just like Brandon. I should be helping him, giving him what he wanted. Instead, I was enabling his problem. Except, he hadn't asked for my help, didn't seem to know he had a problem at all.

The thought occurred to me that I'd been in the same boat once, and that I might be again once I got James back. But I suppressed that idea ruthlessly.

I took one of my ball gags and draped it over his neck. "I'm putting this here as a reminder that you're not allowed to speak again. If you make a noise, even a groan, I'll have to gag you. Nod if you understand."

He nodded.

"All right." Only then did I realize I'd been delaying this moment. I hadn't needed more lubrication, hadn't needed to masturbate, hadn't needed his rim job. I'd been doing all of those things only because doing so let me delay plunging that huge dick into me.

I'd been a virgin when I'd met James. I'd blown other men on his orders. I'd given dozens of men handjobs. But James's was the only dick I'd ever had in my twat—and that not very often. Brandon was much bigger, much harder than James had been in his wildest dreams. A part of me feared he'd hurt me. A bigger part suspected he could only disappoint me. Even with the strap tight around his balls, he might come the second I slid his dick into my pussy. He might lose his erection when he realized that a woman had actually let him penetrate her. Or it just might be just another man, just another dick.

I took a deep breath, then turned around to face him, grasped his cock in both hands, and lowered myself onto it.

I hadn't had a dick in my twat for over a year and my muscles had tightened. Despite all of my body's lubrication, despite my masturbation, despite all of Brandon's tonguing, he filled me, stretched me, practically split my body in half.

"Don't move," I said.

Sweat gathered in beads over his strong chest and on his forehead and he licked his upper lip, gathering more salty drops that had to be flavored by my own juices.

I grunted as I thrust myself down on him. Finally, my vagina accommodated him, stretching to take all of him into me.

Despite my warning, he groaned—which drowned out a squeal of my own. It took will power to slap the quirt down on his muscular pec. "I told you to be quiet."

It took only a second to fasten the ball gag—I didn't even have to fully withdraw his dick from me.

Once I'd gagged him, I settled down to the serious job of delaying my orgasm.

I'd masturbated a few minutes earlier partly to let Brandon feel my butthole quiver when I came, and partly because his tongue felt so good that I could hardly do anything else. A third reason, though, was that I'd been *too* prepped. Weeks spent around him, weeks inspecting the boys, retying the straps on their dicks, timing their spunk release in our Friday cum sessions (we'd picked Friday because it was date night at Cambridge State and I wasn't letting the guys date) had changed me.

All that time surrounded by all of those dicks and all of those increasingly hunky male bodies left me in a constant state of arousal.

I bit down on the quirt handle again, this time to prevent an orgasm from sweeping me away.

James would have said something—maybe about my tits being smaller and droopier than one of his students—a student I now recognized as Amber. Or maybe about how my twat was getting old and stretched out—something to keep me in my place.

I searched my brain for something to tell Brandon but came up empty. Luckily for me, my head was the only empty thing in my body.

"Don't come." I suspected my warning was unnecessary, but I didn't know what else to say.

"Mmmah."

I grinned. No wonder James kept me gagged so much. Even though it meant I couldn't lick his cock or ass, being able to speak while others had to remain silent was a major power rush.

I raised myself on my knees until the swollen tip of Brandon's dick was barely inside my pussy lips, then drove myself downward.

He groaned again, but I didn't whip him—I'd save that for later. Instead, I leaned my body forward so I could support my weight with my arms and used all of the muscles of my upper body to pull him out, then shove him back inside myself.

After a few huge strokes, I found a rhythm and let the pressure build inside me once more.

Brandon bit down on the gag ball, the muscles of his jaws bulging as he fought for control.

I reached behind me, grabbed the tie that circled his balls and pulled. Brandon sighed and smiled, regaining a bit of control.

Not me, though. My arms trembled although I'd done thousands of pushups since undertaking the transformation of the Pi Iota Sigma fraternity. My thighs twitched, threatened to cramp and my breasts spilled out of the tight bustier. "Not yet," I growled.

I couldn't understand Brandon's words through the gag, but I knew he was encouraging me, telling me I could take more, could drive myself harder, could ride through the smaller orgasms that shook my body like earthquakes, and continue on until I achieved my goal.

I sobbed for breath. A ten-mile run was nothing compared to the exertion I now unleashed.

Again, I found the rhythm, but my need didn't retreat. Instead it accumulated, like lead weights being piled one after another on a barbell already too challenging to lift.

I passed through the point of no return without really noticing, moving faster and faster, pumping myself up and down on Brandon's huge cock, tears and sweat falling from my face to his beautiful chest.

Finally, like a crystal ball shattering, my body gave way to the orgasm.

It started deep in my womb, shook through my clit, and exploded in my breasts. My spine reverberated like a too-tightly strung piano wire.

Without warning, my muscles turned to jelly, my thighs and arms refused to support me, and I collapsed forward on Brandon's chest, shuddering and gasping.

He spit out his gag. "There, there."

I willed myself to push away. I couldn't become dependent on Brandon, of all people. Not only was I going to get my husband back, I simply couldn't count on a submissive. He'd run from the first sign of trouble, leaving me hanging.

Only when my muscles refused to move me did I realize that the strange gasping sound I heard came from my own lungs, and that the moisture on my face wasn't from the sweat on Brandon's chest. I was crying—crying in front of a submissive.

Brandon's pecs bulged and his right arm trembled, then he wrapped it around me. "It's all right, babe. You've had a rough time, but it's going to be better now."

From somewhere, I sucked up a bit of strength and pushed myself away from his chest although his still-hard dick remained buried deep inside my pussy.

"How'd you do that?" I demanded.

He looked at my gag, which he'd bitten completely through, then at the broken leather straps that had once bound him to my bed. "I couldn't just lie there while you were hurting, Nicole. Guess they don't make leather as strong as they used to."

Or maybe they made men a lot stronger than they used to. I'd felt that surge of pure power when he'd jerked free. "You call me missus. Or mistress." I couldn't summon up any anger, not even the fake kind, but I needed to reassure Brandon I was all right—even, maybe especially, if I wasn't.

"Of course, mistress."

"I crawled off of him, torn between my own submissive side that wanted to please him, and what I knew of his own needs. A good dominatrix would give him a couple swats with the whip for breaking free of his bonds and for witnessing my breakdown. But I couldn't bring myself to do that.

Instead, I inspected his cock.

Incredibly, he hadn't come. I hadn't imagined he could summon that much willpower and had anticipated being able to punish him for violating my orders while simultaneously knowing I'd given him a guilty treat.

"I don't see any way out of this, Brandon," I said. "Unfortunately, I have a craving to see your cum. If there were some way I could get it without allowing you to orgasm, I'd do that. But since there isn't, I'm going to allow you to stroke yourself now. Since you've freed one of your arms anyway, you can go ahead and use that hand."

He obeyed, bringing his big right hand down toward his swollen rod.

"Stop," I commanded him. "You've got my pussy juices on your dick. You're not allowed to touch those. I'll wipe them off first."

I craved that big dick in my mouth, wanted to lick those nasty girl-lubricants from him and then take him all the way to where he gagged me. Instead I struggled to my feet, found a washcloth, and carefully wiped him off.

"Thank you, mistress," he said when I finished.

"I want to feel your spunk on my belly," I said. "You may jerk yourself now. But when you come, don't dare let a single nasty drop near my nice top, my pretty breasts, my face, or especially my pussy. Just my tummy, do you understand?"

"Yes, mistress." His voice came out as a harsh whisper.

I didn't even need to try and remember a time when James had wanted me this badly—he never had. He'd pursued me as an eighteen-year-old virgin because I'd been the prettiest woman in my class and because, as I now guessed, he'd dumped his previous lover and needed a fresh one. But he'd never trembled just from seeing my breasts, never shook when I'd brushed my hand against his thigh or dick. I wondered if my time with Brandon was just what I'd needed to be an even better wife to James. Perhaps a bit of dominance—just when James wanted it, of course, could add a bit of variety to our sexual lives.

Then I caught a glance of Brandon's swollen cock and forgot about James.

"May I begin?" he rasped.

"Just a moment." I untied the loop I'd fastened around Brandon's balls, taking that soft sack in my hands and squeezing it gently.

I pulled up my new bustier so it covered my breasts again, but also so it exposed about six inches of my abdomen between it and my hip-hugging leather skirt. "You have thirty seconds to come," I said. "You may begin now."

I tightened my grip on his balls as he drove his hand down on the velvet skin of his dick, then jerked it back up. He groaned deeply, his bronzed body flushing an even deeper shade as his pulse accelerated.

"Twenty-five," I counted. "Twenty-six."

Before I got to the next count, a boiling hot spurt of liquid poured over my belly. A second jolt followed, then another. Only after those three squirts, which together had produced at least a cup of hot cum, did he slow down to what I considered a normal load.

I hoped he'd splash my new leather outfit so I could punish him, but he'd somehow controlled himself, using his white-knuckled grip on his dick to keep the pressure under control and his aim precise.

I dabbed my fingers in the lake of semen on my belly, then deliberately untied my bustier, let my breasts pop free, and painted the tip of each nipple with a hot dollop of his wad.

"Look at me," Brandon. "Do you see what you did? Didn't you hear me order you not to let any get on my tits?"

He looked. He stared, his pupils dilating like it had gone midnight black outside. I'd thought his face was flushed before, but it became even more so now. "I'm sorry, mistress. I have no idea how that could have happened."

Brandon wasn't stupid. He wasn't blind, either. Since he'd watched me unfasten my top, dip my finger in his cum, and then dribble it on my nipples, he had to have a pretty good idea exactly how it had happened.

"Bad boys who make messes have to clean up after themselves," I said. "Lick this nasty spunk off my nipples."

He rattled his left arm against the headboard. "If you could free me, mistress, I'd have an easier time cleaning you."

"If I wanted you to have an easy time, I'd tell you. Bend. You exercise, don't you? That should improve your flexibility."

While he contorted himself and reached his tongue toward my breasts, I grabbed the washcloth and wiped his cum-bath off of my belly. If he'd been James, I would have had to swallow every last drop of his precious semen. My mouth watered at the pure waste of throwing it into the washing machine, but Brandon didn't need to see me as a needy and desperate woman. I had to pretend to be strong to provide him what he needed.

I moved around a little, making it more difficult for Brandon to reach me. Finally, though, I thought he'd had enough and let him do his job.

His tongue, soft, moist, yet strong, laved my nipple.

Although I'd already orgasmed twice, my hand sought my twat again and I masturbated in time with his warm licks.

He finished cleaning my second nipple just as I shivered back into orgasm.

"I'm dirty from your disgusting male juices," I told him. "I'm going to take a shower now. You may crouch on the bathmat and hand me soap or towels as I command."

"Of course, mistress."

The tub had a transparent glass door. Naturally I blindfolded Brandon, but I made sure the blindfold slipped a little so he could watch. I was girlie enough to want the sexy guy who was the closest thing I had to a lover to watch me and enjoy what he saw while I showered.

As I adjusted the flow, I put down the plug, letting the water accumulate around my feet.

I made sure Brandon saw me cleaning my twat and ass, as well as washing the remains of his cum from my belly and his saliva from my tits.

"You may wash my back," I told him.

"May I climb into the shower with you?'"

"Did I order you into my shower? You may stay crouched down and wash me with this." I handed him an exfoliating sponge. "Make sure you clean out my asshole, completely. I'm afraid I may have left some of your disgusting spit on it."

"Yes, mistress."

His strong strokes felt wonderful. I savored them as long as I could, then stepped away and turned off the water. "Towel now," I ordered.

He handed one to me.

"Wipe me down," I said. "What's the point of a servant-boy if he won't dry me off?"

"Of course, mistress." He dried me with long gentle strokes, treating me like a priceless piece of furniture he was giving a polish to.

"Make sure you dry between my toes," I said. "And don't forget my twat."

His hands shook as he gently brushed the towel along my lower lips, picking up not only drops of water left by the shower but also my own juices.

I grabbed the towel from him and wrapped it around my breasts, putting the knot in my cleavage. "I left the water in the tub for you to bathe," I said. "You may masturbate again before getting out of the tub."

"Will you watch me, mistress?"

"Why would I want to watch a man squirt his juices? Don't you think I get enough of that in our weekly timed jerkoffs?"

"Then, with your permission, I'll wait until I can give you pleasure with my orgasm."

I shook my head. "You do *not* have my permission." I hunted under the sink until I found a near-empty mouthwash bottle. I dumped the remainder of the mouthwash down the sink and rinsed out the bottle. "Squirt your semen into this so I'll know you followed orders. Bring it to me when you're done. I'm going to go back downstairs and see how the preparations are coming."

"Of course, mistress."

Chapter Eight

The preparations for the party had advanced a long way, and I didn't like them.

"This looks like a low-rent stage version of *The Story of O*," I complained.

The guys had hung chains from the ballroom walls, placed fake torches in sconces outside every doorway, and covered the windows with bars.

"We're broke," Russell admitted. "We can't afford a high-rent version."

"Aren't you worried you'll scare away every guy on campus?"

Stretch pulled a cardboard box from the hallway. "These are RSVPs. Every guy we invited has accepted.

"You're kidding." On my advice, they'd invited some of the cooler types as well as the crowd of losers they were used to getting.

"We may have to buy the building next door as an annex." Russell grinned at me. "It would mean a substantial increase in your salary as our house mom."

"Not to mention we could hire someone else to do the cleaning," Stretch added. "It hasn't escaped our notice that you assign your cleaning jobs as punishment, and there always seems to be enough punishment to leave you off the hook."

That wasn't completely fair. I was working full-time for the guys, but I'd spent more time on their exercise and diet routines than I had on basic cleaning and scrubbing. Besides, these guys might want to get married one day—even if they persuaded their sweet Mississippi wives to do all the cleaning, they'd at least recognize what a hassle it could be and do a lot better at not leaving extra messes around. Sort of like tasting their own cum. I wondered if James would have eaten as much mustard if he'd had to try out the nasty way it made his spunk taste.

"Why don't you take tonight off?" Russell asked. "We promised you two nights a week when you signed on and you haven't taken one in the four weeks since then. So, make your boyfriend take you out on a date."

I looked at him with honest puzzlement. "What boyfriend."

Brandon turned the corner just as I asked. He took one look at me, a second at the guys, then headed out.

"That boyfriend," Stretch said. "I think you hurt his feelings."

"He's a submissive. He likes it when I hurt him."

"Maybe when you spank him," Stretch admitted. "Maybe when you humiliate him sexually and make him lick your nasty body parts. But he's been coming around every day to help us out with our workouts. He's helped a lot of the guys figure out how to dress so their new muscles look good rather than like extra flab or something. And he's a good guy."

"You owe him an apology," Russell finished. "Now get out and do it."

I went back to my room and sat on my bed.

Brandon's scent hung heavy in the air—soap, a deodorant that made him smell especially lickable, and the distinct odor of his cum.

I picked up the mouthwash bottle and held it to my nose, inhaling deeply. Okay, the guy was sexy. I wanted him, not just for his help around the place, but also because he turned me on. But I really should let him go, considering I intended to be back with James within the next few months.

The thought of never seeing him again, though, pushed me into motion.

I stripped off my leather skirt and bustier, hanging them in my wardrobe, then grabbed a cropped Pi Iota Sigma t-shirt and pair of running shorts. I still didn't have a car, so I jogged across the campus to the library.

He wasn't there, of course. If this evening had been a work night for Brandon, he wouldn't have been at the fraternity house to help out with the preparations.

Unfortunately, I didn't have any idea where he lived.

A part of me wanted to give up, to return to the fraternity house and just hope that Brandon would get over whatever miff he was going through and show up, as usual, in the morning.

I recognized that as the coward's way out. I needed to find Brandon, to tell him something. Admittedly I wasn't sure what I'd tell him, but one I found him, I figured I could decide.

Phone books seem to pile up everywhere—except when you need one.

I jogged to three separate dorms before I finally located a fairly current Cambridge area directory.

Brandon's number was unlisted.

The county seat was twenty miles away—a long run under the best of circumstances, but city hall would be closed anyway. I had no way to check tax records, and no way of knowing whether he owned his own home or rented an apartment.

Which said something else about me. What kind of woman asks the kind of favors I'd asked from Brandon and doesn't even find out where he lives?

I wouldn't admit defeat, though. I assembled everything I knew about him, looking for something that would give me a clue. The only thing I remembered was the co-ed who worked with him at the library.

I'd never paid much attention to her. She had mousy hair, a cute but unspectacular figure with a bit of a bubble-butt. She didn't have enough in the chest department to pull off the hourglass look, and her glasses that hid big brown eyes that she should have showed the world.

I closed my eyes and visualized Brandon's library. His desk was in the middle, where he could supervise everything. The clerk's normal position was at the front, checking out books and collecting overdue library fines.

I mentally tuned and looked at her desk. Yes, she had a name tag. And the name was Lisa Beckley.

Student directories were a lot easier to find than town phone books. I located Lisa's number and called it within a few seconds.

"Yeah?"

"Is this Lisa Beckley?"

"Who's calling, please?"

"I'm Nicole D'Angre. I work at—"

"Everyone knows who you are, Mistress D'Angre. I'll tell Lisa you're on the phone for her."

Everyone knew who I was? Then I remembered the rumors James was spreading. Lisa's roommate probably thought I was looking for a human sacrifice.

"Mistress D'Angre. How can I help you?"

"Lisa?"

"Yes, it's me."

"I'm looking for Brandon. I thought, since you work with him, you'd know where he lives."

"You mean because I've humiliated myself by practically throwing my body at him. Or did he tell you that I've been riding my bike up and down his street. I might have done that once or twice, but I was lost, besides he wasn't there anyway—he's always with you. So, who did I hurt?"

"I'm not trying to trap you, Lisa. I just want to find Brandon."

"You messed with his feelings, didn't you? Women like you never know what you're doing to men, and men just lap it up, accept the humiliation, and never even see the perfectly nice women around who'd treat them with respect."

"How about this, Lisa? Next time I want a sexual ethics lesson, I'll call you first. Right now, though, I want to find Brandon. I'm afraid he'll hurt himself."

I threw the last in as motivation, but the second the words left my lips, I wondered if I wasn't being precognitive. Maybe Brandon *would* hurt himself.

"Ohmigod. You did screw him over, didn't you? We've got to save him."

"Brandon isn't the kind of man who can be saved by a nice woman," I said. "That's why he likes me. Tell me where he lives and I'll do what I can."

I heard muffled shouting in the background, then the first voice I'd heard returned.

"Mistress D'Angre?"

"Yes?"

"One of our sorority sisters is holding her hand over Lisa's mouth. We'll let her give you your answers, but only if you do something for us."

"I don't like threats."

"Learn to live with it. If you don't wangle us invitations to the Pi Iota Sigma rush party, we're just going to sit on Lisa until you give up and go away."

I thought about all those whips and chains hanging around the fraternity ballroom. "You don't have a clue what you're asking for."

"We've been hearing rumors about the new Pi Iota Sigma ever since school opened. Everyone is talking about the sexy housemom who's turned a bunch of losers into complete hunks. Half the guys on campus are planning on rushing. I think I know exactly what I'm asking.

"You and Lisa can come. That's all."

"Ten of us."

"Five."

"Ten."

"All right, ten. But don't blame me if you don't like what you find. Now put Lisa back on."

"Mistress D'Angre?" It was Lisa. "I'm so sorry they did that to me. I wouldn't have let them, but they're stronger than me. I'd never do anything to hurt Brandon."

"I will do something to hurt you if you don't give me Brandon's address right now."

"Will you tell him I gave it to you? Please."

"Sure, Lisa. Whatever you want."

She gave me an address about two miles from downtown and three miles from where I was—a nice section where a lot of professors and professionals live. James, of course, would never consider living anywhere but the most elite neighborhood in the city, but Brandon was less concerned with appearances than James.

I ran the three miles in barely over a quarter of an hour, passing a couple of track runners on my way.

Brandon's house wasn't fancy, but it was nice. A two-story probably dating from before the war, he had a great lawn and landscaping. His car, a late-model Ford, sat in the driveway.

I was panting as I approached his door and my hands were shaking enough that I missed the doorbell on my first try.

On the second, though, I connected and listened to the chimes ring through his house.

From somewhere in his house, I heard footsteps.

Panic flooded adrenaline through my system. I'd never stopped to ask Brandon if he was married. Maybe I was setting myself up to walk in on a perfect family scene.

As the footsteps neared the door, I sucked in a breath. If Brandon had a wife and kids, he should have told me. Despite what James had always said, I wasn't responsible for everything that went on around me, just for my own actions.

Still, when Brandon, rather than the mythical wife, opened the door, I failed to restrain a little gasp of relief.

"Hi Nicole. What brings you here?"

"I thought...," I paused a second to catch my breath. "I thought we might chat about our relationship."

"Why?"

Why indeed? Both of us knew that I'd have to leave Brandon behind when I won James back.

"Are you going to invite me in, or are you just going to treat me like a door-to-door salesman you want to get rid of."

The answer should have been automatic, especially for a submissive like Brandon. Instead, he stared at me for a painful thirty seconds. "It seems to me that you said everything back at the fraternity house. You've been happy to use me to whip your boys into shape, no pun intended. But I'm looking for something more than just being another boy in your harem."

"You expect me to quit my job?"

"I didn't say that. I'm not talking about what you do with the boys. Hell, I think you're a good influence on them. I suspect you get a bit more pleasure from watching fifteen guys jerking off as they look at your fabulous body than you've ever admitted, but you've forced them to become aware that women aren't just passive receptacles for their dicks and sperm, that they have responsibilities to their women as well. You've also taught them that women can't all be ordered around, just because most of them have always ordered around their moms and what few girlfriends any of them have ever had. Why would I want you to stop that?"

"All right. What *do* you want?"

"I want you to apply some of your lessons to yourself. You've been working so hard to be a dominant that you've forgotten—"

"Forgotten what, Brandon? Forgotten what it's like to be chained to a bed? Forgotten what it's like to eat out of a dog bowl because I'm treated like another animal around the house. I'd never admit it to the guys, but I still sleep on the floor in my fancy bedroom with my hands and feet tied together. I still pour my morning cereal into my Fido bowl and eat it with my face down and arms behind my back because that's the way James taught me to be. Yeah, I work hard at being a dom. I do it because that's what you need, because that's what the guys need. Do you remember what they were like the first time you saw them? They needed someone to give structure to their lives and I only knew one way to do it. Maybe it's not a good way. Hell, I'd be the first to admit that James isn't the greatest role model in the world. But it's all I know."

His hand trembled as he fought what had to be a powerful urge to reach out and stroke my cheek.

"You're messed up, Nicole. I'm sorry. I thought I could help—that's what subs want to do, you know? We want to help others feel better about themselves. But you don't know where you are. Until you can make up your mind, you're going to hurt everyone around you—and that includes your boys. You've got to get over your crazy dream of getting James back. You've got to—"

"Shut up," I commanded. "Getting James back is not a crazy dream. I've got a plan. I'm going to get him back and when I do, I'm going to make him understand that he'll never find another woman who can serve him as well as I can. We're going to be happy together, just the way things were before Amber stepped between us."

"Amber isn't the problem. If it weren't her—"

I laughed. "That's where you're wrong. If Amber dumps him, accepting another co-ed would be admitting he was settling for second best. I've got him trapped."

Brandon shook his head. "I wish I could help you, Nicole. But you've got to want to help yourself first. I'll swing by and work out with the guys—it would be like deserting them if I didn't. But don't give me any more orders. I'm not going to take them."

"Or else what?"

He stepped closer to me. For just an instant, I peeked beneath his submissive role and saw another side—Brandon wasn't just a hunk, he was a powerful man. If he wanted to, he could pick me up and break me across his thigh like a rotten piece of driftwood. At that moment, I suspected he wanted to. "Don't push me, Nicole. I'm not playing your games any more."

My mind felt like it was tearing into pieces. A part of me wanted to throw myself on him, beg him for forgiveness. Another wanted to order him down on his knees and demand that he lick my toes and grovel while I whipped his sexy butt for defying me. A third part insisted that I walk away, hold my head high, and pretend that he couldn't affect me.

Instead, I said what I'd come there to say. "I'm sorry for the times I've taken you for granted, Brandon. I'm even more sorry that I can't be the woman you need. We both know I belong to James and that he'll never accept you as my lover or personal submissive, so whatever attraction we have between us is ultimately not going to matter. Regardless, I know I hurt you by my careless words and I regret that most of all."

He shook his head. "If you go back to James, you'll be pissing away the best chance at happiness you'll ever get. Haven't you learned anything about yourself during the past few weeks? James was holding you down. Since leaving him—"

"James would never hold me down. He gave me the strength I've been relying on—"

"I'll see you around, Nicole. I'd offer to drive you back to the frat house, but… I just don't want to. If you need cab fare, I'll lend you—"

Anger forced the next words out of my mouth. "I don't need anything from you, Brandon. Except one thing."

"Yes?"

"I promised Lisa I'd tell you I got your address from her. You…" I choked up for no reason and started over. "You have my permission to fuck her."

He stared at me for a second, then turned and closed his door. When it was only an inch ajar, he stopped. "I'll see you, Nicole."

Then he closed it the rest of the way.

* * * *

Back at the frat house, I had to consciously slow down. I wanted to strike out at anyone available, but I'd tried to set rules and limits with the guys. I didn't mind punishing them, but only when they could connect the punishment to undesirable behavior.

After a cold shower, I slipped on a clean pair of shorts and a halter and headed down to the ballroom.

The decorating was about done, the dungeon look now included simulated stone walls, rushes on the floors, and tin plates that would hold our party food, as well as the chains, whips and bars I'd seen earlier.

"I've got bad news," I announced after I'd assembled the fraternity. "I've been forced to invite ten co-eds from the Delta Phi Beta sorority."

"Bad news?" Stretch looked at the point of hyperventilating. "Amber is in Delta Phi Beta. What if she comes?"

"Exactly," I said. "What if she comes? I've been working hard to get you guys ready to face age-appropriate females, but let's get real—this job didn't get done in three weeks. It also isn't going to get done between tonight and tomorrow."

"Okay," Russell said. "If we're not ready, why did you invite them?"

"I made a deal. It was a good deal for me, but a bad deal for you guys. That's what I do."

"Even if we're not ready for them," Russell mused, "the prospective pledges will be excited to see chicks around."

"And you were the one who said we should focus on what we are—no lies, remember."

"What we are and what we're becoming. Uh, missus."

I led them into the dining room and tossed a couple of blankets on the table. "As I said, you're not ready for real women yet, but I suppose it's my job to get you as ready as possible.

I climbed up on the table and lay flat on my stomach.

"All right, guys. Who thinks you know what women like."

"Big fat dicks," Chuck suggested.

"Muscle?" That was Russell.

"Guys who spend lots of money on them." Stretch sounded distinctly unhappy about that guess.

"Guys who do exactly what they say," Peter added. "I've noticed that's what makes *you* happy and any one of us would kill to get between your legs."

I laughed. "You guys crack me up. First, none of you is getting between my legs. You're way too young for me. Second, despite everything I've taught you, you still act like women are just like you. Sure women like nice dicks and nice muscles. And who wouldn't like someone to spend money on her or take her suggestions seriously? But let's get real—a guy might marry a woman because he fell for her rack, but few women are going to make a decision about more than a single evening based on the size of a dude's cockring."

They waited with bated breath, doubtless expecting me to unleash the secret of the universe.

"Russell," I said. "Untie my halter."

"You're kidding, missus. You won't punish me. Everyone knows we're not allowed to see your naked tits."

"That's why I'm face down on the table, idiot. You're not going to see my boobs."

"Well, okay." He grabbed the bow and yanked.

"Anyone want to guess what he did wrong?"

"How could he have done anything wrong," Stretch wanted to know. "He did what you told him."

"You're right—sort of. Women are sneaky that way. A lot of the time, there's what you college types call *subtext*. They say something, but there's more hidden beneath the message. Suppose I told one of you to play with my nipples and you yanked on them like you were trying to get milk out of a stubborn cow. You think she'd go for it?"

"I'd sure like it if I could get a chick to see what kind of milk she could pull out my dick," Peter said. "Instead of having to do it for myself on our Friday timed jerkoffs."

"Again, you're thinking women are the same as you. I've been teaching you control because women can't climax after five seconds of friction the way guys can. So, lesson one. If you ever get a chance to take off a woman's top, do it slowly, as if you were unwrapping a present but you didn't want to rip the wrapping paper. Get it?"

Russell nodded.

"Okay, redo my halter."

"Do I have to? With it off I can see the sides of your—"

"You have to."

He grumbled a bit more but followed orders.

"You're next, Stretch. Think you can do better? Undo my halter."

I made all of them practice.

Because they were naked except their cock-straps, I had no problems seeing when they started to get it. One after another, their dicks perked up, then stood at attention as they practiced the subtle art of untying a woman's top.

After everyone had managed the trick twice without hurting me and without yanking hard enough to stretch the fabric, we moved on to lesson two.

"Dudes," I said, "are dick-focused. Rub their dicks and they come. Leave their dicks alone and you need really extreme measures to get any reaction at all. Women aren't built like that. Rub a woman's twat without warming her up and it feels unpleasant. Which is why dominant males have to work so hard to train women to respond to them. They want women to get instantly wet, without all of the normal warm-ups."

"That's why we play with their tits," Chuck suggested. "My big brother told me chicks have a nerve that runs straight from their nipples to their cunts."

A collective gasp met his word choice. He'd just uttered one of the two words I'd forbidden, along with 'no' in response to any of my commands.

"That's what he said. Not what I said. I would never..." Chuck trailed off.

"Fifty pushups," I said.

"Fifty?"

"Seventy-five. Want to go for an even hundred."

"Thank you, missus." Chuck dropped down and started counting out his set.

I raised myself off the table just enough to show them cleavage without actually putting my tits on display.

"You'll never get to a woman's breasts, let alone her pussy, if you don't take it slowly. Think of it this way—all of you have trained hard to control your quick releases. But how's a woman supposed to know you won't spray cum all over her thighs and get soft before you get inside her? So, women go by clues. The rule is, if you've got a slow hand, you just might have a slow squirt, might give her a chance for her own orgasm. Now line up. Russell, you go first. I want you to stand at the foot of the table and rub my feet."

I needed that after my run. Because I was stressed over my disagreement with Brandon, I was tense. Foot rubs, back rubs, and scalp rubs would help relax me. They'd also excite the guys.

By the time I'd had enough, there wasn't a fraternity brother in the room who wasn't standing at full attention.

"We're talking zones of intimacy," I explained. "If you want to get into a woman's pussy, you need to start somewhere she'll find unthreatening, but pleasurable. Not many women would turn down a foot-rub from a guy she was halfway interested in. I'm not suggesting you should walk up to every woman on campus and offer them pedicures, but if you do manage to persuade one to go on a date with you and you want a chance at a second date—and maybe even that magical third date where you're most likely to get at least a handjob, a footrub and some nice kissing is more likely to open the door than if you rush things and tried to get inside her pussy before she's ready.

"About nice kissing?" Stretch demanded. "I'm not sure I know--"

"Twenty pushups," I said. "If you seriously expect that I'll let you kiss me, you really haven't learned anything."

"Good try, bud," Russell whispered as Stretch walked past him to find an empty bit of floor on which to do his pushups.

"If it was so good, maybe you can do some of my pushups for me."

"I've got an idea for the party I want to work on. Otherwise I would."

I retied my halter, went upstairs, stripped, and got into my tub, putting my clit directly under the water stream. I'd had fifteen guys working on me, playing with my body, waving their dicks inches from my face. This should be easy.

For the first time since James had tossed me out on my ass, I couldn't make myself come.

Maybe James was right. Maybe I really was getting older, becoming less than a whole woman.

Before going to bed that night, I tightened my bonds extra tight and removed one of the blankets I used to soften my pallet.

Chapter Nine

Normally, about three of the guys would want to sleep in. The morning of the party, I wanted to sleep in myself—but I forced myself out of bed. Not a single guy was willing to move.

"There are women coming," I reminded them. "I've yet to meet a woman who really wants to date a lazy slug."

"One day won't make any difference," Russell complained.

I went back to my room, grabbed my new riding quirt, and started applying it to naked butts and dicks.

The third bed in, I noticed a trend. By the time I'd awakened everyone, I'd confirmed the pattern. To a man, the guys had managed wet dreams.

I wondered if I should feel guilty about it. After all, I'd ordered them to touch me, to rub my feet and my shoulders. While I'd certainly touched all of the guys during our weeks together—what with frequent spankings and adjustments of the leather straps on their dicks (I didn't want to create any sores, after all), I had never let any of them touch *me*. Possibly as a result of my disagreement with Brandon, I'd changed the rules on them.

While there was nothing really wrong with teaching the guys to rub a woman's feet or massage the kinks out of her shoulders, the evidence of the sheets said that the guys had been overly aroused.

I called them together in the dining room. The co-eds they hired to help with the serving didn't show in the morning, so I ordered them to stay naked. They'd learned to stay naked until I gave them permission to dress.

"I am not your lover," I announced. "None of you will ever stick your dicks inside my twat. None of you will ever shove your penis up my ass. I'll never take any of your cocks in my mouth, I'll never suck you dry, swallowing every drop of your cum. I want you to—"

Russell groaned. His dick had turned a vibrant purple and it pulsed like some sort of horror film monster.

"Did you have something to say, Russell?"

"Yes, mistress."

I'd expected him to cower rather than speak up. But I had asked. "Spit it out."

"You're the best looking woman most of us have ever seen, mistress. Getting between your legs may not be any more likely than getting into Jessica Simpson's bed, but that doesn't keep us from thinking, dreaming about it."

I shook my head. "Sometimes I wonder why I'm wasting my time with you. You're in control of your thoughts, aren't you? Why would you want to waste your time fantasizing about me when you could be learning to improve yourselves so you'd be able to attract an age-appropriate female?"

"You're not *that* much older than us, missus."

I'd asked a question, so I couldn't really complain that he'd answered it. Besides, I'd asked a question I didn't want to think about myself. If we really were in control of our thoughts, why did I spend so much time thinking about Brandon when I should be concerning myself with James?"

"We're not just talking about thinking here, though," I reminded them. "We're talking about rules violations. Was last night group jerk night? Had I scheduled a mass masturbation that I forgot to put on my phone calendar?"

"Uh, no missus," Stretch said.

"That's funny. Because there's cum on all of the sheets."

"Sorry, ma'am." That answer echoed from every guy there.

I stared into their grins. I might have been wrong, but those guys all looked to me like they were wishing for x-ray vision.

It was up to me to reset our boundaries. "I don't really think any of you are sorry at all. Grab your ankles, all of you."

A forest of naked male butts, with dicks and balls dangling beneath them, sprung up like mushrooms after a rain.

"I take it the guys aren't ready for their workouts." Brandon stepped into the dining room wearing a cute pair of shorts but no shirt.

Why was it that the one man I couldn't have turned me on more than a baker's dozen young butts?"

"I'm going to have to hold you responsible," I lied. "Your workout routines must be too easy because every single man here shot his wad into his sheets last night."

"Can't say as I blame them. I'd have a hard time controlling myself if I lived with you."

"Maybe you should grab your ankles, too, then."

I wanted him to rebel. What I really wanted, I realized, was for him to become James, to put me in my place. If I'd told James to grab his ankles and present me his naked butt, he would trip the quirt from my grasp, whip my bottom with it until I couldn't sit on it for a week, then make me lick out his ass from behind while giving him a reach-around handjob.

A woman, James had told me a thousand times, *needs* to be dominated by her man. But Brandon just wouldn't dominate me. Which wasn't at all fair considering he'd given me the best orgasm I'd ever experienced only about fifteen hours before.

Instead of turning the tables on me and punishing my butt, Brandon smiled, dropped his shorts so I could see he still wore the straps I'd tied to his cock, and bent over.

I walked around the circle of males flicking my quirt to leave red stripes across buttocks, to tease their ball-sacks, or to flick their dicks.

The guys groaned, their knuckles whitening as they held their ankles, but put up with the punishment. Brandon, when I got to him, did the same.

"Did you enjoy that?" He asked me when I'd finished.

"It's completely perverted."

He shrugged. "Maybe. But that doesn't mean you can't like it."

"Well, I don't."

"Too bad." Without permission, he straightened, stepped toward me and brought his lips to my ear. "I guess," he said, "that wet spot in your shorts comes from sweat."

"You've got two minutes to put on shorts, shoes and socks," I announced. "Anyone who doesn't make the deadline is banned from the party tonight. Whoever finishes your five-mile run slowest has to wash all of the sheets. Move it."

Brandon shrugged his shorts over his slim hips and tossed me a towel. "You might wrap that around your waist."

"I don't get turned on by a bunch of twenty-year-olds. That's sick."

"Why? Your wonderful ex-husband gets turned on by twenty year-old co-eds. Why is it normal when it's him and sick when it's you?"

"Because he's a guy."

"You're a very sexual woman, Nicole. It's normal that you'd react to the huge load of testosterone these guys generate. You keep them revved to such a sexual peak that it would be hard not to respond."

"If you're trying to tell me something, I'm not hearing it. But don't worry. I don't think I want to hear it. Besides, you made it perfectly clear *we* have no future."

Brandon shook his head. "Don't put this on me, Nicole. You're the one who decided we had no future. You're the one who insists on ruining what just might be the best thing that ever happened to either of us just to chase some weird fetish that—"

"The best thing that ever happened to me was James pulling me out of the crowd of co-eds and making me special. The worst thing was when he dumped me."

The fraternity brothers piled back into the room and I assumed the discussion was over. Brandon surprised me, though, by brushing his callused palm against my cheek.

"You were already special, Nicole, before James walked into your life. James didn't make you special by picking you, he picked you because you are special. And when he dumped you, he sabotaged the best thing that ever happened to him, but he gave you exactly what you needed. You were stuck in a rut, but now—"

"But now I'm a figure of fun for the whole campus and a wet dream for the guys in the fraternity. Didn't you hear what I said? Every single one of them shot their wad in their sheets last night. I woke up this morning to the smell of semen."

He brought his lips back to my ear. "I shot my wad in my sheets last night thinking about you as well. What do you think the odds are that James did?"

"Zero. He's got Amber to swallow his spunk. He doesn't need to have wet dreams."

Brandon shook his head as if he'd made a point and I'd been too dumb to miss it. I didn't think so, though. James had what he wanted. I didn't have what I needed. To me, that sounded like I was the one who'd lost out and who needed to regain my place.

"No weights today," I announced. "Pound out the miles, though. If I don't hear that at least half the guys came down with dry heaves from running too hard, that wasn't good enough."

"Yes, missus!" The assembled brothers headed for the door with Brandon tailing behind.

"At least think about what I said," he told me as he followed hit the front porch.

"Sure, Brandon. Whatever."

From outside, I heard high-pitched cheeps coming from Cambridge State co-eds who increasingly gathered to see the nearly-nude Pi Iota Sigma fraternity brothers set off on their runs. I wondered if they knew about the dick-straps the guys wore under those shorts, and whether they'd find them sexy or disgusting.

With the guys gone, I grabbed my Fido bowl, filled it with cereal, and enjoyed a quick breakfast.

Brandon was right about only one thing—James had picked me because I'd been special. But what had made me special was my high-slung rack, my glossy-black hair, my perfect complexion in a world where so many other girls had zits, and my long legs. And I'd been a virgin, someone looking to a man like James to teach me what to do with that above-average body.

My body might still be above average—certainly I'd gotten more positive feedback over it during my weeks with the boys than in the last decade with James. Still, I was no virgin, and younger women with bigger tits, blonder hair, tighter assholes, had replaced me. Just as they'd soon replace me in the minds of my fraternity boys.

I finished my breakfast, washed out the bowl and hid it under my bed, then walked through the house looking for work to assign out to the guys. As Stretch had pointed out the previous day, I didn't really need to do much cleaning--there was always a fraternity brother who'd snuck a milk shake at the student union, who'd jerked off in the shower, thinking I wouldn't notice, or who tried to skip out on a class.

Unfortunately, I couldn't find anything other than the cum-soaked sheets I'd already assigned to whomever ran the five miles most slowly.

The guys had worked their buns off getting ready for the party, scrubbing the floors, walls and ceilings before decorating them with the dungeon effect. I thought about letting the shower pound down on my clit for a while, but that still didn't have much appeal.

"I'm getting ready to go back to James," I told myself. "It's natural that I wouldn't want to masturbate because James hasn't given me permission to have an orgasm."

I was profoundly unconvinced.

* * * *

"Just sit on the chair," Russell told me. "You've *got* to be on display. After all, you're our chaperone. We can't have a fraternity party if we don't have one."

The guys had waited until ten minutes before the party to explain the role they wanted me to play, which went with the black leather outfit they'd bought me. I was supposed to sit on a throne, and let potential candidates suckle my toes.

"If they won't lick your toes, they probably aren't right for us," he pointed out.

"Fraternity guys are supposed to want their chaperones to disappear," I said. "Who ever heard of putting one on display?"

"You're our key feature," Stretch argued. "Of course we're leading with you."

I knew some guys were subs. Brandon proved it, Stretch proved it, Russell proved it. But that didn't mean anything—the Pi Iota Sigma fraternity had attracted Cambridge State's biggest losers for years. Unfortunately, the guys couldn't understand that putting an old woman dressed as a dominatrix in front of the crowd would scare the cool men on campus away.

Of course, I was probably the only one who cared that Stretch was unlikely to unhitch Amber from James unless we fooled Amber into thinking that he was one of the in crowd.

Still, a bad plan was often better than no plan at all, and it was too late for me to come up with an alternate. I climbed onto the throne-like chair the guys had built on a pedestal, hiked my tits a bit higher in the bustier, then pressed my legs together because the microskirt put my naked twat at eye level.

"You look great." Stretch's dick strained against his skin-tight black leather pants. His open leather vest, a sort of harem-style design but with an S&M feel to it, showed off his well-built chest and his abs—now showing a six-pack of muscle rather than the six-pack-generated flab I'd seen when we'd met. "I can hardly—"

What he could hardly do, besides hardly keeping his cum inside his dick, we never learned.

The doorbell rang, signifying that the first of our guests were five minutes early.

"Don't they normally visit several fraternities on rush night?" I asked Russell. "Who would come here first?"

He laughed. "Sometimes, ma'am, you come across as a hardass. It's hard to remember that you're as big a mass of insecurity as any of us."

"You dare laugh at me. One hundred pushups."

He was counting them out when Stretch walked into the ballroom with a group of ten males.

If these were freshmen, freshmen had gotten a lot better looking since I attended school.

Stretch solemnly collected invitations, read off their names, jerked off their shirts and slapped nametags on their now-naked chests, and commanded them to hit the floor and do pushups with the fraternity president. From Chuck's whisper, I picked up that this was the rugby club, a group not known for joining anything.

For a moment, I let myself wonder whether Brandon had been on the rugby club. These guys were in the process of developing the hard muscle, fierce good looks, and, from the way they started nailing out pushups, the same easy-going attitude Brandon had.

Stretch joined the guys doing pushups, while Chuck brought in the next group of guys.

These weren't all hard-body types like the rugby club. They seemed, however, to include a mix of just about every kind of guy on campus. A short kid with thick glasses looked like a cartoon version of a genius. A fat kid looked around for food. An obviously gay kid with a perfectly accessorized outfit blinked at me. All, though, surrendered their shirts, accepted the name tags stuck to bare skin or hairy chests, and dropped to the floor to keep Russell company a he counted out his hundred.

A couple of co-eds had arrived by the time Russell shouted "one hundred." He used the momentum from his last pushup to stand, literally pushing himself all the way from the ground.

I was impressed. After a hundred pushups, I didn't think *my* arms would be able to lift a cock ring, let alone show off like that. Considering the bulge in his tight black jeans, it was a definite shame the residual sense of decency James had never been able to train out of me marked him as ineligible to me.

The potential pledges weren't doing nearly as well. The rugby players had made it to fifty, but of the rest, the best of them had only done twenty pushups and one had collapsed after five. Still, they high-fived each other as they struggled to their feet.

"You will beg for permission to kiss our mistress's toes," Stretch commanded. "On your knees."

One by one, the potential pledges crawled up to me and whispered their requests to be allowed the honor of kissing my feet.

Russell hadn't cleared this with me but I went along with the gag. If he wanted to make his fraternity look like a bunch of sissy-boys, that was his business. Besides, even if I couldn't imagine taking any of these boys into my bed, what woman would complain about a lineup of cute college boys begging permission to grovel at her toes?

They didn't just grovel, either. As I gave them permission, they tongued my toes, lapped at my instep, and purred when I rubbed their spit off in their hair.

"I see we have some female visitors," Stretch announced when I'd finished with the early arrivals. "At Pi Iota Sigma, Mistress D'Angre is training us to satisfy females fully. If you young ladies would care to take your seats in the chairs along the north wall.

Those chairs were outfitted with wrist and ankle restraints. I knew at least some of the co-eds would get into being subdued. Women who grew up in the south were taught that seeking pleasure is unnatural in a woman. Being restrained, given no choice but to submit to the male, allows a woman to savor sex without taking responsibility for it. That, I realized, had been my story. The co-eds might love it, too—but nobody was getting forced, even if they partly wanted it, on my watch.

"Stretch," I said. "Get over here."

He whirled to face me, jogged over, and knelt at my feet. "Yes, mistress?"

"If you think you're going to tie those girls up and screw them, think again. I don't care if they voluntarily sit in those chairs and beg for your cocks, it's not happening."

"That isn't the plan, mistress. I think you'll approve of what we do but if not, we are your slaves to command."

I nodded. "I'll be watching."

"Of course. We know that you're always watching us. I have to say, I had no idea how sexy it could be to imagine that a beautiful woman has her eyes on you no matter what you're doing or how humiliating it might be. With your permission, I'll return to the party."

"Yeah, whatever."

The fraternity brothers adjusted the arm restraints, then secured blindfolds over the eyes of the half-dozen co-eds who'd taken their seats.

"Other women will get the treatment," Russell announced. "But because you went first, trusted us when you had no reason to do so, you'll always be remembered as special women by the brothers of Pi Iota Sigma. If you ever need anything from one of us, you have only to ask."

The co-eds giggled and whispered. I noticed that two weren't wearing panties and crossed their legs a little obviously, as if trying to cover up, but actually drawing attention to their smooth-shaved pussies. I wondered about that—we'd worn thongs to parties when I'd been a freshman twelve years earlier, but I'd never have dared risk displaying my twat on the dance floor back then—not until James had broken me of the habit of wearing underwear.

When the co-eds were restrained, Russell and Stretch pulled the line of chairs out from the wall.

A few squeals came from the six co-eds secured to those chairs. More came from the second group of co-eds who'd arrived. The party was definitely starting to fill up the place.

Chuck knelt next to me. "We have another group of pledges who wish the privilege of kissing your feet, Mistress."

I settled back into my chair and savored the tongue-work as each of the young men attempted to out-do the others with their oral caresses.

One of the guys looked up, obviously trying to grab an upskirt glance at my snatch.

I brushed my quirt across his cheek. "There's a line between bravery and idiocy," I told him. "You just stepped way past that line."

He dropped his gaze back to my feet. "Sorry, mistress."

While he licked my feet, I checked out the girls on the chairs. A line of brothers carried Iron caldrons from the kitchen, placing them in front of the co-eds.

"They're going to rape and sacrifice them," one of the guys in line whispered. "Brother Bob at the Whole Bible Church was right about this place."

"Don't be an idiot," his friend whispered back. "First, Brother Bob is a good Christian, but he's also a paranoid moron. Second, these are some of the prettiest girls in the school. If they were going to sacrifice anyone, they'd do ugly girls since nobody would notice."

I wondered if I should correct the two guys, but decided they wouldn't believe me. After all, if we were a cult group worshiping the father of lies, could we really be expected to tell the truth?

The fraternity brothers lowered the caldrons in front of the co-eds, stripped off sandals and heeled shoes, sliced away the stockings of the one co-ed who'd worn hose despite the Mississippi heat, and plunged the women's now-bare feet into the caldrons.

I halfway expected to hear shrieks—these were guys, after all. Three weeks earlier, when the semester first began, they would definitely have filled those caldrons with something that felt like worms or human eyeballs or something equally disgusting. From the cautious looks on their blindfolded faces, the co-eds had the same concerns. Instead of screaming, though each co-ed breathed a sigh of relief when her feet descended into her caldron.

"Pledges one through ten, please step forward," Russell announced.

Ten guys, running the gamut from obese nerd type to some seriously cute, if under-age for me, crowded up to Russell, anxious to see what came next.

"Odd numbers on the right, even on the left, by numbers. You will now wash their feet. Clean them thoroughly, then a brother will bring you pumice, polish remover, and polish."

While the potential pledges pedicured the surprised and overjoyed co-eds, a current brother stood behind each co-ed, massaging her shoulders and upper back.

Again, I was suspicious. I watched for what I felt sure would be the inevitable 'accidental-on-purpose boob-grab. But that didn't happen.

By the time the first group of co-eds had been pedicured and released from their restraints, the other girls who'd wandered into the party were anxiously pushing their way to the front of the line and on their phones calling all their friends to come and get it.

Girls tracked down Russell, Stretch and the others, begging to cut in line. A couple even tried unfair inducements—unfastening extra buttons on their tops or flipping their hair and touching the guys' faces while they talked.

I wasn't sure how the guys would handle it. They'd had weeks of me lording it over them, treating them like peons barely worthy of licking my ass.

They grinned like imps, but didn't succumb to temptation.

The guys did paint tiny Pi Iota Sigma's on the girls' big toes—but I made sure they offered to strip that off and replace it with plain polish.

None of the girls accepted that offer, though. And none put their shoes back on. By ten, the ballroom floor was a nosh-pit of hormone-ridden co-eds, dancing wildly in bare feet—and increasingly bare bodies as their body heat overwhelmed the house's air conditioning and they stripped everything non-essential, exposing bare arms, tummies, cleavage, and thighs.

A few of the fraternity guys and pledges danced, too, so the girls could pretend they weren't strippers, but I recognized their dance for what it was—a mating display.

From their grins, Stretch, Russell and the others recognized it, too. "I've seen pictures from the fraternity archives of the eighties, back when we were cool," Russell shouted over the hard rock drive of the sound system. They never had anything like this." He held out his arm, letting me see the line of names and phone numbers girls had written there.

Only one of the girls had given me her phone number and she was obviously drunk and willing to try anything. Still, plenty of co-eds had cornered me to ask whether I really did beat the guys, whether I'd beat girls if they went out with any of the fraternity brothers, and if it was true that the guys trained in sexual endurance.

I answered their questions truthfully. Yes, I beat the guys when I thought they needed it, but I found making them tongue-clean the bathrooms to be far more effective when I wanted to change their behavior. Yes, I'd beat anybody who dated one of my guys, but only if I thought she needed it. And yes, I did train the guys in what it took to satisfy a woman—with learning to hold onto their wads only a small part of that.

At eleven thirty, people were still arriving, the massage chairs were still in operation, new potential pledges were still ripping off pushups, and it looked like the party might go on all night.

I spotted Stretch and called for him.

He hurried over and crouched by my side. "Yes, Mistress."

"Time to shut this down."

"You're kidding. Chicks are still arriving."

"You've read about those fancy clubs in New York, right? Where the bouncer has to let you in and there are always lines of people who just hope to get in."

He rubbed his chin. "So?"

"So, think about it. Would the party be better if everyone wished they'd gotten there earlier, or if we let everyone party until they got sick of it?"

"Yeah, but..." his voice tailed off and I lost his attention.

I didn't put up with being ignored and had my quirt ready. Before letting him experience the touch of whip against bare stomach, I decided to check what he was looking at.

James had arrived at the party.

My ex-husband wore that condescending look he'd put on for those rare occasions when he'd decided to humor me, but he wasn't humoring me this time. Amber danced on the end of her leash, getting into the beat, her hips shimmying, her bouncy twenty-year-old double-Ds rotating to the music like cement mixers.

"Dance with me, James," she squealed. "This is so cool."

I couldn't say anything. For the first time since James had kicked me out of his house, I felt his gag in my mouth, even though I knew it wasn't really there. Then again, I really had nothing to say. In the twelve years I'd been with James, ten of them as his wife, he'd never danced with me—and I must have begged him a hundred times before I'd finally given up.

"You go ahead." He unhooked her leash.

He hadn't noticed me until then and his eyes widened when he saw me. "I'll just talk to Nic, here."

"I'm a good dancer," she protested. "I'll bet I'm better than her."

"I'm sure you are," he said.

"Tell you what, Amber," I said. "Stretch here would be willing to take you out on the dance floor. Have a good time."

Stretch looked like he might kiss me—or kill me. But when Amber grabbed his arm, he went.

Women love guys who dance. Unfortunately, I'd had mixed success beating any sense of rhythm into my crew. They were willing when I told them that dancing was a socially acceptable chance for women to rub their bodies all over a guy they hardly know, and who they couldn't justify touching anywhere else. But most of my guys moved like someone had taken a broomstick and shoved it up their ass until it hit their throat. They just couldn't seem to find joints in their hips, waist, or back. I'd hoped our workouts would improve that—but there's a difference between improving and non-horrid. It was a distance few of the guys had traveled.

Since I'd promised Stretch I'd help him get Amber, I'd spent a bit of extra time with him, and with Russell as well. Unlike most of the others, Stretch had actually learned something about his body. I wouldn't say he could dance, but he faked it better than most.

The sound system switched into an ancient Z-Z Top tune and Stretch and Amber hit the dance floor.

"Too bad you had to settle for a cleaning job," James said.

I shrugged. "You know I didn't have a lot of skills. And this job has kept me busy."

"That's what I've heard." He practically sprayed me with his sneer. "Do you really think the alumni and administration will put up with an S&M fraternity on campus?"

"Nobody's objected so far. They certainly don't object to their faculty practicing bondage and discipline on co-eds."

He stuck his face inches from mine. "What *I* do is different. I'm a man. It's unnatural for a woman to dominate a bunch of kids. You're going to turn them into faggots or something."

"If any of my guys are gay, they were that way a long time before they pledged the fraternity. And it may not be natural for a forty-something man to be dominated by a woman, but my guys are barely more than kids. They've spent their lives following their mothers' orders. I'm taking over that role, but giving them orders a mother only wished she could enforce.

"Are you talking back to me?"

"Of course not, James. I'm simply pointing out some facts you might be ignorant of."

A vein pulsed on his forehead. "You, a college drop-out is calling me, a full professor, ignorant? You're definitely off your training since I tossed you out on your ear. I guess I shouldn't be surprised. After all, after ten years, I was still disciplining you like you were a novice. Anyway, your feeble excuses won't do you any good when the University shuts down your cheap little whorehouse."

My brain felt like it had gotten caught in one of those old-fashioned wringer-dryers and was being contorted out of shape. "This isn't is a whorehouse, James. There's no sex here at all."

James prided himself with his calm, but I didn't see any evidence of that calm now. His face morphed to the ugly red of an overripe radish. "You stupid bitch. You know I'm not speaking literally. Whips, mandatory masturbation, strapped dicks, even making those boys swallow their own semen. This is Mississippi, idiot. The powers that be here think of sophistication as a dangerous influence."

Since I was from Mississippi, I thought James's slam was a bit unfair, if not completely inaccurate. Then again, James had spent most of our twelve years together making light of my state, its supposedly moronic population, our accents—which he claimed reflected slow thought processes—and our hypocrisy about sex.

"It's funny that you always have something negative to say about Mississippi, but you're still working here after twenty years. What's the problem? Couldn't find another jo—"

"That's enough, slut." He balled a fist and swung it at my face.

James had beaten me with whips, spanked me, and pinched me so hard the bruises hadn't faded for weeks. He'd never punched me before, no matter how frustrated I'd made him.

He didn't punch me this time, either, but only because a suntanned arm got between me and James, redirecting that punch into the wall.

"Stay out of this, library-boy."

I'd invited Brandon to the party back before our fight but I hadn't seen him and I'd been certain he hadn't come. I'd been wrong.

He pushed me away from James, putting his own body between us.

"There are," Brandon said, "a lot of negative things you can say about Mississippi culture, Professor. I'd even agree with you on a few of them. But there's one thing we're taught that you might want to pay attention to. We don't hit women. Ever. For any reason. You want a fight, I'll—"

"You fight me?" James's laugh seemed incredibly genuine. "Grovel at my feet is more like it, little submissive."

"Come on, you two," I said. James trained at a boxing studio twice a week. He was good enough that his trainer pitted him against guys half his age—and won money on the bets. "This is a fraternity party, not a prize fight."

"I'm not looking for a fight," Brandon said. "But I'm not letting him hurt you. He did enough of that while you were married."

"That's redic—`"

James planted a hand in Brandon's chest and shoved. "What I do to Nic is my business."

Brandon gave way with the shove. Instead of reeling backwards, though, he twisted his body so James stumbled past him.

"Maybe," he said, "it was your business when you were still married. But you divorced her. As far as I can see, that means you have no right to do anything to her."

"I guess I do have to teach you a lesson." James put his fists up and stepped into a boxing stance.

I scuttled from behind Brandon and tried to get between them, but Brandon seemed to have eyes on the back of his head. He kept his body between me and my husband.

When James finally struck, he moved so quickly I couldn't follow his fists.

Brandon didn't stop the punch, he simply shifted his weight, stuck up a hand, and allowed James's fist to pass a fraction of an inch from his face—and then did the same thing with James's follow-up punch.

"Think you're fancy, do you?" James launched himself into a flurry of attacks.

I lost count of how many fists Brandon made miss, but he couldn't do it to all of them—James was too fast and Brandon wasn't hitting back.

One strike bent Brandon's straight nose to the right side of his face. He grunted when James landed a punch to his gut.

I squealed and grabbed for James's arm.

James punched me in the stomach.

All the air rushed from my lungs and my vision blurred with tears as I fell on my butt, my legs going straight into the air. My naked pussy was on display—at least it would have if anyone had been looking at me instead of the two angry men.

Brandon hadn't fought back when James had attacked him, even after James landed those two punches. I'd about decided James was right about poor Brandon. As a submissive, the librarian was incapable of doing more than defending himself, especially of attacking a dominant like James.

When he'd hit me, though, James had changed the rules.

Brandon blocked James's next punch high, stepped under the taller man's reach, and drove an elbow into James's ribs.

Z.Z. Top failed to hide the distinctive crack of breaking bone.

James stared at Brandon for a moment, tried to bring his fists back to eye level, then sagged against the wall.

"You hurt him." My voice came out in a shrill squeal.

"Your ex-husband is a loser and an abusive jerk." Brandon pulled a handkerchief from his black jeans and wiped blood from his broken nose. "I shouldn't have just hurt him, I should have put him down like a rabid 'coon."

I ignored my stomach's complaints, struggled to my feet, and rushed over to where James sagged lower against the wall. "Are you all right, master? Is there anything I can do?"

James glared at me. "Yeah there's something you can do. Help your pathetic boyfriend with his resume. The University is the biggest employer in this town and the mayor knows it. You can bet that library-boy has just earned his last paycheck."

The song ended and James shoved himself away from the wall, grabbed Amber by the collar, attached her leash, and dragged her away from the party.

"You want him back?" Brandon demanded in the sudden silence. "Even if you have no respect for yourself, I'd think you'd want to set a better example for your guys."

"I don't know what you're talking about."

"Do you want them to turn into miniature versions of James? I thought you were teaching them something different—to cherish women, to care about their happiness. If you run back to James, you'll prove exactly one thing—that the biggest and most abusive jerks are the ones who get the prettiest girls."

"James isn't a jerk, he's masterful. Anything I've taught the guys, I learned from James. I shouldn't have made that crack about why he's still in Mississippi since he has nothing but bad things to say about us—that set him off. But he's still a wonderful man."

"Just about every abused woman blames herself. The best thing that ever happened to you was when he dumped you."

"You're wrong, Brandon." I made myself take a deep breath. "I don't want you to think I'm not grateful for stopping him from hitting me because I am, although he ended up hitting me anyway. But I think you should leave."

Brandon glared at me, his jaws biting down so hard the muscles stood out from the side of his face. For a moment I actually thought he'd throw me over his shoulder, drag me to my bedroom, and take out all of his frustrations by nailing me on my bed. Then he turned on his heel and headed for the door.

When he reached it, he turned to face me. "When James was wrong, you were brave enough to tell him. Now you're wrong and I'm brave enough to tell you. You're pissing away something special here for a man who's not worth licking mud off your feet."

"I appreciate that you think I'm so wonderful, Brandon. I wish I could live up to the perfection you think you see in—"

"I never said you were perfect, Nicole. I said you were special."

Sending him away felt like I was reaching into my gut and ripping out a kidney or something equally important. I squared my shoulders and made myself do it. James had always promised me that pain made me stronger. After what I was going through here, I suspected I'd be strong enough to get a job in the circus. "Good-bye Brandon. I'll do what I can to stop James from getting you fired."

"If you want to do me a favor, do it by staying away from that man."

"That's the one thing I can't do."

He shook his head like I'd connected with a punch. "Bullshit."

Before I could answer that, he was gone.

Chapter Ten

"The party was awesome," Stretch shouted.

The other thirteen existing fraternity brothers yipped out their agreement.

I'd been tempted to snooze my alarm, but I'd decided the guys would be better off with another long run. I'd thought it would be a way to teach them to control their partying, to show them that late nights don't match with real life.

I hadn't calculated for the resilience of twenty-year-old young men.

Eight miles into it, they were still exchanging knuckle knocks, drooling over the hot babes who'd graced the fraternity with their presence, and running down the list of guys who'd requested application forms to join the fraternity.

A golden SUV roared by—for the fourth time that morning. Once again, I caught sight of blond hair blowing from the open back window. Instead of continuing on, this time the SUV pulled over across the street from our group and waited.

As we approached, a half-dozen female voices called out suggestions, mostly involving dropping shorts.

"Amber's sorority," Stretch whispered to me.

I was impressed that he could still whisper after eight miles at a six-minute mile pace. Just a few weeks earlier, he'd been scrawny with a bit of a beer belly. Again, the resilience of the twenty-year-old amazed me. Again, I wished I could develop some level of sexual interest in the boys. I really could have my own harem of cuties. Maybe Stretch preferred Amber, but the others would sell their souls for any sort of sexual encounter with me, even if they had to share that encounter with the dozen fraternity brothers.

When we jogged past the co-eds, though, the back door opened and a tall blonde form hopped out, running to catch up with us.

"Slow down," I ordered. "Seven minute mile pace."

Amber was already panting, and the sorority sisters drove alongside her, probably worried her double-D's would knock her unconscious.

"Hi, Stretch," she said.

"Oh, hi Amber. I didn't know you were a runner."

"James has been making me run some." She fingered her chrome choke-collar. "I had to see a special designer to get something that could keep these from getting all torn up." She gestured to her oversized tits.

"Definitely wouldn't want those to get injured," Stretch agreed.

"I wanted to tell you I had a good time last night. James isn't much for dancing."

"Mistress Nicole has been teaching all of us to dance," Stretch admitted. "I'm surprised she didn't teach James, considering they were married all those years."

"James isn't much for letting anyone teach him anything," Amber admitted. "He has a definite way about him, though—`something that makes him stand out from the students here. Most of them, anyway."

I suspect my face fell as completely as Stretch's had. Sure, I didn't expect miracles. Still, I didn't need Amber to be quite so enamored.

"Being a professor and all—" Stretch began.

"I was real surprised," Amber interrupted, "when I met the guys in your fraternity. I don't know what it is, but you guys have it too."

Every male chest in our little running group puffed out.

"Thanks, Amber." Stretch's grin made him look like he was in immediate danger of the top of his head falling off.

"There was just one question I wanted to ask you."

"What's that?"

The giggles from the SUV paralleling our run gave me a clue what was coming.

Amber smiled. "Actually, it wasn't me who was interested. Some of the other girls were curious, and they asked me to find out for them."

More giggles.

"Okay. What do they want to know?"

Stretch was buying Amber's story about asking for the other girls, which made one of us. In my opinion, she wouldn't have asked if she hadn't been interested in the answer.

"It's your nickname—Stretch. I've never known anyone named that, except one guy who was almost seven feet tall. And you're less than six feet."

"Too true."

"There's a rumor going around the school that the guys named you that because of your enormous, uh, schlong.

"Really? Well—"

"Frankly, Stretch, the girls won't take words for an answer. After all, we all know guys who lie about their size.

"You're kidding? Why would they do that?"

"Can you hold still for a second?"

I called the guys to a halt. I thought I knew where this was going I also thought it could do us some good.

Sure enough, the moment we stopped, Amber plunged a hand down inside Stretch's shorts.

"It's definitely eight inches," she shouted to the girls in the SUV. "Thick as a rolling pin."

The giggles didn't let up, but they sounded a little awestruck as well.

I'd seen Stretch's dick. Eight inches was about right, but the girth of a rolling pin was a definite exaggeration. Maybe after a few weeks with James's dick, Amber's standards had been lowered.

"Guess that answers their questions," I said. I noticed she didn't release her grip on Stretch's cock.

"Ask him about staying power," one of the sorority girls shrieked.

Amber pushed her hand up and down on Stretch's rigid dick. "About that, Stretch. Has Mistress Nicole really trained you guys so you're no longer quick-shot artists like most of the other boys around campus?"

Stretch nodded. From the look of his gritted teeth, there wasn't much else he could do.

"Interesting. I'm sure some of the sisters will find that to be excellent news over the next few months.

"Yeah." He managed the one word, then fell silent.

Amber slowly drew her hand from Stretch's shorts, licking her fingers when her hand was free. "Nothing like hot sweat from a sexy guy, huh, girls," she called as she climbed into the SUV.

I know I wasn't the only one who noticed she wasn't wearing panties.

* * * *

"She was just asking questions for the other sorority girls," Stretch whined.

A couple of days had passed since our run. We'd heard rumors James was politicking against the Pi Iota Sigma fraternity, he had gotten Brandon fired from his job at the library, and Stretch hadn't heard a word from Amber.

My plan didn't seem to be working—none of my plans seemed to be working. If Brandon hadn't punched out my husband, and if I hadn't hurt Brandon's feelings, I would have brainstormed with the sexy submissive. My librarian had the incredible ability of helping me make decisions, as well as a charming way of making my decisions actually work out the way I wanted them to. In contrast, James had generally made sure any decision I made was wrong, making me rely on him for everything.

Not that I'd minded, back when we'd been married, I reminded myself. I'd enjoyed letting him take responsibility for everything—especially my sexual fulfillment. That didn't mean I didn't also appreciate the different way Brandon had made me feel. Now, I had neither of them.

"I can't believe," Stretch continued, "that I was dumb enough to believe Amber could be interested in me. Even with what you've done, I'm still a loser.

I might go into pity-sulks once in a while, but I wasn't going to put up with that kind of behavior from my boys. "Don't be an idiot, Stretch. Amber wouldn't have put her hand down your pants for her girlfriends' benefit. She did it because she wanted to feel what you had hidden there. And what you've got is a lot more impressive than what James has to offer."

He shook his head. "It's been days."

I took out my quirt and flicked it up against his balls. "Nobody likes a whiner, Stretch. If I hear any more, you're going to be cleaning my bathroom again--with your tongue."

His dick twitched, getting even harder.

We were in the fraternity house, so he was, of course, naked except for the leather straps tied to his dick. As usual, Stretch's naked dick pointed at the sky like a nuclear missile. Nakedness meant less laundry, and the guys had gotten to the point where they were pleasant to look at.

"If licking my toilet sounds sexy to you, Stretch, you definitely have an overactive imagination."

I wasn't going to take any of my boys to bed, but I certainly didn't mind the eye-candy of a couple of dozen increasingly attractive naked males, every one of whom looked at me as if I were their ultimate sex dream come to life. For perhaps the millionth time since I'd moved into the fraternity, I had to resist the urge to drop to my knees and take a hard dick into my mouth.

Damn. I needed Brandon to help me take the edge off—at least until I got James back.

But getting James back was the problem.

"Sorry about the whining, missus."

"I understand what it's like to want someone so bad you can hardly stand it."

He laughed. "You're kidding, right? Look at you. You could walk across the mall on campus, crook one baby finger, and a thousand guys would line up to serve your every whim. You're even hotter than Amber, and if someone had told me that was even possible before you took over our fraternity, I would have called them a liar."

"It isn't that simple, Stretch."

"You mean because of that asshole, Professor D'Angre? I'm sorry Brandon got fired, but I'll bet even he thinks it was worth it to punch D'Angre out. I've been talking to him about adding martial arts training to our fitness program here and—"

"You've talked to Brandon?"

He shrugged, a gesture that gave his erect boner an extra little jiggle. "Sure. Brandon and I talk all the time. He's a good guy."

"Yeah." He was a good guy. He'd even given me my best orgasm ever. He just wasn't a guy whom I could trust to fulfill my sexuality—because he wasn't the dominant I needed.

"Anyway, I just don't know what to do about Amber. It's been days. I don't get why you don't let me call her. What's the worst thing that could happen?"

"You could piss away your chances. Amber is a woman. No matter how interested she might be, she'll run as fast if she senses that you're desperate, and you are—completely. You'll never get a second chance."

"Okay, so I'm desperate. I've wanted her for over a year now. My balls feel like they want to crawl up inside of me when I think about her."

"That's really romantic, Stretch—not." He didn't get it, but that was because he was a guy. James hadn't really understood what made women tick either, but he'd gotten the head-game thing down to a science. When we'd dated, he'd timed his calls to perfectly coincide with when I'd gone from anxious to worried and was just at the verge of talking to one of the other guys who hung around.

"You boys can be so completely stupid," I said. "Aren't you taking sociology this semester? Haven't they talked about the way dating works? Women send out the signals. Men only think they're asking. If you ask without getting a signal first, that marks you out as a loser."

He blinked at me, his dick softening under the impact of my words. "So all those co-eds who shot me down last—"

"No big surprise, Stretch."

"But I hate to wait."

I hated to wait too. "I'm not saying there's nothing you can do. I'm just saying you can't call her until you get the signal."

"How will I know it, assuming it does come."

"I'll help you recognize it." I glanced at my watch. Five in the afternoon was way too early for serious partying, but the Student Union would be crowded with kids and grad students coming out of their last classes or looking for a cup of coffee after a hard day in the library. "Grab your cue stick and bring Barney. Time to send some phernomes into the environment."

* * * *

James needed to be an expert at everything he tried. That, I abruptly realized, had to be why he never danced—the man had about as much rhythm as a log. His mathematical mind, though, was perfect for billiards. He'd installed a table in our game room, and he used me for a practice opponent. He'd never learned that I often polished my game while he was teaching or screwing one of the department wives—I'd never been foolish enough to beat him. Still, I'd spent an hour or two a day playing pool for ten years. All in all, I was a fair hand with a stick.

As I'd expected, the Union was crowded.

Still, we created something of a stir when we arrived--partly because of the skintight black leather pants I wore--a close match for the tight black jeans Barney and Stretch had poured on over their naked butts and strapped dicks.

All three of us wore thin black wife-beater tops--mine tight enough that my C-cups pressed my air-conditioner-chilled nipples straight forward and the guys showing off impressive pecs and arms.

Half the tables were unused, but nobody was going to be impressed if we played a quiet game by ourselves. I stared around the pool room and settled on a pair of football players matched off in an eightball game. From the crowd around them, they definitely seemed to be the class of the outfit. And at least one of the girls oohing and ahhing their shots was from Amber's sorority.

"That one." I gestured to Stretch. "Put your money down."

"They're better than me."

"Then you'll lose. And I'll have to punish you. I'm counting on you to win Amber and I won't accept failure."

His dick perked up when I'd said 'punish,' but he grew a little pale as I completed my thought. We both needed him to win.

At the Union, the rule was that the challenger puts down two bucks—one to pay for the game and the other to repay the the winner of the previous game. If he wins, he keeps playing for free. If he loses, he buys the winner a beer, coffee, or whatever.

Stretch sucked it up, stalked over to the table, and plunked two one dollar coins on the side of the table.

We'd generated a little attention when we'd walked in. Challenging the school's masters went beyond that. A flurry of whispers mixed with the sound of thumbs clicking out text messages on mobile phones.

The two football players looked up from their game. One of them quickly returned to his shot. The other reached out a hand. "Stretch, right? And I suppose this is the mistress of darkness."

I shrugged, letting my tits do their little dance and watching to see if he tried to crush Stretch's hand when the two shook. That didn't seem to be the plan.

"We heard about your fraternity." Joe Football shook his head but kept his eyes firmly on my boobs. "Nice plan. Too bad you're going to be run off the campus. You've been good for recruiting—all the high school football players want to check out Cambridge State now that the rumors have gone around. If you were still here, you'd have a bunch of pledges this time next year and we'd be able to recruit some potentials."

"We'll survive," Stretch said.

"Well shit," the other football player announced. "At least I didn't leave you anything."

"I'm Harry," Joe Football told my breasts.

I nodded. "I've found that waxing helps with that."

"Very funny." He moved closer but shifted his gaze from my boobs to my face. "Listen, Mistress of Darkness or whatever you want to be called, I got a question." He lowered his voice to a whisper. "Do chicks really go for that dick-shaving thing?"

"Would you rather eat oysters with seaweed growing out of them?"

He jerked as if I'd poked him in the butt with his cue. "I see your point. Plus I hear it makes you look bigger. Not that I have any—"

I traced a single finger along his jeans zipper. "It couldn't hurt."

"You'd better be kidding. Every girl I've dated has told me I was the biggest she's ever—"

"This might come as a shock to you but women aren't all stupid. We know what our guys want to hear and we play it back to him. It's what we tell our girlfriends that counts."

"Huh. I never thought about that." He grabbed his cue, then cleared the table, finally calling the left center pocket for his eightball and sinking it with just a hint of English.

He might not be much in the dick department, but he could play eightball.

"I'll get us a couple of beers," the loser announced. "Sorry I won't get to see you play, Stretch, but having a big cock won't help around the pool table."

"Unless he wants to rack up a different kind of score," a co-ed faux-whispered to her girlfriend. "If I didn't want to piss Amber off, I'd let him do me right there on the table."

Stretch was all ears. "Did you hear what she—"

"Rack the balls," I told him. "We've got a game to play."

Harry broke, sank the eleven, and then rattled off three more stripes. I wouldn't have minded too much if he beat Stretch—as long as Stretch got a chance to show off some good shotmaking. But getting skunked wasn't going to do the job.

I checked out the way Harry was lining up his next shot, figured out where he'd place the cueball, and walked over to the other side of the table.

By the time Harry had sunk the shot and was lining up next, I was there, leaning over the ball to give him a nice angle on my tits.

James had often had me do this—not that he'd needed a distraction considering how bad most of the other faculty members were at pool. A player had every right to ask me to step away but I'd never met a male who wouldn't rather look at my tits. Harry proved to be no exception—not only did he miss, he scratched.

"You did that on purpose," he growled while Stretch placed the cueball.

I jiggled the girls. "Want to make something of it."

"I can beat the shit out of you."

"Oooh—you can beat up a girl. That makes you a powerful man."

"I'll whip your butt in eight-ball."

"Straight pool. Playing for what?"

"I win, you suck my dick. You win and I'll eat your twat."

I laughed. "Got to admit it, Harry. You've got one hell of a sense of humor. How about, I win, I shave Pi Iota Sigma into your buzz-cut. And you spend the weekend as my servant."

"All weekend? Okay. But you not only suck my dick if I win, I get to play with your big tits. That would serve you right for distracting me with them."

I licked my lips. "I'll not only suck you off, you can even squirt on my face."

"Shit. You'll swallow?"

"Unless you've got a girlfriend you want me to spit into."

Sweat beaded on his forehead. "Better dust off your kneepads then. Because you're going down on me tonight."

"After Stretch clears the table."

Which he proceeded to do. The kid might not be the brightest student in the school, but he'd put his time pining for Amber to good use.

Beating Harry was a piece of cake. Every time he made a shot, I puckered my lips and sucked in my cheeks.

He'd really wanted that blowjob, but he got into the spirit of his loss well. In addition to the Pi Iota Sigma shaved into his skull, he'd insisted on wearing one of my collars. He even asked me to tie up his dick the way I tied up the dicks of my guys. Naturally I refused—he wasn't part of the fraternity, and besides, I recognized it as a feeble attempt to get me to squeeze his cock and balls.

Still, he walked like a guy with a raging hard-on as we headed back to the challenge table and I didn't think that was an act.

We got there just in time to see Amber arrive along with a quartette of sorority sisters.

I'd counted on James coming along—had timed our outing for when I knew he'd be out of class and in the area. Apparently, though, Amber was less fully in his thrall than I had been at the same point in our relationship. She'd only brought giggling girlfriends.

Stretch had disposed of the second football player without needing me to create a distraction and now battled Barney, who'd won our fraternity pool tournament the previous week.

Amber watched with apparent interest but she couldn't disguise her growing frustration—like any woman, *she* wanted to be the center of attention and Stretch was stealing it.

Unlike most women, Amber generally got her wish. I doubted a guy had ignored her since the moment her tits started popping out.

She had to be seething that Stretch hadn't even noticed her arrival—especially as she'd obviously gone all-out for him. She'd pulled her tight shorts straight up into her crotch, showing off the distinctive camel-toe lines of pussy, and her double-Ds threatened the integrity of her top, displaying just the slightest hint of nipple-pink.

It was a perfect look—as if she'd just come from a workout. I suspected she'd been working on that look from the moment she'd gotten her first text message. How galling to her that Stretch didn't notice. How anxious it must make her to be noticed.

I grabbed the eight ball from the table. "Maybe Amber wants to challenge in, guys."

She shot me a grateful look. "Oh, I couldn't. I don't even know how to play."

"No problem." I plunked two bucks into the machine and spilled out the balls. "Stretch is a patient teacher. I'm sure he'll be happy to show you the moves."

"You wouldn't mind, Stretch?" She practically purred out the words.

"I—uh"

"He doesn't mind," Harry said.

I pinched one of Stretch buttocks, pulling him away from Amber. "Do *not* cop a feel. If she wants to rub against her, let her. But don't you dare come no matter how hard she rubs. And don't take those popping out tits or shrink-wrapped twat as invitations."

"Why would she show—"

"You ever go fishing?"

He nodded, not sure where I was going.

"You jerk the line when they're still nibbling, you won't catch a thing. The tits and pussy on display show she's nibbling, but that's just the tease. But if you want her to nibble on your cock, if you want a chance to go round the world with her, you've got to wait until she gives you a full bite."

He nodded. "I'll try."

"Do more than try. Go ahead and show her how to play. But don't be too smug—I'll bet she knows more than she's admitting. She's fishing, too, remember? Except she knows she's the lure."

He looked confused, so I let go of his butt-cheek and gave him a push toward Amber. She wasn't a fool. As long as he didn't completely blow it, she wasn't going to let him get away. She'd keep him dangling if for no reason other than to keep James on pins and needles. And James would hate that.

"Your fraternity still taking pledges?" Harry whispered to me as we found an unoccupied table. "My dating life would be a hell of a lot easier if I had someone to help *me* navigate the hard spots."

"Your dating life would be better if you didn't get distracted by thirty-year-old ladies."

He groaned. "Give me a break. I'd kill to have a shot at a chick like you. Most of the co-eds giggle and can't figure out what the hell they even want. With you it's no nonsense. If you wanted me, you'd have had me strapped to your bed, my cock at your command, an hour ago. I could only be so lucky as to find someone with a tenth of your sexual charisma."

"If you say so."

He cocked his head. "You're not really going to stay here and play pool, are you?"

I shrugged. "I told him that because I didn't want him to freak. But you're right. It's time for him to fly on his own—or crash and burn. As long as he keeps her simmering a bit longer, Amber will be begging for his dick."

"Do you really think that's fair to her?"

I'd actually wrestled with that question. Sure Amber had been part of what had happened to me when I'd hit thirty. But I knew James, knew he'd spotted her, hunted her down, attracted her with the same type of techniques he'd used on me—techniques a lot more powerful than the simple understanding of woman's psychology I was giving Stretch. She wasn't the villain in this story.

"I'm taking care of myself. Besides, Stretch isn't that bad."

He shook his head. "So, is it true new fraternity brothers get to take you to bed for their initiation?"

Chapter Eleven

"She kissed me." Stretch burst into the fraternity ballroom, his hands held over his head, obviously looking for high fives.

"Sit down, Stretch," Russell said. "We're in trouble."

"*You* may be in trouble. Thanks to Mistress Nicole's advice, I'm practically into Amber's pants.

"How interested do you think she'll be when you're living in a dorm again?"

Stretch opened his mouth to answer, then slammed it shut when he caught Russell's meaning. "They can't possibly remove our accreditation. We're the only fraternity on campus on schedule to have its members pass all of their classes."

"Professor D'Angre claims he was assaulted by drunk fraternity members when he passed by our fraternity house during our rush party," Russell explained. "Drunk students and assaulting a full professor are both justifications for decertification."

"But Brandon isn't even a member of the fraternity. He just helps out."

"Professor D'Angre claims several students helped Brandon," Russell explained. "He said there was no way a wimp like Brandon stood a chance against him in a fair fight."

"Yeah," one of the brothers grumbled. "Like he's so tough. The reason nobody takes his classes is because he's a complete nerd."

"He's not a nerd." I'd been thinking about what to do since getting back from the pool game and finding the notice of proposed decertification on the fraternity house's front door. It seemed possible that James was reacting to my relative success. If I agreed to give up the fraternity, surely he'd back off on his plans.

When I explained that, every single head in the place shook. "Without you, I wouldn't have a shot at Amber," Stretch confided. "And I doubt a single pledge would stick with us. Which means, if you leave, we shut anyway and d'Angre gets what he wants. You've got to stay."

"If I stay—"

"We need Brandon," Russell announced. "No offense, mistress, but when it comes to fighting, Brandon outranks you."

"But he's a sub." A lot of things came to my mind when I thought about submissives. Expertise in fighting back wasn't high on the list.

"I'll get him on the phone," Stretch announced.

Brandon showed up early the next morning, in time to take the guys for their run.

I needed the exercise and wanted to see Brandon, so I went along. The first thing I noticed was that he'd lost his collar.

"Considering everything, I didn't think the collar conveyed the right message," Brandon told me before I could even ask.

I thought about the way I'd reacted to the fight.

I'd blamed Brandon, even though James had started it, and even though Brandon had only gotten in the middle to keep me from getting hit.

Clearly I'd been in the wrong. I couldn't be happy about poor James being beaten, but I could still recognize that he had asked for it.

"I'm sorry I lit into you for beating up James," I said.

"Are you really?"

I had to be truthful. "Sort of. I spent a lot of years with James and it hurts me to see him in pain."

He shook his head. "It hurts me to see how badly he twisted you from who you really are."

My mouth gaped open and I stopped so suddenly that a couple of fraternity guys crashed into my back. "What are you talking about?"

He waved his hand. "Look at you with the boys."

I knew what I'd see, but I followed his direction, checking out the fourteen guys on the run. They looked better, healthier than they had when I'd taken them under my wing, although there was still obvious room for improvement. They looked sexy in their ultra-thin racing shorts, no shirts, and leather collars but, as I'd suspected, none of them did anything for me. "So?"

"You've turned their lives around. Do you really think James trained you to do that?"

"Of course. He trained me—"

Brandon sighed. "I know what he trained you. He trained you to bring him his paper in your teeth, to lick his butt while he banged whatever other girl he chose, to tease and distract the other members of the math faculty, and to eat out of a Fido bowl."

"How'd you know the bowl says Fido?"

"You're the number one topic of conversation around the fraternity house, Nicole. Do you think the guys wouldn't notice something like that?"'

"Okay, but that's the point—I'm passing on James's training to the guys."

Brandon laughed. "You may think that's what you're doing, but you're wrong. James beat you down, made you think *less* of yourself so you wouldn't be a threat to his own over-expansive ego. You're building the guys up, helping them become more—"

"But you're wrong. James made me more."

Brandon turned the corner, picked up the pace, and led the pack back toward the fraternity house. "James couldn't make you better if he had a recipe book. He made you weaker. Since you left him, you've discovered the strength you had all along."

I closed my mouth and concentrated on the run. Maybe I should have been complimented that Brandon thought I was so wonderful but I knew better. I was a weak woman who needed a master—all Brandon's words meant was that he had an unhappy relationship with reality.

The guys must have felt equally let down when they dumped the accreditation issue on him and he just shrugged his shoulders.

Hell, even though I'd known all along that fighting with James could only lead to defeat, a part of me was let down that Brandon couldn't step in and solve my problems.

"In general," he finally said, "the best defense is an attack. If you can ruin d'Angre, you eliminate his credibility and his ability to destroy you."

Russell raised a hand. "How can we—"

"You can't," I interrupted. "First, James is a Full Professor and you're only undergraduates plus one unemployed librarian. And second, even if you *could* hurt him, I wouldn't let you. He'd never take me back if I lost him his job."

Brandon gave me a strange look and I abruptly remembered that he'd come back after I'd cost him his job. I told myself that it wasn't the same but a part of me wasn't convinced.

Stretch pulled off his shoes and then stripped off his shorts, leaving him naked except his cock-straps and his leather collar. "*You* can get him, Mistress. You know his secrets. If you went to the faculty board and described how he stalked you when you were an undergraduate, how he insisted that you drop out so you could serve his sexual appetites, they'd fire him. If you explained how he made you eat your breakfast from a dog bowl, how you had to lick his ass and pretend you liked it, how he beat you every day, he'd probably never be able to get another teaching job in the country."

"Who told you that?" I demanded. "I've never admitted to any of those things."

"Amber told me." Stretch took a deep breath. "And she showed me. You've spanked us with your quirt, but the worst any of us have ever gotten is a red butt. Amber had deep bruises on her ass and tits from where James hit her, and scars on her arms and ankles from where he'd chained her. And he's trying to make her drop out of school, just the way he made you. He uses you as a model for Amber, telling her that if she doesn't perform, she won't be living up to your level, and that he just might invite you back."

My heart felt like it was going through a roller coaster ride. For weeks, I'd wanted nothing so much as for James to realize that I was his perfect slave and to call me back into his arms. But a nagging sense of incompleteness interfered with my happiness at hearing he might call me to return. Not just incompleteness because he hadn't actually invited me back, but the sense that I couldn't abandon the fraternity. They'd taken me in when I'd had nothing. I owed it to them to be sure they could carry on without me before walking away.

"I've got to talk to James." I stood and headed for my office. "See what I can negotiate."

Brandon grasped my arm as I passed him. "You don't negotiate with a cockroach, Nicole. You stomp him flat."

"Don't worry, Brandon." It was crazy, but I ran my fingers along his naked shoulders, taking strength from his heat and from his hard muscles. "I'll see if I can get your job back, too."

He clamped a hand down on each of mine, pressing my fingers deeply into the hard muscles in his shoulders. "That's bullshit, Nicole. First, James is a jerk. He'll never give up punishing anyone who gets in his way, no matter what he promises you. And second, do you think I care about my lousy job when you're talking about sacrificing your entire life to go back and be some sort of slave for that asshole?"

"James is not an asshole," I fired back. "And of course he'll keep his promises. James has the strongest sense of honor of any man I know."

"Wow. I know when I've been shot down," Russell whispered, sotto voice.

"You be quiet, too, Russell. Now leave me alone. I'm going to see if I can cut a deal to keep you on campus."

I closed the door to my office and sank into the glove-leather chair the guys had bought me. Pictures of the guys on their first outing, charts recording their progress in weight lifting, distance run, strokes before orgasm, and hours studied lined the walls.

I closed my eyes and tried to remember the clean modern lines of the house I'd shared for ten years with James and came up empty. To an incredible degree, the fraternity house had become my home.

It even took me a moment to remember James's number, although that wasn't a huge surprise. He'd never allowed me to call him—instead, he'd insisted that I stay in range of my own phone, letting him call me whenever he wanted to demand anything. Finally, though, it came to me.

I dialed, then waited. A breathy female voice I barely recognized as Amber's finally responded. "Stretch? Is that you?"

"It's Nicole d'Angre," I told her. "Would you like to talk to Stretch after I'm done with my own conversation?"

"Could you? He is so funny. I can't get over, though, the way he treats me like I'm a princess or something. I mean, James treats me like I'm a sewage treatment plant, just engineered for him to fill me with his cum, to kneel there and let him piss all over me, and to lap up his asshole."

"I'm not much interested in what you've been doing with my hus—"

"Okay, okay. What do you want?"

"I need to talk to Professor d'Angre. Put him on, please."

"I'll check to see if he's here for you, Nicole. It won't surprise me if he says no, though. He's been real busy lately.

"Do your best."

Although I'd closed the door, Brandon opened it while I waited for James to pick up the phone.

I'd worn a tank top for my run and he slipped both straps off my shoulders, poured a dollop of some kind of oil into his hands, and then rubbed it into my back.

I really intended to tell him to go away, but the instant his strong thumbs hit a pressure-point in my back, I knew the effort was pointless. I let his clever hands explore my muscles, moaning with pleasure as he found one erogenous zone after another.

In ten years of marriage, I'd rubbed James's back hundreds of times. At the time, it had seemed natural, appropriate, that he'd never returned the favor.

Now that I knew what I'd been missing, I understood why James had so frequently demanded massage—Brandon's hands felt wonderful as he discovered and slowly untied the many knots tension had tied through my shoulders and back.

"That isn't going to help," I whispered.

From behind me, I felt Brandon's muscular shoulders shrug. "Neither is calling James. I guess we've both got to do what we've got to do."

I had the uneasy suspicion that if I ordered him out, he'd simply refuse. Which wouldn't be good for either of us.

"I'm fairly busy right now." My once and future husband's voice wasn't quite as deeply pitched as Brandon's, and for the first time I could remember, it didn't send instant quivers through my pussy.

"I want to know the deal."

"Deal?" He didn't quite laugh but I didn't miss the mocking tone he put into that one word.

"You've made life rough on Brandon and on the fraternity all because of your little snit. So, tell us what it'll take for you to back off."

"I would hardly call assault a snit."

"We have at least two dozen witnesses who saw you throw the first punch, James."

His sharp intake of breath told me I'd said the wrong thing. What had he expected? That I'd call him master even after he'd dumped me?

"Witnesses consisting of a group of drunk teenagers attempting to circumvent their just punishment and a faggy librarian. I hardly think the university will bother considering their self-serving lies."

I gasped when Brandon's hands found another knot in my back and rubbed it out. My twat had begun to respond, although I wasn't prepared to decide whether it answered to my long-time conditioning or to Brandon's strong hands.

"You were trying to shut down the fraternity even before you assaulted me, with your rumors of satanism. So, tell me what you want."

"What I want is for you to give up your weird dominance fetish. Just look at the difference between men and women. If you open your eyes at all, you'll see that the male is designed to be dominant, designed to lord over a harem of weaker females. What you're doing with that fraternity is obscene."

"I *had* to get a job."

"I realize now that I may have been… abrupt in the way I severed our relationship. So I've arranged for your sale to Professor Sloane in the Philosophy Department. He doesn't mind that you're older and—"

"Sloane is already married." Married to a woman who'd been the hot campus co-ed of a couple of years earlier.

James laughed. "At your age, you can't expect to find another *husband*. You offered to serve as my servant, keeping the house, cleaning, cooking, serving as occasional sperm bucket, when Amber moved in. Obviously that won't work for us but you can serve that role for Sloane."

"You're telling me that you won't back off on the Pi Iota Sigma Fraternity unless I become a slave to a seventy-year-old professor who already has a hot twenty-three-year-old wife?"

Even over the phone, I could see that little head-quirk James thought was so charming. "Did I say anything about letting your unnatural boys off the hook? If I had my way, they'd be castrated and made harem guards. Unfortunately, the University won't allow that, but I will make sure they're expelled from the university—and blackballed from any other reputable college in the south.

"Tell him," Brandon's breath tickled my ear and sent shivers of pleasure down my spine to my soaking-wet pussy. "Tell him where he can shove his offer."

"There's no deal unless you back off on the fraternity and get Brandon his job back."

"Really? Perhaps you'll reconsider when you see what happens next."

"I think you've already done everything as you can, James. You've ruined the fraternity, gotten Brandon fired, and you're likely costing me my job. Whatever else you're planning is what we technically call anti-climax."

His mocking laughter echoed over the phone line. "What a charming description. I can hardly wait until you see it. Ta-ta."

"He's a bully," Brandon said when I set down the handset. "You can't back down to a bully and you can't reason with them. You've got to stand up for yourself."

"Like you know so much about standing up for yourself. Strip down, naked."

"Nicole, you don't—"

"Don't tell me what I want or what I can do." I swept my arm across my desk, sending fraternity paperwork, pens, a stapler, and the calendar flying. "Get naked now, and lie down on my desk."

"Of course, mistress."

He wore only a pair of silky shorts and his running shoes. It should have taken maybe five seconds to get completely naked. Instead, he made a production out of it.

Outside the closed door to my office, a couple of the brothers had been tuning up and now the throaty sounds of a pair of jazzy saxophones filled the air.

Brandon slid his clever hands down his legs, highlighting hard muscles and the cut, almost flayed, length of his legs.

Removing his shoes shouldn't be sexy. The man was nearly naked, anyway, his broad chest tanned a golden brown, his shorts barely rising high enough on his abdomen to keep the swollen mass of his cock from escaping.

It shouldn't have been sexy, but I almost came when he finally removed the second shoe and stood before me with only that thin silk separating us.

"I'm going to use you," I told him. "This has nothing to do with affection or relationships. If the guys weren't too young, I would use one of them instead of you."

"Of course you would. Maybe you'd even use all of them," he suggested. "Fill your hands, your mouth, your ass, your pussy with their hard young cocks."

"Are you teasing me?"

He shrugged. The gesture created a beautiful and stunningly sexy play of muscle across his shoulders and chest. "Why would I tease you?"

Why indeed? Considering he definitely was teasing.

"If you continue to harass me, I will punish you."

He grinned. "As you wish."

"You're right—that would be what you want, you submissive."

"Your ex is wrong, you know?"

"Wrong about what?"

"About most things, probably. Specifically, though, he's a math professor. I doubt he's taken a single class in anthropology in his life. Dominance is not a male-related feature. There's nothing feminine about being submissive. In a healthy relationship, dominance and submissiveness are about trust and intimacy."

"I suppose you're trying to say that James and I didn't have a healthy relationship."

He shrugged again, then looped his thumbs under the elastic of his running shorts and pulled them down—but just enough to expose another inch of lower abdomen. "I believe your fraternity boys would say something like 'you said it, not me.'"

I swallowed, hard. I'd really had something clever to say—something that would affirm the wonderful relationship I'd had with James and put Brandon in his place. But the line where his tan met paler skin called attention to the hard ridges of his stomach—and to the even harder ridge of his dick, swelling like something monstrous just below the surface.

Then he grasped the front of his shorts and pulled, ripping the strong fabric like it was Kleenex, stepped out of the rags and closed the distance between us.

"I ordered you on the desk." My voice was a hoarse whisper.

"I'm getting there."

But he wasn't getting there—he kissed me.

James had kissed me—I felt certain of that. But I could find no memory of his lips on mine. Once Brandon's tongue teased my lips open and plunged into my mouth, I couldn't call up any of my past at all. My mind perceived only the touch of his lips, firm but with a surprising softness, the taste of coffee, chocolate and Brandon on his tongue, the sensation of his arms on my shoulders, drawing me into him, and the incredible hardness and size of his cock pressing against my belly.

Without conscious thought, I committed all of that to memory.

I'd known Brandon was strong.

I'd spent more time than I would admit to anyone trying not to stare at his muscles, pretending to coach the guys when my guts were tying themselves in knots trying to keep my cream from staining my shorts.

Still, when he lifted me off the ground, I felt like I weighed nothing in his arms. I wasn't fat—more than a decade with James had rid me of my freshman fifteen and kept my body honed. Still, I was solid. Brandon picked me up as easily as he'd raise a glass of sweet tea.

For just an instant, his lips lost their lock on mine.

My brain whirled from the impact of his touch, his muscles, his taste. For maybe the millionth time, I wished he were a dominant, could control me, order me on my knees to take his rigid cock in my mouth and swallow that enormous wad of cum I knew he'd built up. For at least the millionth time, I cursed whatever fortune made him submissive. No matter what he said, James had to be right—a real man could only be a dom.

"I don't kiss," I told him.

"Really." He paused, holding me lightly, his dark eyes probing mine. "Here I thought you were doing fine. Maybe you need more practice."

"That's not—" But I couldn't talk any more because his lips descended on mine once more.

I told myself to resist, to clench my teeth, to seal my lips, to refuse to allow him entry. I already liked him too much, was too attracted to him. But once again, James proved right. My dominant act for the guys was only that—an act. Trying to stay dominant, attempting to satisfy Brandon's needs, would ultimately tear both of us to pieces.

So, my body betrayed me. My mouth opened and my tongue met his, explored his mouth, echoed his thrusts with my own.

I'd thought the sound was the guys outside with their saxophones, but when I caught a belated breath, I realized I'd accompanied them with moans dragged up from deep within me.

Brandon had no right to have a free hand. Yet, with no warning, he slid his fingers between my legs.

Blood surged to my thighs and twat. Moisture flooded my swollen vaginal lips as his fingers brushed against my own running shorts.

I felt Brandon's smile against my lips, then he pulled his mouth from mine. "You ordered me on the desk. I think I can comply."

"Good. On your back, th—"

He set me down on the desk, face-up, grasped my shorts, and ripped them off far more quickly than he'd removed his own.

"Brandon. You don't have to carry on with this act."

His smile looked predatory. "Don't I?"

Before I could answer, he'd ripped my shirt down the center, exposing my breasts to the air.

Between my breasts, drops of sweat beaded.

When he bent his head and licked first one breast, then the other, my entire body shuddered. I knew he was acting. Brandon was no dominant and this act must have torn him apart. Still, I could no longer protest. I craved him, needed him inside of me, more than I'd ever wanted anything in my life.

"You may untie my bonds," he told me.

The only bonds he wore were around his cock—those leather straps I used to remind him who was in charge, to make him ever-aware of his sexuality, to stand in for my touch when I couldn't, or wouldn't actually touch him.

I reached for that glorious cock, but he caught both of my hands in one of his own. "With your teeth."

Who was this man?

I struggled, fearing I'd ruin his act, even though I would be doing him a favor if I stopped him before he hurt himself.

His one-handed grip shouldn't have been strong enough to hold me but, even though I strained every muscle in my body, I couldn't move him.

"I bite," I warned.

"You'll do what you have to."

A real dominant would have punished me for the threat, made sure I was aware of truly dreadful consequences if I resisted his force. But in that moment, Brandon showed his submissive side—and I found it sexy. James never would have trusted me without threatening, without complete control, without a dominance that stemmed from power and fear. Brandon trusted me, yielded his body to me, brought the most sensitive part of his body close to my snarling teeth.

In my brain, thoughts chased themselves around like straw caught in a tornado. Brandon was a dom. Brandon was a sub. Brandon was teasing me. Brandon trusted me. Brandon's kisses were like nothing I'd experienced. Brandon's big dick smelled of sex, of soap, of and of his need for me.

He deserved better than me, but at that moment I didn't want him to do better—I wanted him to do me.

I licked my lips, then bit down on the leather strap, letting my moistened lips caress his swollen cock.

Brandon groaned and his dick throbbed. Bubbles of sweat popped up on his ripped abdomen and I brushed my cheek against them as I held the strap with my teeth and pulled the end of the leather chord.

His huge dick sprang free.

"Tell me you want me." His lips against my ear sent ripples through me, feeding on one another until I was awash in sensation.

No true dominant would have asked. Once again, Brandon's fundamental nature betrayed him. Once again, though, I couldn't bring myself to object. "Take me."

He brought his face to my twat, his tongue making wonderful circles on the very tip of my clit.

I'd been trained to control my orgasms, to come only on command, but all those years of training went out the window when he slid two fingers into my pussy... and his thumb up my ass.

Sensations that had flowed through my body like mighty rivers suddenly converged, centering in my sex and they swept all of that training away.

I groaned and spent myself on his hands and tongue.

"That was—"

He raised his lips from my twat and smiled. "If you're going to say something negative, I won't believe it and I'd just as soon not hear it."

"Get on your hands and knees and let me take you in my mouth."

"Tempting." His teeth glistened white against his beautiful tanned face. "But this time, I think I'm going to come inside of you. Just out of curiosity, you are protected, aren't you?"

"Implant."

"As I thought. Your ex-husband is far too self-centered to even consider allowing a child to gain your attention."

"It was *my* decision."

He nodded again. "A wise decision, considering who you were with. He would not be a good father."

And Brandon would. That he could play the dominant meant that his children wouldn't run roughshod over him. That he was submissive in his heart meant that he'd never hurt them, never leave them unprotected.

For an irrational moment, I wished I wasn't on the implant, that I could bear a child by him. A part of him would be better than none at all, and my clock was ticking. Once I got James back, I wouldn't have anything.

"You can take me in my ass," I told him. "I'll be nice and tight for you."

One of his fingers tickled my twat. "You *will* be nice and tight for me, but I'll save your ass for another day. Today, I want your pussy."

Without waiting for an answer, he joined me on the desk, raised my knees to his shoulders, and pressed the tip of his cock against my wet twat.

"I won't be able to come again," I promised. "You're just wasting yourself."

"First, it's my self to waste. And second, I think you underestimate your capabilities. When I first felt your tight pussy, I knew your asshole of an ex-husband didn't properly appreciate you. How could anyone be married to a woman like you and not want to fill you with cock?"

"Why fill up on bread when there's caviar available? My butt and mouth are—"

"Why quote your loser of an ex-husband at a time like this? He wanted his pleasure, and he wanted to make sure you didn't get too much enjoyment yourself."

I couldn't think of an answer, and then, when he plunged into me, I couldn't think of anything at all—except for the way our bodies fit together, the way Brandon filled me completely, the way his hard dick felt like it would split my entire body in half—and made that feel wonderful

He groaned when he entered me.

For a moment, I thought he'd lost control, spent himself like one of the fraternity brothers. But his grin dissuaded me of that. Brandon was no college boy. He was an experienced and strong man.

I clamped down on my pussy muscles, willing myself to be tight for him.

He groaned again, then rested his weight on his strong muscular arms and partially withdrew, only to plunge into me once more, his balls slapping my sensitive bottom as he fully sheathed himself.

I pushed against him, gaining an extra fraction of an inch of penetration. If he went any deeper into me, I worried his big cock would come out my throat.

Then he was moving, pumping himself into me.

My first orgasm hit me around his tenth surge. My second just two minutes later.

At first, it wasn't easy matching his rhythm, which should have made the experience less intense. Instead, though, our occasional fumbles made our lovemaking feel more authentic—less the product of the virtuosity James had sought as he'd played my body like a music instrument for his own pleasure and ego gratification and more like a man and woman learning about each others' bodies.

Then I realized we weren't quite firing together because we were both trying to accommodate the other, both letting our submissive sides take charge.

I wasn't going to change Brandon so I decided to change myself. I lifted my knees, planting my feet firmly on the desktop, and pressed, picking the rhythm that matched the pounding need inside my pussy, the jackhammering of my heart, and my shuddering, gasping breath.

Brandon groaned, then instantly accommodated my new rhythm. He kept his weight on one elbow, but freed up his hands, one to stroke and gently squeeze my breasts, tweaking my nipples into rigid points which he slid the other between our bodies, finding my clit and drawing small circles on it with the tip of his thumb.

I bit down on his shoulder, concerned I was hurting him but unable to help myself. My body felt wrung out and I was simultaneously certain I would never come again and that I'd yield to another orgasm too quickly, before the pressure fully peaked within me.

Brandon's breath came nearly as fast as mine. Despite the air conditioning, sweat from both of us lubricated our bodies, making them slide together like—well, like all of Brandon was dick and all of me pussy.

Then the wave swept back powering everything before it.

I thrust a finger into Brandon's muscular ass and felt his explosion.

The sensation of his hot semen shooting into my pussy pushed me over the edge. Darkness washed over me and my arms suddenly felt as if they weighed more than the grand piano my mother had kept in her home and never let anyone play.

Chapter Twelve

"Nicole. Are you all right?" Brandon's voice sounded a million miles away.

"Huh?"

"I think you fainted."

I had magically moved from the desktop to my office couch.

"Of course I didn't faint. I just, uh, dozed off." I got my arm under me and tried to push myself to a seated position.

Brandon gently pulled my arms from beneath me. "Don't try to do too much."

I pushed him away. "Give it a rest, Brandon. Thanks for the great sex, but it doesn't make you my mother.'"

Hurt crossed his handsome face and I wanted to take back my words, but I couldn't let Brandon believe what we'd done changed anything.

"I'm definitely not your mother. But I think a lover has a right—"

"We're not lovers. We just happened to experience a moment when we needed--"

He shook his head. "If it happened only once, maybe I could buy your bull. But this was the second time, remember? That makes it a pattern, a relationship, if you will."

More than anything in the world, I wanted to humor him, agree we had a relationship, promise that we could continue to explore the weird desire that drew us together even though we were so obviously wrong for each other. But doing that would only hurt him more in the long run, and I didn't want to hurt Brandon. Or rather, I knew I was going to hurt him and I needed to find a way to limit the damage.

"I'm a sexual woman, Brandon. Maybe you're not used to women like me. I spent ten years having cum for breakfast every morning, getting spankings every night before James would tie me up, blindfold me, and make me sleep on a doggy pallet on the side of his real bed. It's natural that I'd want to try you out more than once, especially as I'm horny from hanging around naked fraternity boys all the time."

"You're a capable woman, Nicole. I'll bet you know how to masturbate. If all you wanted was sexual release, you could find that without any help from me."

"Don't kid yourself. A full-body dildo is better than a couple of fingers in the twat. Why wouldn't I use one if I had the choice."

"A full-body dildo?"

"Uh—" that had come out a lot harsher than I'd intended.

"That's how your ex-husband saw you, isn't it." He didn't raise his voice, but his tone changed, grew almost frightening. "To him, you were a set of holes he could stuff his dick into. Only he didn't like to use your pussy-hole because he knew you're a sexual woman, that you'd find pleasure if he fucked you there. So he contented himself with your asshole and mouth and hands."

"There's nothing wrong with my asshole, mouth and hands. There's nothing perverted about giving a blowjob or taking it up the ass. You should know how good it feels to have something up your ass, you certainly liked my finger there. It's just—"

"It's just dessert, darling. A nice change from the main course. But it's—"

"This isn't about James, Brandon," I interrupted. It's about your need for someone to reassure you that you're all right even though you're just a submissive. Well—`"

"There's nothing *just* about being submissive. I get happiness from making you happy. What's wrong with that?"

"You're a man, Brandon. Everyone knows—"

"Stop quoting your ex-husband at me. If he had any intelligence at all, he would have held onto you like you were a precious gem. Instead he spit you out like overchewed bubblegum. He's a loser, and idiot, a fool."

"I think you'd better go now, Brandon."

He glared at me for a good ten seconds. For the first time, I saw the man who'd faced my husband down, who'd taken a punch for me, who'd handled James as easily as Hulk Hogan might handle an angry two-year-old. Then he grabbed his ripped shorts, pulled them over his legs and cock, and stalked out the door.

I waited until the door closed, then picked up the leather straps I'd taken off his dick.

They were still warm from his body, slightly moist from his sweat, and, when I pressed them to my nose, I smelled his soap and his sex.

I hadn't, I realized, handled that scene very well at all.

* * * *

"We've got to get Amber free of him."

Two days after Brandon and I had sex, my body was demanding more—and was increasingly unsatisfied with what I could do with my fingers.

The university's processes were grinding away toward evicting the fraternity from the college—and us from the fraternity house.

And Stretch couldn't get Amber out of his mind.

"Amber's a big girl," I reminded him. "She went to James voluntarily."

"She may have *gone* to him that way, but she sure isn't staying voluntarily. He ties her up every night."

We were sitting in the game room, Russell and Harry were playing pool, and most of the other guys were pretending to study—which I insisted on even though it wouldn't matter if we got tossed out of the school—but really listening to Stretch and me.

"James," I explained, "uses bondage to enhance the sexual trust between himself and his woman. He tied me up every night for more than ten years."

Stretch's long slender dick picked up, making me wish I'd never introduced the 'all-nude inside' program at the fraternity house. I didn't want Stretch's dick, but looking at it made me think of Brandon.

"I'm not saying," Stretch said, "there's anything wrong with ropes and handcuffs. I mean, not that I've ever done anything like that—"

"Not that you've done anything at all," Harry pointed out.

"That wasn't nice," I said.

"But it is true."

Stretch sighed. "My point is, he keeps her tied up for hours and she can't leave. He even took away her cellphone so we can't talk any more."

"Maybe she's just not returning your calls," Russell suggested, unhelpfully.

"She's not returning the calls from any of the girls in her sorority either, and one of them says they saw her phone in Professor d'Angre's laptop bag."

"If he really is holding her captive," Harry suggested, "he's breaking the law. Get her out and trot her in front of the faculty association and he'll be drummed out of the university—at least."

I'd talked to a lawyer, who'd told me that the police and the faculty association would ignore any of my claims as those of a disgruntled ex-wife. If my own accusations were backed up by my replacement, James's current girlfriend, though, they'd be given at least some credibility.

On the other hand, if we broke into James's place and learned that Amber was enjoying her time in bondage, we'd be the ones going to jail.

"Is she still attending classes," I asked.

Stretch shook his head. "Russell talked to a work-study student who does data input for the registrar. She says Amber dropped everything."

"Good job, Russell." Harry slapped him on his naked butt and then looked horribly embarrassed. "Uh, sorry."

"You didn't ask my permission to have sex with a co-ed," I pointed out.

Russell blushed. "She and I haven't done anything, but she seems interested in the Pi Iota Sigma fraternity. The point is, even if we get kicked out of school, what we did with the fraternity, with missus, will have been worth it for me. When I walk by, chicks notice me, check me out. Before, I was the invisible man."

I'd never been invisible, but the entire time I'd been with James, I'd been James's wife, not Nicole, not a person of my own. I thought I could understand how intoxicating it must be to have people notice, to be thought sexually attractive for himself.

In an *ah-ha* flash of what seemed obvious wisdom that had escaped me until then, I realized my feelings toward Brandon must stem from that same desperate human need to be noticed, to be thought worthy.

"Seems to me," Harry offered, "that if you're getting kicked off the campus, you might as well nail her if she likes you. You might not have another chance."

I understood the logic. How many times had James come home stinking of pussy, telling me that he'd had just that one chance—that a visiting lecturer was heading back north, that a co-ed was getting near graduation, that an administrator was leaving to take a job in the private sector? Of course he'd had to nail her while he had the opportunity. He was a male, after all. Why should he deny himself?

"You can do that," I admitted. "With what you've accomplished, most of you guys could line up a one-night stand or two. That's not what I signed on for, but we're losing the fraternity and I won't be able to give you orders any more. If the occasional hookup is what you want, I guess I can't really blame you."

Russell looked uncomfortable. "Maybe you could explain our alternatives in a little more detail. Even with our Friday jerk-offs, I'm getting blueballs from being around co-eds all the time and not being allowed to hurry home and masturbate, not being allowed to touch them, and then looking at you, all hot and sexy. I mean, Stretch dreams about Amber but for the rest of us…"

He had a point. I knew what I *didn't* want for the guys, but I'd never put what I *did* want into words. Sure it would be great for them to be popular and they shouldn't have to spend their lives horny and frustrated. But an occasional one-night-stand wasn't it.

Then again, they were guys. As James had repeatedly informed me, guys are happy to take one-night-stands when they can get them. And it didn't mean anything about their relationships.

Another thought hit me. I'd taken James's words about male as gospel truth. What if he'd been wrong, though? In the previous month, I'd been around more guys, in more desperately intimate situations, than James had ever dreamed of. Maybe he was, as Brandon had repeatedly told me, full of shit.

"Fair question," I said. "What I want for you guys is real girlfriends. I want you to spend time with women and enjoy their company, even if you're not in bed with them. I want you relaxed around them enough that when sex finally comes, it's a part of your relationship, not a lucky score that would have been just as good if you'd stuck your dick in a glory-hole and let a stranger get you off."

"Yeah, but—"

"Girls are easy, Russell. If you want one bad enough, you can probably get one—once. But girls talk, and any female that you'd want to spend time with her doesn't want to feel used."

"So, how come you're using Brandon?" Stretch demanded.

I decided it was time to change the subject. "So, how are we going to get Amber free?"

* * * *

The first half of freeing Amber turned out to be ridiculously easy.

I checked James's schedule and had one of Amber's sorority sisters agree to sit in his lecture with a cellphone to call us in case he decided to end early. We were waiting outside his place when James pulled his Jaguar out of his attached garage and pulled away.

The second James turned the corner, Russell tossed a brick under the descending garage door.

To my surprise, it worked—the child safety mechanism on the garage door opener sensed something blocking its descent and reversed itself.

Russell, Stretch, Harry and I hurried into the garage, then removed the brick and let the door close just in case some neighbor got suspicious.

I'd never locked the door between the garage and the house and twisted the knob with some confidence, but it didn't move.

"Let me try something," Harry said.

He slipped a flexible sheet of plastic between the door and jam, explaining a nerdy friend in high school had given it to him in exchange for Harry's protection from the other football players and a good word to one of the high school cheerleaders.

Less than a minute later, the door swung open.

"Amber?" I shouted through the open door. "I'm just coming to pick up some of my stuff."

I'd come up with that excuse in case she didn't want rescuing—James wouldn't believe it, but I didn't think the police would arrest me for it, especially as I really had left most of my clothes in James's closets.

Nobody responded—not a good sign.

"I promise she's not at her sorority house," Stretch said. "She's got to be here."

"Maybe she was in James's car," Russell suggested unhelpfully. "If I had a hot chick like Amber, I'd have her suck my dick every time I went for a drive—just to sort of keep the lubrication fresh, if you know what I mean."

I certainly knew what he meant. I'd lost count of the times James had made me suck him off in the car. I'd often had to sit in the car for hours while he attended faculty meetings or whatever, just so I'd be available to suck him off on the way home. More than once when he came out of those meetings, I'd first had to lick off the taste of another woman's pussy or another woman's ass before doing my job. So, yeah, it would not be beyond James to handcuff Amber to his Jaguar car while he gave his lecture.

Fortunately, we had a second string of fraternity brothers. I got on the phone with Chuck. "He's on his way. You know where he parks.

Check out his car and see if Amber's in it. Look in the trunk, too. When he thinks a woman needs discipline, he locks her in the trunk for a few hours, especially if it's really hot or really cold."

"Jerk," Stretch said.

"We don't know he did it to Amber."

"He's a jerk for doing it to you."

I tried to think of words that would explain why it was all right for him to treat me like that—and came up empty. "It's how he is."

"How he is is an asshole."

"Since we're here, let's look around and see if we can find anything we can use against him," Russell said.

While the guys headed for Russell's office and computer, I felt drawn to the bedroom he had allowed me to share for all those years.

Trussed like a turkey, with a huge ball-gag in her mouth and an expander up her ass, Amber stared at me, her blue eyes wild.

I'd spent uncounted hours like that, completely helpless, trusting that James would return, that he'd free me, that he'd feed me and take care of my needs. I couldn't tell if Amber was enjoying this and feared my intrusion, or if she wanted her freedom.

"I've come to pick up some stuff," I lied. "If you want, you can come with us. If you'd rather stay, we'll leave you."

She shook her head frantically, which told me she had strong feelings but didn't tell me what they were. James would have done a better job asking yes-no questions.

"No you want to stay?" I started over.

She shook her head even more frantically.

"I'm taking that as, you'd like us to free you?"

She nodded.

"Okay. I'm taking out your gag so we can talk like people."

James had padlocked the gag to the back of her head, but I attacked it with a pair of scissors and the leather fell away.

I looked at the worn gag and wondered if he'd even replaced the old one he'd used on me. I didn't think so.

"Can you take that thing out of my butt," Amber whined. "It hurts like the devil."

"James sometimes doesn't get hard enough to push his way into tight spots," I explained.

"I don't care *why* he does it. Take it out."

From the red stripes on Amber's ass, that wasn't the only thing she hadn't cared enough about. James liked to spank, but some of the marks on Amber looked like serious discipline rather than friendly correction.

Tight chains circled her body, fastening her to the bed and holding the plug up her butt.

I fumbled with the chains that bound her in place but came up with a hefty padlock that held in all the slack. She wasn't going anywhere.

I felt a bit cheated. He'd always used rope and leather straps to hold me in place. Why did Amber deserve steel chains?

"Do you know where the key to this is?"

"Like he'd tell me that."

"We're pretty much done here." Stretch burst through the bedroom door with the impetuosity typical of a college-age male. "Oh. Oh! Uh, hi, Amber."

"Get him out of here," she whimpered. "He can't see me like this."

"Stretch, see if you can find a padlock key or something. We've got to get Amber free."

"Yeah, sure."

I pulled a couple of pillows off James's bed and put them under Amber's side so she could lay down and relax a little, then I got some salve from the bathroom and rubbed it into her sore butt and back.

"He hit my tits, too." She rolled over.

I *really* didn't want to rub her breasts, even with Neosporin, but the poor girl was hurting. James had drawn blood with a couple of his strikes.

"I tried to get away from him," she explained when I asked why James had her so firmly secured. "He said a few weeks of this and I'd be more amenable."

"James knows how to get people to see things his way," I agreed.

"He's an asshole."

"That seems to be the consensus. Does that mean you want us to help you escape from him?"

She didn't answer right away but a couple of tears ran down her cheeks.

It wasn't fair. When I cried, my face got blotchy. When Amber cried, she just got more beautiful.

I tried not to hold it against her.

"He'll come after me and punish me more," she said.

"We'll protect you."

"Ha. You want to go running back to him."

"That's different. I'm—"

I stopped because reality finally penetrated my thick skull. There wasn't a bit of difference between how James treated me and how he treated Amber.

If Brandon was the only one who thought James was a jerk, I could take that as jealousy.

If the guys in the frat house thought he was a loser, I could read that as simple protectiveness for a woman they saw as a mother figure—or maybe a sexy-older-sister figure.

But if *everyone* thought he was a loser, then maybe it was time for me to open my eyes and see the truth.

James had dumped me when I'd turned thirty because I was too old for him. He'd pulled a fast one to divorce me and cheat me out of our shared assets, making the couple of hundred bucks he gave me seem like a huge gift, even though he'd put me through the humiliation of letting a fat and smelly bank manager paw my tits to get access to the account number.

I couldn't, I finally decided, go back to James after all.

Then again, my alternatives sucked. I still had no skills. The fraternity job looked like a short termer, and I'd managed to get everyone who'd trusted me fired or at the point of being kicked out of school.

"I found these," Stretch jingled some keys from the other side of the bedroom door. "No hacksaw, though. Can I come in?"

"No," Amber whispered.

I opened the door a crack, took the handful of keys he'd found, and closed the door.

A five second examination was all it took to prove there was no help here—none of these keys looked remotely the right shape for that big padlock.

I tried the most likely two anyway, with all the lack of success I'd anticipated, then stuffed them all into a pocket and checked my watch.

Incredibly, an hour had gone by since we'd broken into my former home. James was famous for delivering short lectures and abandoning his graduate assistants to answer any questions. He would be home soon. If he caught us, I wouldn't have to worry about losing my job, I'd have to worry about adjusting to prison food and hairy girlfriends.

"Ouch. You're hurting me," Amber whined.

I looked down to see that I'd clamped down on her tits. Gross.

"Call around," I told Stretch. Isn't there someone in the fraternity with a misspent youth? We need someone who can pick a padlock."

"I'll try," was Stretch's not-very-encouraging response.

My own phone rang. "Professor d'Angre has left the lecture hall," Lisa, our sorority spy reported.

"Shit." I hung up. "Hurry, Stretch. James will be home in ten minutes. Why did he have to pick today to deliver a half-hour lecture?"

"Can I come in?" Stretch asked. "Maybe I can do something about the lock."

"Don't let him in," Amber whispered. "I don't want him to see me like this."

She looked pretty good to me. Although she was tied up, the chains provided for easy access to her pussy, mouth, and tits. Still, I understood her reluctance. In a few weeks, she'd learned what it had taken me over a decade to understand—it isn't enough to be sexy. She wanted Stretch to think of her as a person rather than a collection of holes he could stick his dick into.

I didn't want to, but a part of me couldn't help wondering if James had seen me as more than that. Could our wonderful relationship have been completely in my mind?

That, though, was something I would worry about later. Right now, we had a co-ed to rescue.

"Unless you've suddenly developed lock-pick skills, we can't use you," I said.

"Crap."

It was time to stop panicking and start thinking.

The chains were made of hardened steel. The lock was a fancy Master. I wasn't going to break either of them.

But if we could get her out of James's home, we could take our time freeing her.

I jerked on the chain—and heard the solid sound of metal on metal. He'd fastened her to the brass bed so she couldn't creep around.

"Did you find any wrenches or pliers," I called. "If we can take the frame apart, we can roll her out of here."

"Roll?" Amber and Stretch echoed anguish.

I'd been kidding, but I didn't have time to explain. Besides, this probably wasn't the best time for a joke.

"We didn't see anything like that," Russell said. "But I've got a toolbox in my truck. Let me grab it."

"Hurry," I told him.

A couple of minutes later, the door slammed and booted footsteps headed down the hall to the bedroom.

"Any luck, Russell?" I shouted.

"Depends on how you define luck." It wasn't Russell's voice, though. Once again Brandon has stepped in where he wasn't expected, where I wasn't sure he was wanted.

"Hi Amber," he said as he set down a heavy metal box.

"Oh. Mr. Tiel."

"She's chained to the bed," I said. "If you have some wrenches, maybe you can unfasten it."

"Professor d'Angre is two blocks away," Harry reported. "We've got to move out."

"No time for unfastening," Brandon said.

"You can't leave me," Amber whined.

Brandon opened his toolbox, took out a small gasoline-powered chainsaw, jerked the power cord and grinned as the machine shot blue smoke into the air. "Cover your ears."

Without waiting to see if we'd obeyed, he pressed the sawblade against one of the brass uprights at the foot of James's bed.

The shriek of metal against metal had me cringing, and flaming chunks of metal flew through the air to join the increasing cloud of gasoline smoke, but the saw bit through the brass like a sorority girl going through Russell Stovers.

Less than thirty seconds after he'd started it, Brandon turned off his saw, grasped the brass upright with his working-gloves-protected hands, and jerked the whole thing out. Then he put his saw neatly back in his toolbox and handed it to me.

"Huh?" The heavy weight of the box practically yanked my arms out.

"If you can't carry it, get one of the guys to do it." He bent down, scooped up Amber, and carried her out to his Ford.

I tagged along, toolbox in hand, while the guys scrambled to get out of what had been my home.

James's Jaguar passed the pickup full of frat boys as it made the turn into his street.

"Head for the frat house," I told Brandon. "I think we've finally got the evidence we need to save the fraternity and get your job back."

"That's all you have to say?"

"Uh." Oh, shit. Once again I had failed to take into account the sensitivity of the submissive class. "Thanks for your help, Brandon. If you hadn't come and rescued us, James would have caught us, had us arrested, and we'd all be worse off than we already were."

He shook his head. "You may find this hard to believe but I wasn't fishing for your thanks. I'm concerned that you're engaging in crazy behavior, then counting on me to bail you out. From now on, if you do something insane, how about leaving me out of it?"

That was so unfair I had to grit down on my teeth to keep my jaw from trembling. "Sure, Brandon. From now on, you're off the hook."

"Or you might include me in the planning."

"Oh, no. That might still get you into some kind of trouble. We couldn't have that."

"Do you think you could stop bickering," Amber broke in from the back seat where Brandon had laid her. I'd been watching him, certain he'd take the chance for an accidental-on-purpose grope of the beautiful co-ed, but he hadn't. I didn't want to think about what James would call a man who'd ignored that kind of opportunity.

"I'm sorry, Amber," I said. "Once we get to the fraternity house, we'll buy some bolt cutters and get you out of those chains."

"And get this thing out of my butt. No offense, Nicole, but your husband is a pervert."

"Ex-husband," I said. "And he'll have to find new ways to be perverted when we get him locked up in jail."

My words surprised even me. James in jail. I should feel miserable about the possibility. Instead, it seemed… wonderful.

"Just get me out of this," Amber said. "Oh, and if you could find something to cover me up when you carry me in, Mr. Teil. I don't want the guys seeing me like this. Who could look at me like this and even consider taking me home to meet their mothers?"

"No problem," Brandon said.

Fortunately, the drive from my former home to the fraternity house was short, because our silence became a little oppressive.

I did take the opportunity to call Russell and tell him to stop by a hardware store on the way and pick up bolt cutters. I didn't know how James would respond to Amber's escape, but I knew him far to well to believe he'd just go with the flow.

He'd be looking to get back at us. I just didn't know how.

Chapter Thirteen

Russell, with his bolt cutters, beat the police by two minutes.

Despite my anger at him, I had to admire Brandon's muscles looked when he bent his weight on the cutters and snipped through the case-hardened chains James had used to secure Amber.

The second she was free, Amber race-waddled into the bathroom to get rid of her butt stretcher and I found her a tank top and shorts—just about the only clothes I owned.

She was still in the bathroom when the cops knocked on the door.

I opened it, professed surprise that they were there, and didn't invite them inside. The guys hadn't taken down the party decorations and I didn't think the Marquis de Sade theme would incline the police to take us seriously.

Instead, I suggested that they sit on the veranda and offered them sweet tea—the universal southern mark of hospitality.

"Look, lady," the older, whiter, fatter cop said. "We don't want your damned iced tea. We want some answers."

"If any of my boys have gotten into trouble, I definitely want to sort out the truth," I said. "I make them turn off their stereos at nine in the evening. Have there been complaints about the noise?"

Brandon joined me, bringing out a pitcher of tea and a tray of ice-filled tumblers. "Mint, officers?"

"No goddamned mint." The younger, thinner, blacker cop proved he could curse as well as his partner. "Professor d'Angre has sworn out a complaint against you. He says you broke into his house and kidnapped a young woman."

"Kidnapped?" I forced a laugh. James thought Amber was under his control and had made a mistake. I intended to make him eat it. The second Amber appeared and explained the truth, the cops would head his way—and he wouldn't be able to talk his way out of his problems. I doubted they could make a rape charge stick. In Mississippi, if a woman agrees to sex with a man, ever, she's pretty much screwed if she changes her mind ever. The laws may say one thing, but juries judge the victim more harshly than the rapist. Still, James was good for assault and kidnapping. Either of those charges would eliminate him as a threat to the boys.

"James said that, did he? When you hear what Am—"

"Maybe *you* should wait to hear what she says," Brandon suggested.

"Is this your lawyer," the younger cop demanded. "Because if he isn't, he can just—"

"Brandon is my friend," I said. "But neither of you said anything about a lawyer. I thought you were just looking for information. Am I a suspect?"

"Let's not get carried away," the fat middle-aged cop said. "Professor d'Angre reported a kidnapping and suggested you might know something. If you haven't done anything wrong, there's no need to involve a lawyer."

"Fine. Did my ex-husband, the man who, by the way, has been trying to ruin my life since our divorce, name any names, or is this mythical kidnapping victim an unknown person."

"She's known all right." The younger cop got in my face and growled at me. "And I think you know that name because you almost said it. Amber McGill. The girls in her sorority report that she became interested in one of the boys in your fraternity and then vanished. I'd say that was pretty suspicious behavior. I'd say you have a lot of explaining to--"

"Let's hear what Amber has to say for herself." I ignored Brandon's head-shake. Why was he trying to protect James? That didn't make sense.

"So you admit she's here?"

"She may be," I said. "Although we're a fraternity, we do have hours when we allow co-eds into the house."

"It would help matters if you'd trot her out," the older cop said.

"I'll get—"

"Perhaps your boyfriend could bring her out?"

"I'm not Nicole's boyfriend." Brandon's voice could have been a wind straight from the North Pole.

"Just get her out here, whoever you are.

"I'm happy to." He headed into the fraternity house.

I thought I was going to have to send out a search party for the two of them, and the cops were stirring uncomfortably in their seats when Amber strolled out.

She'd found a pair of my shoes, the high spiked heels combining with the short shorts and too-tight tank top to make her look like a hooker. I could have told her that wasn't her look, but it was a little late.

"The police are—"

"We'll handle the questions, Mrs. d'Angre," the younger cop interrupted.

"Okay, but—"

"If you can't keep your mouth shut, we'll have to ask you to leave."

I drew myself to my full five-foot eight height. "I'm responsible for what goes on in this fraternity and that includes protecting both my young men and their visitors. You can either talk with me here or we will call a lawyer and you won't be talking at all. Your choice."

"Jeez, lady. Your husband said—"

"Ex-husband. I admit I was married to that jerk, but our marriage is over."

"Fine. Your *ex*-husband," he put the emphasis on the 'ex,' "said you were trouble. I guess he knew what he was talking about."

"I believe I already mentioned he'll do anything he can to ruin my reputation.

"Just shut up. You can sit and listen," the older cop said.

I nodded.

"So, Ms. McGill. Can you tell us what you've been up to today?"

I grinned. So long, James. Be sure to write us from prison. Because you're going to be spending a lot of time there.

Amber fluttered her eyelashes. "I was at Professor d'Angre's house but I got bored so I decided to visit Stretch."

I choked on my own spit. What the hell? 'Decided to visit?' We'd freed her ass—both figuratively and literally.

"So, your claim," the younger cop said, "is that you weren't kidnapped."

Say it, I projected. Tell them you were kidnapped, held captive by my ex.

"Kidnapped?" She laughed horribly convincingly. "I should have left a note for Professor d'Angre, but once I decided to leave him, I just didn't think of it. Of course I had no idea he'd panic like this."

"Of course not," the fat cop agreed, completely taken in by Amber's lies.

I couldn't hold myself back. "How about—"

"Ms. d'Angre," the younger cop interrupted. "You agreed to keep silent. One more outburst and we'll evict you and request that the D.A. find some basis to indict you.

I nodded, feeling numb. Ten minutes earlier, Amber had been in chains with a plug up her butt. We needed only about five words of truth from Amber and our troubles were over.

I glared at her and she batted her eyes at me. Could James have set this up? Was I sucker enough to fall for the pathetic girl routine?

"Professor d'Angre claims you were kidnapped from his home earlier this afternoon," the fat cop said. "Why do you think he said that?"

Amber giggled. "Like I said, I should have left a note. I *was* dating him, but he's so old and really, well, it was a fling. I never thought he'd go nutzo on me, though. I mean, calling the police. Really."

"If this woman is putting pressure on you," the younger one pointed his whole hand in my direction, "we can protect you from her."

"Could you do that?" Amber batted her eyes at the cops. "Mistress D'Angre is so mean. She hardly lets me spend any time in Stretch's room—Stretch being my boyfriend. Maybe you could tell her to lay off on the maternal thing. I mean, Stretch is over eighteen and I'm—"

"That isn't what we had in mind," the fat cop said. "If you'd like to speak to us alone, just nod. Ms. d'Angre has no right to—"

"Don't be silly. I already told you I should have left a note for Professor d'Angre. He can be a little possessive, you know."

And Martians can be a *little* green. I gripped the tabletop hard enough to turn my knuckles white, but managed to keep my mouth shut. Whatever James had told them, those cops definitely didn't trust me.

The old fat cop took out a business card, handed it to Amber, and told her to call him if she had anything to add to her statement.

"Can we give you a ride back to your sorority, Ms. McGill?" the younger cop asked. "I'm sure your sorority sisters would be reassured to see you healthy and unhurt."

Amber giggled again. "I'm hanging out with Stretch right now. Don't worry, I'll see the girls soon enough."

I collected the tea glasses and went inside, motioning Russell to keep an eye on the cops. I'd been so confident our troubles were over,

I hadn't thought to ask them for proof of identity. Were they really police at all, or could they be men James had hired to bring Amber back?

A few minutes later, though, Amber joined me in the kitchen. "You probably wonder why I didn't tell them what Professor d'Angre did to me."

"That question crossed my mind," I admitted. "Don't you know that James already cost Brandon his job and now he's shutting down our fraternity? All you had to do was tell the truth and all of our problems would be over."

"*Your* problems would be over," Amber agreed. "But what about my problems."

"You're nineteen years old. What problems could you have? Tell the truth and James will never bother you again. Even if he somehow managed to stay out of prison, you could swear out a protective order against him. He wouldn't dare come after you."

She waved sculpted fingernails in front of my face. "All I have to do is go on national TV, admit that I volunteered to let James tie me up, beat me, fuck me in the ass, squirt his cum all over my tits, my face and my hair, lick out his dirty hairy ass, and eat like a dog from a bowl marked Prince. Is that what you're saying? What happens to me if I do that, Mistress d'Angre? That reputation would stick to me for the rest of my life. The only dates I'd ever get would be perverts who wanted to tie me up and use me the way James did.

"I want to help you, mistress. But look at me. I've got tits the size of gallon cartons of ice cream. Guys already think I'm a slut just because of that. I'm not going to confirm it for them."

I nodded. Amber had a point.

"Besides," she continued. "He made videos and he'll post them in two seconds. How would you like it if every guy in the university was jerking off over an asshole professor taking a dump on your tits?"

"I understand," I said. And I meant it. "I'm sure we'll figure out another way to stop him. One thing we can do, though. We *can* stop him from releasing those videos."

"How?"

"Watch me."

I took out my cell and dialed James's number.

"Nik," he said, obviously reading the caller identification. "I've been meaning to call you."

"Calling the police was dumb," I said.

"I confess that my thinking hasn't been the same since you left me, Nik. Maybe we should try again."

"I beg your pardon."

"Come on, Nik. You know we had something special together. I admit Amber's mammoth jugs and her youthful body distracted me, but you're the woman I married. For better or worse, right. I want to make it up to you."

"James, you're not making sense."

"Okay, I'll be more clear. I want you back. I want us to be married again. I want things to be back the way they were when we were both so happy."

I'd wanted exactly that for so long that I couldn't speak.

"We'll even take a second honeymoon over the Christmas holidays."

Our honeymoon had been wonderful. We'd gone to one of those clothing-optional resorts and I'd run around wearing nothing but my brand new leather collar the entire time. James had tied me up of course, but only during sex. And he'd probably used my vagina more during that week than he had in the ten years we'd been together afterward. "That isn't—"

"I already made reservations for us at the same club where we had our first honeymoon."

When I'd seen Amber trussed up like a Thanksgiving turkey, I'd told myself I would never go back to him. But James could be so thoughtful, so sexy.

"What about other women?"

I hadn't seen Brandon enter the kitchen, but I sure noticed him when he dropped the chains he'd cut off of Amber into the trash.

"Don't push it, Nik. I'm already humbling myself way more than I'm comfortable with. You know I have needs that go beyond what even you can deliver."

"Don't worry about it," I said. "I don't even know why I asked."

"I can be at your fraternity house in five minutes. And tell Amber that if she doesn't want her videos of her sucking shit out of my ass all over the Internet, she'll be waiting with you. The two of us have unfinished—"

"You misunderstood me," I told him. "I'm not coming back. I wouldn't come back even if I thought you *could* be bothered being faithful to me. As far as those videos go, they're the only thing that's keeping Amber from telling the truth to the cops. Post them, ruin her reputation, and watch out. An hour later, you'll be introducing yourself to new boyfriends—in prison."

"Nik. I know you don't mean—"

I got mad. "For ten years, asshole, I let you tell me what I meant. You persuaded me that I was no better than tissue for you to wipe your semen off after you'd masturbated, or toilet paper to clean your butt when you took a dump. Well, guess what? I'm done with that. A dominant is supposed to help me enjoy my own sexuality rather than gratify himself while letting me go months at a time without an orgasm of my own. So, here's my advice to you, James. Call the dean, tell him you've decided to resign. Then head for South America or someplace else far away. Because if you stay here, I'm going to destroy you."

For a moment, all I heard was silence.

Finally, James laughed. "You can't get Amber to testify, can you? Unfortunately for you, we're not really at a standoff. Once your fraternity is disbanded, you'll be out on the street. Your only choices will be begging me to take you back as anything I want, or to sell yourself for twenty bucks a screw on the street. One thing you can count on—you're not going to get a repeat of my offer to re-start the marriage."

"I can't find the words to tell me how grateful that makes me," I told the man I'd thought I loved.

* * * *

"We're worse off than ever." Russell called the fraternity to order, Amber and I being the only non-brothers attending the evening meeting.

"We're not worse off," Stretch said. "We freed Amber. She was—"

"I don't want to hear anything about that," Amber interrupted.

"Yeah, sure," Russell said. "We were good guys. But Professor d'Angre is still destroying the fraternity and he's getting all of us expelled. I doubt my parents will belly up the money to pay my tuition at another school if I get kicked out of this one, even assuming I could get into another with something like that on my record."

"We just need to find something to blackmail him with," Stretch argued.

"Like what?" Russell demanded. "Nobody will believe our Mistress, and Amber can't talk without destroying her reputation."

I was proud of the way the guys had accepted Amber's decision. Despite everything, they were sons of the south. Sure a southern upbringing had its drawbacks. It also included some definite virtues. Nobody in the fraternity would pressure Amber to ruin her reputation.

Unfortunately, nobody in the fraternity had come up with any alternatives.

Amber wriggled on the couch. I couldn't tell if she desperately needed to go to the bathroom, or if she was prepping to strip off her clothes and do a pole dance.

As it turned out, she did neither. "I've got an idea."

She blushed when all of the guys stared in her direction, most of them with the kind of look they would have given a monkey if he'd stood up in the zoo and explained Einstein's General Theory of Relativity.

"That's very nice," Russell said. "But—"

"Just because I'm blonde and I've got big tits doesn't mean my brain is worthless."

"I'm sure nobody was thinking that," I lied. "But hey, guys, tell me if I'm mistaken and you were thinking that. If anyone thinks women can't be smart, now's the time to let us all know. I'm sure I could think of something to let you think that through."

That sent a lot of heads shaking. "No disrespect," Russell insisted.

"We've got this really smart girl in the sorority—Kara-Sue. I figure, since Professor d'Angre lost both his ex-wife and me, he'll be looking for a new—"

"How would fixing him up help us?" Stretch demanded. "And do you really hate this Kara-Sue chick?"

"That's the thing. She's a college freshman, but she's only sixteen. Wouldn't he, like, get arrested if he made a pass at her. She wouldn't have to do him or anything."

The idea had its appeal, but I didn't think it would work. First, no matter how careful we were, we couldn't guarantee that we could stop James from abusing the girl. Second, sixteen was the age of majority in Mississippi. James would have his way with the poor girl and send us a thank you note. Third, he'd probably sue us for entrapment and make us look like the badguys.

I pointed out the issues, but praised Amber for her creative thinking.

"Creative maybe," Chuck grumbled. "But we're still going to get kicked out of the school for something we didn't do."

Russell slapped himself in the forehead. "Speaking of creative, d'Angre is a professor with a Ph.D. and we're all undergraduates with C averages. Am I the only one who sees the problem here? It's stupid to think we can outsmart him. But what about if we corner him somewhere, beat the snot out of him, and then tell him if he doesn't back off, we'll do it again. I mean, he's already accusing us of assault, right? If we're going to do the time, why not do the crime?"

I thought Russell had the cliché backward, but the rest of the guys were all over the idea, suggesting places they could find James alone, special punches and kicks they'd read about in martial arts magazines, and smacking fists into palms and making male grunting sounds.

I waited for the noise to settle down, but Amber rained on their parade before I could. "After Mr. Teil punched him, Professor d'Angre bought a gun. If you tried to mug him, he'd shoot you."

"And don't suggest we shoot first," I said. "Getting kicked out of school is one thing. If you murder him, you've ruined your lives."

Stretch snapped his fingers. "Let's ask Brandon. He always has good ideas. How come he isn't here, anyway?"

"I, uh, might have hurt his feelings again," I admitted.

"You've got to stop doing that," Russell lectured me. "The two of you are really good together."

We *were* good together—in bed. Unfortunately, the only reason we worked well in bed was because I pretended to be someone I wasn't.

"I don't *mean* to hurt him."

"It's what you do, not what you mean to do," Russell said.

"Until you stop denying who you really are," Amber said, "you're going to keep messing up like that."

This was all I needed. Relationship advice from a guy with leather straps around his dick and a girl who'd had a plug up her butt a few hours earlier.

"Can we stick with the program here? We're trying to figure a way to head James off, not to improve my sex life."

"If they shut the fraternity down," Russell said, "you're going to need someplace to stay. Making up with Brandon—"

"How about we figure a way to keep the fraternity going so I don't have to sell my body for shelter? Because I don't see myself moving in with Brandon and turning into a little wifey."

"Like you were with James?" Stretch wanted to know.

I guessed that was fair ball, even though his question made my cheeks burn with embarrassment. "I was a kid when I met James and he sort of kept me in arrested development. Since I've been out of the cage he kept me in, I've been forced to grow. It hasn't always been comfortable, but I no longer want to return."

Stretch held up a hand. "Getting back to Professor d'Angre. We know he's an asshole. Now, being a jerk might not be against the law, but a lot of the things people like him do are against the law. Like what he did to Amber—"

"Don't go there," Amber said.

"I was just using it as an example. Here's the thing. Mr. Tiel is a librarian. Which makes him an expert at tracking down information. We need to get him on the job, have him research Professor d'Angre's past, find out what women he's abused that might have turned him in or at least be willing to testify against him when the discipline committee hears our case next week. If we can prove he's a liar, a pervert and a sneak, we have a chance."

Amber abandoned her seat on the couch and plopped down next to him, sliding her hand up under his shorts. "You are so smart, Stretch."

"Amber," I said, "When I was in school, my teachers would say, you can't bring candy into the room unless you bring enough for everyone. Unless you want to give a handjob to all the guys here, I suggest you take your fingers off Stretch's dick."

Amber licked her lips, then fluttered her eyes at Stretch. "Would you mind, Stretch? They are your fraternity brothers. I've never had more than one dick in my hand at a time."

He grinned. "No problem. As long as you save me for last."

So much for my being less than direct. "You did say you were worried about your reputation, remember."

"Oh, don't worry," she said. "They're just hand jobs. And no touching my boobs, guys. Looking only. And if you think I'm cleaning up after you squirt, dream on." She winked. "Except you, Stretch."

"Yes, ma'am," came a chanted response from every male in the room.

She kept one hand under Stretch's shorts and put the other under Russell's. "As president of the fraternity, I guess you get to come first."

I got up. I'd intended to head this off but I had said she could do it. And, in a way I was glad for the guys to get a little release. Amber probably needed to be the center of attention again after the abuse she'd been through. Still, I didn't need to stay and watch it.

"I'll call Brandon," I said, "and see if he can help with the research. But every guy who squirts had better clean up their own messes—and that includes Stretch. And Amber, if I hear you swallow one drop, from Stretch or any of the other guys, you're not coming back, ever."

"Yes, Mistress," she said. "Oh, you might tell Brandon I'll do him, too if he wants it. I really owe him for the way he came through for me."

I smiled as sweetly as I could. I'd pass that message on—when hell froze over.

I did my best not to think about why I felt so possessive all of a sudden.

Chapter Fourteen

I didn't completely buy Stretch's theory that James's treatment of Amber would be reflected in past complaints. In all the faculty meetings I'd attended, I'd never picked up so much as a whisper that he'd had troubles. For sure, with his looks, he didn't have to break any laws to get a willing woman in his bed. Dozens of times, I'd taken down phone numbers from faculty wives, grad students and co-eds throwing themselves at him. Still, at least it was something to do. With Amber going silent, it was the only plan we had.

Once Russell came down from his handjob high, and I judged him fit to get behind a vehicle wheel, I had him drive me over to Brandon's place, then pounded on Brandon's door until he finally opened it.

"What?"

"Do you want me to apologize again?"

He practically growled at me. "Apologize for what?"

"For not being the woman you need me to be, I guess."

He shook his head. "Nicole, you *are* the woman I need you to be. You just won't admit it to yourself."

"We've had this discussion."

"Is that what you call it? I call it you sticking to an untenable lie no matter how often the facts bite you in the ass."

I hadn't thought talking would help. Obviously I'd been right. "I'm following up on an idea Stretch had. Would you be willing to research James, see if you can find out anything we can use against him, any women who might be willing to testify about the kind of things he does."

Brandon shrugged. He looked perfectly edible in a tight pair of jeans and a muscle shirt that really did show muscles. His shrug moved those muscles across his chest and shoulders in perfectly delightful ways.

My eyes drifted down from those sculpted pecs past his six-pack abs, finally focusing on the hard ridge making his jeans stick out in front like he'd stuffed a two-by-four down there. I was pretty sure, though, it was all him.

"And stop doing that," I added.

He grinned. "Doing what?"

"You know what. The muscle thing. I've got to keep my thoughts straight, which I can't do if you keep flexing your pecs at me."

"Was I doing that?"

Damn, when he got all cocky, I wanted to do something about it.

I thought about turning around and running as fast and as far as I could, but I had to look a little more. "If you won't help me," I told that rigid cock, "I guess—"

"I never said I wouldn't help. Come on back to my office and I'll fire up my search engines."

I froze when we reached the doorway to his office. The biggest computer monitor, the one facing the door, held a picture of me as its screensaver.

I'd given Brandon plenty of opportunities to get a nasty picture of me. He could have gotten one of me in a jogging outfit, sweat gluing the thin nylon tops to my tits and my shorts sticking to my shaved twat. Instead, this photo had to have been shot that first day I'd met him in the library. I'd halfway turned from him, my head hung down like I was just waiting for someone to beat me, and my shoulders were slumped so bad I looked like I was fighting a crippling disease.

"Guess that's why you didn't take a blowjob that first time I offered," I said.

"You looked like you'd come near breaking." He sounded like he thought he was agreeing with me, but that hadn't been what I'd meant at all.

One tiny move of his mouse cleaned my picture off his screen. Brandon pushed up a second chair for me, then sat down himself and started clicking.

I watched for a while. I'd used Google and Yahoo, but what he was doing didn't look anything like the ordinary search engines I'd grown up with. Instead, blobs with words and pictures merged and separated on the screen like some sort of Venn diagram videogame.

It was interesting for about five minutes, then I got bored of the display and started thinking about the man.

"When James worked on the computer, he'd always have me get between his legs so I could suck him off," I said.

Brandon clicked something. "Hey, I've got news for you. If you're trying to turn me on, comparing me with James is not the right way to do it."

"I'd be happy to—"

"To what? Pretend to be some kind of bedroom appliance rather than a human being? So what if your husband liked to come in your mouth while he did his research or, more likely, looked at pornography on the Internet? What's that got to do with me?"

"Actually, he didn't come *in* my mouth," I admitted. "He liked to cum on my face and tits."

"I really don't want to hear this, Nicole."

I got frustrated. "Why not? I like you. Can't you understand that I'd *like* you to cum on me?"

"And you want me to do that while I'm looking at all the women your husband has done, thinking about his perversions? Don't you get it? When I have sex with you, I want it to be about us, not something I do because I'm too lazy to masturbate myself."

His anger completely surprised me. "Is that what you think I'm doing?"

He drove his fist into the solid oak of his desk. "That's what James did, how he molded you. Now, since that's what you know, it's what you're trying to replicate the same destructive behavior. I almost vomited when you whined to him about finding a dominant who'll let you have a safe word, who'll allow you to experience your own sexuality. You don't need anyone's permission to experience your sexuality, you've got everything you need already."

"But I'm a sub. I need—"

"A real submissive could never have whipped that fraternity into shape."

"Come on, Brandon. I *had* to do it."

"A real submissive would have found alternatives. Got it."

"I hear what you're saying, but I—"

"I wasn't clear. I didn't mean 'got it' as in 'do you understand what I'm telling you?' I said 'Got it' as in, 'I've found something on your darling ex.' Did you know he left Harvard after his second year?"

"He told me he wanted to try—"

"A female student complained he was stalking her after they broke up. He was asked to leave the University."

Despite Brandon's air conditioning, sweat condensed on my palms. "That's what we need. Print it out and—"

"It's not so easy. He'd say we forged it, and Harvard would never allow that kind of information out. Especially since, if it happened today, they'd never let him off so easy."

"You got into Harvard's internal database?"

He shrugged, once again showing me his sexy muscles. Damn, if he didn't want me caressing him and sucking him, I wished he'd stop tempting me.

"So, what can we do?"

"I've got the name of the woman who accused him. We can call her."

Ten o'clock in Mississippi was only seven o'clock at Berkley where Professor Maggie Cotton, one-time stalker victim, served as Associate Professor of Abnormal Psychology.

Her office phone rolled over to voicemail, but Brandon did some more of his search magic to track down her unlisted cellphone number, dialed it, and handed the phone to me.

"Who is this?" The woman might live in California, but the accent was all Boston.

"Dr. Cotton? My name is Nicole d'Angre. I'm the—"

"d'Angre? If you're calling on behalf of that perverted bas--"

"I assume you're talking about my ex-husband, James. I'm definitely not calling on his behalf. He's trying to ruin me and the University won't believe my unsupported claims."

"Join the club. Harvard didn't believe mine. Not that I can really blame them. First, I let d'Angre do things I'm not very proud of. And second, some of the things he did are, frankly, unbelievable."

"If you could testify—"

"d'Angre is still in Mississippi, isn't he? Cambridge State, right?"

"Uh-huh. Why?"

"d'Angre wasn't the only jerk I called out. I've got a reputation as a ball-buster. Your university president there owns two of the balls I've busted. If he hears my name, you've already lost your case."

"Crap. Do you know anyone else James may have abused— anyone who would be willing to talk?"

"I don't know of any, but I can assure you they're out there. I've made my career out of studying narcissistic misogynistic assholes and James d'Angre is a classic case. He can't help himself."

"I guess I knew that. I was hoping—"

"If you were his wife, you would know it. Why don't *you* testify against him? My bet is that he kept you essentially terrorized—classic Stockholm syndrome."

"A disgruntled ex-wife? Everyone would assume I was trying to get back at him for dumping me."

"You're discounting yourself, Ms. d'Angre. There's a lot more understanding of abusive behavior now than there was thirty years ago when James had his thing with me."

Right. Which was why she wouldn't help. Despair crept over me like kudzu, choking me under its weight.

"Okay, there is one other thing," she said. "Narcissistic personalities like James like taking trophies. At Harvard, he was famous for his underwear collection. In the digital age, he probably also takes pictures."

"I know that. He's blackmailing one of his students to stay silent."

"I guarantee this… where there's one, there are others."

Although I'd discouraged television viewing in the fraternity, I'd bowed to pressure and made Thursdays 'movie night.' One of the favorites we'd seen had been *Revenge of the Nerds*, an ancient but funny movie that definitely related to the situation my Pi Iota Sigma fraternity brothers faced. In the final scene in that movie, the nerds had gotten revenge by selling nude pictures of the co-eds. I wondered if we could similarly get our own revenge.

"But you can't name any names," I probed one more time.

"Look, Ms. d'Angre. I cut my deal with Harvard. I've already said more than I really should have and if you're some sort of spy, I'm in trouble. I'm not going to say anything else."

With that, she hung up on me.

"From what I overheard, that didn't go well," Brandon said.

"Could have gone better. Still, she gave me an idea."

"Hum?"

"She said James's personality was that of a trophy-hoarder. According to her, the pictures he took of Amber aren't an exception. He probably has nasty shots of every woman he's done."

"How does that help us?"

"We are still in Mississippi, Brandon. While everyone nods and winks when a man steps out, anything seen as perversion will have them up in arms."

"Which is why they're trying to close your fraternity."

"Fight fire with fire, Brandon. If we can get access to those pictures, we'll shatter his reputation and run him out of here."

Brandon shook his head. "I don't like it."

"Why the hell not?"

"Because his isn't the only reputation we'll destroy."

I hadn't thought of that. But if it came down to protecting my boys or protecting some strange women who should have known better than to have sex with a married man, I knew which side I was coming down on.

"Wake up, Brandon. Any pictures he took over the past ten years were of women he was screwing while he was married to me. Am I really supposed to cry over a bunch of women who couldn't keep their panties on when a married man slimed on them?"

"Considering that you were willing to go back to that man while he kept Amber as his sex slave, you sound a bit hypocritical to me."

"You know, Brandon. Sometimes you're a real pain in the butt."

He grinned. "If you brought your riding crop, you can get me back. I don't mind if you're a pain in the butt."

I wanted to tell him I wasn't in the mood.

Then he took off his shirt.

Crap, was I ever in the mood.

* * * *

I woke Brandon up by straddling his face, clamping my thighs around his ears and lowering my twat into his face.

He made a few complainy noises, but only until he woke up and realized the situation. Then he put his clever tongue to work, licking at my clit like it was a Smokey Mountain-sized lollypop he'd been ordered to suck a tunnel through.

Some woman had spent a lot of time training Brandon, and I was getting the benefit. It didn't seem fair, but then again, James always told me fairness was a myth invented by those too weak to carve out their place in the world.

Within a minute, my stomach tied itself in knots, my thighs were quivering, and I was at the point of orgasm.

I wanted to come, but I didn't want it to be so fast. So I looked for something to hold my attention.

Brandon's stiff dick not only held my attention, it filled my hands.

Considering that I'd planted my twat right on his mouth, and my butthole on his nose, Brandon couldn't be getting a lot of excess oxygen, but he had enough to groan when I grabbed his cock.

A liquid pearl drop of cum formed at the end of his shaft as I squeezed it, so I tugged on the leather strap I'd tied around his balls while we'd been sexing it up the previous night.

The distraction provided by the straps kept him from coming too soon. Now it kept me from coming as well.

My high school science teacher had once given us a lecture on how water in the microwave can super-heat, getting well above the boiling point without actually boiling, until something touches it, at which time it explodes.

I felt something like that happening to me now.

James kept licking my clit, occasionally dipping his tongue into my twat while his clever fingers kept up the pressure.

His nose, stuck right up my ass, engaged all sorts of nerve endings polite women pretend don't exist but that definitely added to my sensual overload.

My entire body hummed while my eyes took in the treat of Brandon's huge engorged dick, his sexy, leather-wrapped balls, and his sculpted stomach.

He groaned again, his breath simultaneously heating and cooling my pussy. I couldn't help myself—I groaned too.

I squeezed my thighs together even tighter, holding back the explosion I knew was now inevitable. Every second I could keep control, though, superheated me further, compressing that knot in my center even more tightly.

I grabbed the leather straps around Brandon's balls and tugged.

His whole body responded and he raised his legs, giving me a perfect view of his hard-muscled ass and pressing his dick up between my tits.

His cock felt good there, like it belonged. I grasped his butt with my hands, using my elbows to tighten my cleavage. With all the sweat, I thought it would give him the sensation of a hot, wet pussy.

His butt looked so delectable, I didn't bother resisting temptation. I tugged it a bit closer, then bent down and bit—not hard enough to draw blood or anything, but hard enough that he noticed.

He definitely noticed.

He lost control, spraying semen all over my breasts.

The smell of his jism was like the touch exploding superheated water. The feel of Brandon shooting hard against my boobs, and the sudden bucking of his face against my twat pushed me off the cliff.

My thighs, which had been trembling for what seemed an eternity, abruptly gave out and I fell forward on Brandon, letting his man-juices smear all over my front.

He kept licking, his tongue now flicking more than seriously probing, as he nursed explosion after explosion out of me, long after I'd reached the point where I knew I had nothing left to give.

Finally, I rolled the rest of the way off of him. My body was hypersensitive. Even Brandon's soft zillion thread-count Egyptian cotton sheets felt like sandpaper against my skin.

Brandon smiled at me. "You do have a wonderful way of waking a man up."

I couldn't help myself. I grinned back. Brandon had been the first man I'd slept with in years—unless you count sleeping in a doggy-bed shoved up against James's king-sized real bed.

He gently rolled me back, letting me reclaim the soft feather pillow, and licked every inch of my torso, paying special attention to my breasts.

"I'm pretty sure you got all your semen off the tips of my nipples," I told him as he caught the hard nub of one of my tits gently between his teeth and proceeded to flick my nipple with his tongue until I started to wonder if I could come again.

He kissed it, then pulled back, grinning at me again. "I don't mind cleaning up after myself, but that really isn't the purpose of this. You've got an amazing body, Nicole. I'd happily kiss every inch of it."

I didn't want to think of James. Not then. But when we'd been dating, James had used those exact words—'you've got an amazing body.' Then, when I'd gotten too old for his tastes, he'd tossed me out like yesterday's used condoms.

James had been infatuated with my eighteen-year-old body. While I kept it up as best I could, running, lifting weights, eating healthy foods, a dozen years had aged me. How long, I wondered, before Brandon looked at me and wanted to trade me in on a newer model. Or maybe it was even simpler than that. How long would I be able to keep up the dominant act he needed so desperately? How long before he found a true dominant who could give him all of what he craved?

"You're sabotaging yourself," Brandon said. "Don't do that."

I smiled. "You're right. I need to learn to live in the now."

It wasn't like Brandon had asked me to marry him. It wasn't even as if he'd suggested we were an item, that he'd be faithful to me.

I grabbed his ears and pulled his face up to mine, kissing him lightly on the lips.

He tasted like me, like his sperm, and like Brandon. It should have been nasty. Certainly I'd never particularly enjoyed the mixed taste of twat and male cum when I'd sucked other women's juices off of James's dick.

Instead of nasty, Brandon's taste was purely sexy.

"I'd like to stay in bed all day," I admitted. "But we really need to get to work if we're going to stop James."

"Why don't you stay here," he suggested. "I'll whip up some breakfast."

"I need a shower."

Chapter Fifteen

By the time I got out of the shower, Brandon had made waffles with fresh blueberry topping, and brewed up just-ground coffee beans, which explained the roar I'd heard while drying myself off.

I wore one of Brandon's white work shirts, unbuttoned enough in front to tease him, over my rinsed-out running shorts.

Brandon was still naked except for the leather strap around his balls—and his leather collar. He'd taken off that collar weeks before and certainly hadn't been wearing that collar the previous night. I felt the pressure of having someone depend on me—someone I cared enough about to worry about how he'd deal with his inevitable disappointment. But I didn't let myself think about that for too long.

I'd been sure I'd wrung his dick dry, but it perked up the moment I stepped into his kitchen, it pointed up at my face like a homing missile.

I resisted the temptation to forget about waffles and have Brandon for breakfast. Time was running out. If we were going to stop James, we needed to do it in the next two days. If we couldn't bust him before the university disciplinary meeting, it would be too late.

It took until my second cup of coffee before I got my mind thinking about something other than Brandon's hot dick and wondering if I could talk him into creaming my coffee with his natural juices rather than with half-and-half.

"The guys were looking at his computer while I was talking to Amber," I said. "Maybe they found James's pictures."

"Does he use a digital camera?"

I shrugged. "He started using one a year or so ago. But before that, he had a scanner."

"I'll check with the guys." He attached his Bluetooth headset to his ear, then rubbed the knots out of my shoulders as he dialed the fraternity.

"Russell, it's Brandon. When you made that computer service call yesterday, did you notice any photos?"

I wouldn't have worried about anyone tapping the fraternity's line, but I realized I should have. It wasn't as if James had any moral compunction.

"Really? How big?"

I purred, letting Brandon dig deeper into my sore muscles with his sexy strong hands. Listening to half a conversation wasn't that interesting, but feeling my tense body turn into liquid made it more than worthwhile.

"Okay. I'll swing by in a few minutes. Yeah, I've got Mistress Nicole here with me.

"There's a huge file that looks encrypted," Brandon told me as he pulled a pair of running shorts over his still-rigid dick. "That's probably got his pictures on it."

"Cool. We're in business, then."

"Maybe. Some encryption packages are pretty good."

It turned out that James used one of those pretty good systems. Which shouldn't be a huge surprise considering he was a math professor.

Fifteen hours later, we'd made exactly no progress.

"We're sunk." Russell pushed himself back from his computer. "We've got the Greek Council Disciplinary meeting tomorrow night, and we have nothing."

Brandon looked as tired as Russell. "I'm sorry, Nicole. But I'm not giving up. We'll think of something."

I shook my head. After Brandon had found about James's indiscretions at Harvard and identified Professor Cotton, I'd been sure we were on track, that we'd be able to show the world who he really was. But once again, it looked like he done just enough to keep himself safe, to make anyone who complained look like a whining baby instead of an abused victim.

"Let's go to bed," I said.

"Bed? But it's Friday night," Russell sounded shocked I'd forgotten.

"Right." I really wasn't in the mood for watching a bunch of college-aged young men jerk off, and I knew that Amber had given most of them handjobs the day before. Still, our Friday orgasm training had become an institution. "Everyone strip."

I made sure all the blinds were down, quickly stepped into the shower so my t-shirt and shorts clung to my tits and twat, then grabbed my quirt and headed back into the ballroom.

Considering they all have the same basic job, dicks are funny. Some were long and skinny. Some short and fat. A couple of the guys had the worst of worlds, cocks that looked like gnawed-off pencils. None had the massive appeal Brandon's did.

Brandon, of course, was nowhere to be seen.

Regardless of the size of their equipment, every guy in the fraternity lay on the ballroom floor, towels under their naked butts, holding their dicks in white-knuckled hands, staring at the door and waiting for me to enter.

The sound as I entered, a kind of gasping for air mixed with low moans, would have stoked the ego of a woman with far less self-esteem than I had.

Twenty pairs of eyes followed every step I took.

"Legs up," I ordered, setting the metronome that timed their strokes. No reason not to have them get a bit of an abdominal workout while they masturbated, plus it gave me access to their butts.

They gripped down hard, jerking faster when I met their gaze or leaned toward one, giving them just a hint of cleavage.

"Nobody comes in less than ten minutes." I set the alarm on the workout timer I'd installed after the disaster of our first jerkoff.

They groaned and a couple of them murmured complaints. Not loudly enough, though, that I felt compelled to take notice. I'd have plenty of chances to whip them into shape as the jerkoff continued.

Over time, we'd increased their stamina, but the base had been low. The first time I'd had them jerk off, the first guy had come after about four strokes. And I hadn't wet myself down for them that time.

Still, Amber's handjobs should have taken the pressure off. The rest of the trick was to help them out.

After three minutes, sweat dripped from all of their bodies, and twenty beet-red faces stared at me, their eyes following every shift of my hips, every small wiggle in my breasts.

Chuck was first to push himself too close to the edge.

I caught him in time, though.

Before he could spurt, I grabbed both of his legs and whipped my quirt hard on his naked butt.

He moaned and I swatted him again.

That did the job. He gritted his teeth and nodded, regaining control.

"Thank you, mistress."

"Your lover can grab your balls and squeeze, helping you delay orgasm," I said, "but you need to let her know you need it. Or him, of course."

With four minutes to go, I reset the metronome to a faster pace.

Almost instantly, Russell moaned, pumping his fist up and down his engorged shaft even more quickly than the new rhythm.

I didn't think he'd really lost control. Still, it looked like this would be the last event in our fraternity. After the Greek Council meeting the following night, I'd be out a job and the guys would be sent back home. If Russell wanted his butt whipped, I didn't mind obliging.

In fact, weeks of running and weightlifting had turned a once-flabby butt into something he could be proud of.

I turned my back on him, spreading my legs so I straddled him. Then I leaned my ass against his legs, pushing them down toward his chest, and lifting his rear off the ground.

I teased his bottom with my quirt first, before raising my arm above my head to bring it down in a whistling slap.

He moaned, but I didn't think he minded the pain at all. He'd reached that point where pain and pleasure mingled, where all of his nerves were overloaded and where sensation fed on itself.

I brought down the quirt again, leaving pink trails on both of his butt-cheeks and his upper thighs.

Finally, the alarm sounded, indicating that the ten minutes had elapsed. Every single guy had made it.

I had to dodge quickly as semen flew through the room.

It must have been a conspiracy. Because every single guy unloaded in my direction. Apparently they'd decided the punishment would be worth it.

None of them hit me, but I must have presented an interesting picture, my ass and tits jiggling as I contorted myself to avoid flying spunk.

"You guys are natural-born kidders," I told them. "On your hands and knees in a long row."

I'd miss this, I realized as I went down the row, flicking those sexy boy-butts with my quirt, making sure they would think twice before challenging my authority again.

When I'd first walked into the fraternity, I'd barely been able to resist following whatever orders Russell and Stretch chose to give me.

If they'd been grown men, instead of college-age boys, I probably would have obeyed them, let them pass me around like a ragged copy of *Hustler*.

We'd grown together. As I'd gained confidence, the guys had learned important lessons about women, about themselves, and about relationships. They'd also been put through a physical training program that had turned them from a mix of scrawny and obese misfits into guys with above-average physiques, even for a college campus.

All of a sudden, I wasn't sad about James tearing this away from me, I was pissed.

Yeah, Brandon had failed to break James's cryptography. Yeah, neither Amber nor Dr. Cotton would talk. Yeah, James had a gun, so I couldn't mug him in a dark alley. But I swore I'd do something. I just didn't know what.

* * * *

Morning came, hot, sticky, and alone.

I stretched out on the bed and realized—I was in my bed. For the first time in over a decade, I'd gotten into my own bed and stayed there, rather than climbing into a doggy-bed at the foot of the adult bed.

Considering I probably won't have a bed by sunset, I realized I'd better not to get too used to the idea.

I wasn't looking when I stepped off the bed and my bare foot came down on something sharp.

"Ouch, damn." I'd stepped on the black jeans I'd worn for Amber's breakout.

I reached into the pocket and pulled out the collection of keys Stretch had found when he'd been looking for a way to unlock Amber.

None of the keys had worked for the padlock, but they had to open something. James was far too organized a person to leave around old keys that no longer had a purpose.

As I flipped through the set, I spotted one that rang a distant bell.

I grabbed the little brass key, squeezed it in my fist, and tried to remember.

I hadn't actively remembered the early days in my marriage for years. Instead, I'd gradually replaced true memories with artificial constructs—assembled out of a combination of facts, James's stories, and wishful thinking on my part.

As I held that key, I made my mind think back to my first years with James.

Reluctantly at first, but then in a flood, my memories returned. So much that I lost my balance, had to clutch at my bed to keep from falling into the doggy pallet that still sat next to the king-size mattress.

I hadn't always been a willing submissive. Like Amber, I'd fought him. I'd tried to escape. I'd schemed for some way to get out of his control. But nobody had come to rescue me.

The tricks James had used on Amber, he'd used on me first. I'd spent weeks with my neck chained between my knees, a ball-gag in my mouth, plugs in both my ass and twat.

He hadn't just tickled my butt with a quirt, he'd beat me hard with a short bullwhip, giving me the scars he'd convinced me were disgusting cellulite.

And, he'd taken me to the bank, made me open a safety deposit box in my own name, just in case someone decided to come looking for any of his stuff.

Naturally he'd made me sign papers giving him power of attorney. He had free access to the box and it wasn't even in his name so no greedy lawyer could locate it.

He always thought he was smarter than the system. I felt certain whatever secrets he'd hidden in the box were still there—and in my name.

And now I had the key.

Unfortunately, it was Saturday.

By the time the bank opened on Monday, the fraternity would be closed and the guys expelled.

* * * *

It took me twenty minutes to find the business card the bank manager had slid down my cleavage.

"Winfield Clay, Vice President and Branch Manager," it read.

He didn't answer his office phone.

I put on my black leather pants and the black bustier the guys had bought for me for the rush party, then headed downstairs.

A couple of the guys were stretching. Others were pulling on running shoes and shorts. A few lounged around naked, their dicks on proud display.

I had to stop myself from looking. These weren't *guys*, they were *my guys*.

"Russell," I called. "I need a favor."

"Sure, missus." He approached me a little gingerly. Well, he deserved a sore butt for that little display the previous evening.

I handed him the business card. "Can you find where this guy lives?"

"No problem." His laptop was already running on the dining room table and he clicked open a browser window and entered the name. "How come you didn't get Brandon to help?" he asked.

"Brandon's a nice guy, but I don't need him to bail me out of everything."

"Especially when you have us to bail you out," he offered.

"With you, it doesn't count as bailing me out. It counts as paying me back a small part of the debt you owe me."

He grinned. "I know you think you're kidding, but it's no joke. Every single guy in this fraternity owes you more than we can ever repay. Sure it's about over but we had a great run. You've changed our lives, made us—"

"Cut the sappy stuff and give me the address," I said. "Besides, I haven't given up on stopping James."

He shook his head, grabbed a pen, and wrote an address on his hand. "Okay, let's go."

"What's this *us* stuff. *You're* going for a run."

"First," he counted off on a finger, "you're going to need my truck and I don't trust you to drive. Second, you're a part of the fraternity. Since when do we let one of us get into trouble without backing them up?"

"What makes you think—"

"Come on, missus. I'm no genius, but I'm not blind. You've got some crazy plan and you're going to get into trouble. Well, I'm an expert at getting into trouble. I figure, I should be able to help."

I sighed and grabbed my quirt. "All right, then. Just wear your shorts. No shoes."

He looked down on himself.

Of all the guys in the fraternity, Russell might have changed the most.

He'd always had potential. He'd been a bit soft, a bit pasty-white, a bit nerdy when I'd talked myself into a job. Now, he was hard muscle, dark tan, and an intimidating presence. He was too young for me, but my body still responded to his closeness. *Just a little,* I promised myself.

I led him out to his truck and piled in.

"Want to tell me what this is about?" he asked as he roared out of the fraternity lot and out away from town.

"I need a little banking assistance."

"The local banks are closed on Saturday."

"That's why we're going to Clay's home."

Clay lived in a housing development about five minutes from downtown.

It was solidly middle-class, with brick houses that seemed all garage from the front, competitively green lawns, and shiny new pickup trucks in every driveway.

Clay's place was almost exactly like every other.

"Stand behind me with your arms across your chest and glare," I told Russell as I got out of his truck. "Whatever happens, don't open your mouth."

"What if—"

I put the tip of the quirt to his lips. "That order started when I gave it, Russell."

He nodded, mouthing the words, "yes, Mistress."

Clay's doorbell chimed out the opening notes to Dixie.

A minute later, an attractive woman of about my age opened the door.

She glanced at me, then stared at Russell. "Uh, can I help you?"

"Are you Mrs. Clay?"

"Uh," she seemed in a daze. "Uh-huh."

"I need to speak to your husband, Mrs. Clay. It's important."

"Can you tell me what this is about?"

I slapped the quirt against my thigh. "I think it would be better for Winfield to explain things to you."

"You don't mean—"

"I'm sure he'll want to tell you himself."

"Well, of all the—"

She started to shut the door, but I gave Russell a quick nod and he pushed it open, sending Mrs. Clay reeling backward.

"Winfield," she shouted. "There are strange and scary people looking for you."

Winfield didn't look any different than he had when he'd been groping my tits and offering me fifty bucks for a handjob.

He obviously didn't recognize me, but he got a silly grin when he caught a look at the way my bustier displayed my c-cups. "Uh, hello."

"Winfield," I said. "You offered to help me with my banking business. I've decided to give you that opportunity."

"Winfield." His wife's voice had gone all shrieky. "What is this about?"

Recognition dawned slowly. "You're Mrs. d'Angre, aren't you. You've certainly changed since—"

"Since we last did bank business," I interrupted. "You're quite right."

"This is my home." His eyes seemed glued to my tits. "I don't think this is really the time or place—"

"You're right about it not being the place," I agreed. "As for it not being the time, I'm afraid you're quite mistaken. We'll just pop over to the bank, conduct our business, and have you back here before your beautiful wife even knows you've been gone."

"But—"

"She really is pretty, isn't she, Winfield." I used my quirt to tilt Clay's head in Mrs. Clay's direction. "I'd think any man would be proud to have her. Russell will stay with her while we do our banking business."

Mrs. Clay's chin trembled, but she also blushed. Compared to the fat and unattractive Winfield, Russell had to look like a winning lottery ticket.

"Mrs. d'Angre and I have some, ah, banking business to conduct, Lucy," he told his wife. "It shouldn't take more than a few minutes."

"But the bank is closed on--"

"For some customers, we need to make exceptions." He winked at me.

I stared at him for a solid ten seconds. The idiot really thought I'd come over to give him his handjob and get my fifty bucks.

"You're off restriction until I get back," I told Russell. "If Mrs. Clay wants to provide you with any services, you may accept."

His eyes widened as he looked from Lucy to me. "Don't you need me to—"

"Do we need company for our banking business, Winfield?"

He looked at his wife and then at me. His dick wasn't anything to write home about, but it sure looked proud of itself standing straight up like pole-vaulting equipment. "Uh, no. Why don't you stay with the lad, Lucy. I'll just give Mrs. d'Angre what she needs and pop back in."

The innuendo was gross, but I let it go. I did need his help to get into my safety deposit box.

His body jiggled like lukewarm gelatin as he grabbed his keys and led me out to his pickup. "I was sure you meant it when you said not to hold my breath," he babbled as he opened my car door. "It's great that you finally came back. I mean, Lucy is great and everything, but she's sexually repressed. Frigid."

"Funny how often that happens to guys like you."

I didn't expect he'd catch my tone and he didn't. "Yeah, you're not kidding. But compared with you, Lucy is second-rate, anyway."

I slapped his hand with my quirt as he reached for my ass and he drew it back quickly, rubbing the bright red streak I'd left across his fingers.

"Damn, lady. That hurts."

"Pain can be so enjoyable." I sank into his soft leather seats. "Let's go to the bank, please."

"The bank? There's a turnoff just a mile up the road. Nobody comes there and you could stroke me off and earn your hundred bucks in just a few minutes."

I laughed. "You're such a kidder, Winfield. I don't know how a fat ugly guy like you ended up with a babe like Lucy. I wonder if Russell will think she's frigid, too."

"What's that supposed to—"

I reached between his legs, unzipped his zipper, took out his dick, and twisted. "Now, drive me to the bank."

"Ouch. Damn. I see what you mean about the pain, though. That's completely hot."

Gross. I tightened my grip. "Drive."

If this is a robbery—"

"It's not a robbery. I just need to pick up some things from my safety deposit box."

"Our office hours--"

"You did offer me your personal banking services, remember."

"I meant my dick in your mouth."

"Sometimes things just don't work out the way you plan."

"You're kidding. You mean you're not going to suck me off."
"Drive."

Chapter Sixteen

Getting into the safety deposit box was a bit tricky. Winfield had to call a security company and give them some secret handshake before he could open the big safe that contained all of the boxes. Then he conscientiously compared my signature to that on the form I'd filled out when James had made me open the account.

I checked and saw that James hadn't signed in since we'd freed Amber.

"I guess it's okay for you to open it," he said. "But maybe I should call Professor d'Angre and get his permission. You have no idea how sticky things get in some divorces."

"I have a pretty good idea how sticky things are going to be if we don't get you back to your wife soon, Winfield. She was looking at Russell like he was an all-day sucker and she'd been on a diet."

"Lucy?" He laughed. "I already told you she's frigid."

"Keep thinking that way, Winfield. But if you call James, I'll call the Mississippi bank examiner. It's my name on the box, isn't it?"

He made a ho-ho-ho sort of laugh. "A matter of convenience. But now that you're divorced—"

"You're saying you knowingly participated in fraud, Winfield?"

"Oh, hell. I don't know. Go ahead and get your stuff. I guess it's okay."

"I'm sure it is."

I'd forgotten that James had selected one of the big boxes at the bottom of the vault.

Like all the boxes, it was locked with two separate locks. Winfield used the bank's key to undo his half, then backed away. "I'm not supposed to look at—"

"Far be it from me to interfere with your duties, Winfield."

He stepped out of the vault, his feelings obviously hurt. Oh, boo-hoo. I just couldn't find any sympathy.

I had a moment of panic when the key didn't fit. But I jiggled it a little and it finally slid in.

The box practically exploded with—panties.

So that's what happened to the thong I'd worn for my second date with James.

If there was an eBay market for used woman's panties, I was on the cusp of a second income.

That was so not what I'd been looking for.

"What the hell—"

"Winfield, bring in a wastebasket. I want to get rid of these things."

"Why do you keep your underwear in a safety deposit box?"

Dr. Cotton had told me that James was the type who'd collect trophies. I guessed I should be glad he'd picked panties rather than fingers or ears.

"My closets at home were getting full," I said. "I could use that trash can any time."

"Do you want me to help with those?" Winfield's voice shook.

"Knock yourself out. But if you find anything other than panties, I want to know about it."

It took a while to dig through the wadding, but at the back of the box, I found what I was looking for: notebooks filled with both contact prints and negatives, as well as a set of SD-RAM cards.

I scooped up the notebooks and memory cards and closed the box.

"I don't suppose—"

"No, Winfield. I really don't suppose it would be a good idea for you to keep those panties."

"But I swear one set belongs to Lucy. What would they be doing in there?"

Poor Winfield. Obviously Lucy wasn't as frigid as she'd led him to believe. Fortunately, I wasn't their marriage counselor. "We must shop in the same stores," I said. "It's not like Cambridge is that big a town."

"I guess that must be it."

"All right. I checked to make sure I had everything, then locked the box. "You can take me back, now."

He stared at my tits. "I don't suppose—"

"Your not supposing is getting tiresome, Winfield. I don't have my account number written on my boobs today, so there's really no reason for you to paw at them."

"That was a really nice thing for your husband to do." Winfield licked his lips. "If you want to know the truth, I've never fondled a better set. Lucy, well—"

"I could have gone my whole life without knowing that. Let's head back."

I loaded the notebooks and memory cards into Winfield's extended cab just as a sleek Jaguar rounded the corner and pulled into the lot.

"Uh-oh," Winfield offered.

"Yeah. I guess I'm going to have to deal with this. Just one thing, Winfield."

"What's that?"

"I want you to get into the truck and wait for me. If you show up at your place without me, Russell will tear off your balls and make you eat them. He's sort of protective that way."

His Adam's apple bobbed like a high-speed elevator. "I guess—"

I didn't have time for his guess. James was out of his car and heading toward me, fists up in his boxing pose.

"Fancy running into you here," he sneered. "Not quite quick enough this time, though, were you?"

"I'm afraid I have no idea what you're talking about, Jimmy."

"You call me Master."

"Sure, Master." No point in getting him mad prematurely.

I knew I'd suppressed a lot of memories, but I felt certain I'd remember if I'd ever seen him that completely pissed. His face had turned a darker maroon than the Cambridge State school colors, and the pulse in his neck had to be beating a couple hundred times a minute.

"I know you broke into my place. I know you kidnapped Amber. I know you stole my bank key. And I know you broke into my vault and took my stuff."

"You seem to know a lot of things that just aren't so, Master."

"Didn't I warn you never to lie to me, Nik?" I'd once thought he was sexy when he lowered his voice that way. Now I recognized it for what it was—an attempt at intimidation.

"Hey. Now that you mention it, I do remember."

"You're forgetting something, Nik."

"What's that?"

"Last time you back-talked me, you had a mob of goons to attack me. Today, you've only got a fat cuckold. And he's not sure whose side to take."

My stomach tightened. He'd threatened me, terrorized me, beat me for thousands of days until my body automatically responded to him. He looked more like Thor than ever and I suspected he was about to launch the kind of attack the mythological Thor was famous for.

"I had noticed you chose your time bravely."

"Oh, aren't you clever?" He launched his fist at my stomach.

I'd been fit before he'd kicked me out. But weeks of lifting weights with the guys and extending my runs made me quicker. I dodged to the side.

"You bitch." He pulled out a gun. "I wonder if you can dodge this."

I didn't stop to wonder if he'd really kill me—to save his blackmail material, he probably would. Instead, I thanked my lucky stars that he'd needed to talk himself into it If he'd simply shot me, I'd be bleeding out in the street.

I put every bit of my body behind my quirt, raking it across his hand as he raised his gun toward my head.

I'd hoped he would drop his gun. That didn't happen but the weapon dangled in his fingers. He reached for it with his other hand, his face contorted into a rage more frightening than anything I'd ever seen.

I hit him again, striking the same fingers.

This time, he dropped the gun and I kicked it away.

"You..." he stuttered. "You struck me."

"Considering how many times you hit me, I'd say you had it coming."

I wasn't so caught up in my comeback that I missed his move.

His eyes tracked my quirt and I knew he was getting ready to grab for it so I waited. Then, when he grabbed, I dropped to my knees and hit him across his calves.

He moaned, faltering just long enough for me to jump back to my feet.

I hit him in his injured hand again.

Mistake. James was strong and didn't let pain stop him. He grabbed the quirt and jerked, balling his other hand in a huge fist.

He might be able to work through pain but I'd hit that hand three times. When I gripped the quirt with both hands and yanked, his injured fingers gave way.

Drawing way back on ancient memories of being a twirler, I spun the quirt in my hands, feinted at his face, and drove the leather thong straight up between his legs.

The look on his face was priceless. But I didn't stop to admire it. James had enough adrenaline going that even a hard strike to his balls wouldn't to slow him much.

I ran for Winfield's pickup, and threw myself in the open window. "Drive."

I was surprised Winfield hadn't run already. I was even more surprised that he peeled out of that parking lot like all the fiends in Hell were after him.

He turned a couple of corners, went the wrong way down a one way street, and then took a detour down a narrow alley I hadn't even realized was there.

"Nice driving, Winfield," I said.

"Thanks. I've always had a fantasy about being in NASCAR."

"One thing I've learned lately—you've got to go for your fantasy."

He nodded slowly. "I can't believe you handled that asshole."

"You *knew* he was an asshole?" How had everyone in Cambridge known about my husband?

"I didn't know before—I thought he was cool. But he just tried to hit a woman. Do you think he really would have shot you?"

"Honestly, I don't know. I doubt he even knew. He thought he could intimidate me, make me do what he wanted. After all, he spent twelve years molding me into a woman who followed orders. I couldn't even go to the bathroom without his permission and I only stopped eating my breakfast out of a dog bowl a week ago."

"Well, you sure looked tough to me." He paused, looking at me with a speculative gleam in his eyes.

"If you're wondering whether that fight made me so horny I want you, I'm sorry. You're just not my type."

"I can be pretty submissive. But that's not what I was going to ask."

Why did he think I'd want a submissive? If I wanted submissive, I'd go with Brandon. "Okay, what were you going to ask?"

"If I asked you a question, would you give me a straight answer?"

"Maybe."

"That wasn't your underwear at all, was it?"

"Huh?"

"In the vault. You said maybe you and Lucy might shop for underwear in the same place. Except you don't wear underwear."

"I think maybe you and Lucy will have some talking to do, Winfield. Considering everything, I don't think either of you is exactly blameless."

He grinned at me. "I can't believe it—this is fantastic."

Huh? "What are you so happy about?"

"You know what this means, don't you?"

"That Lucy has been—"

"That Lucy isn't frigid after all."

Yeah, she just didn't like Winfield. Still, he seemed happy.

* * * *

"How did that go for you?" I asked Russell as we headed back toward the frat house.

"If you mean, did I get laid, no. Not that she didn't offer. And not that I wasn't tempted. Still, she's married. If she gets a divorce, she can give me a call."

I wouldn't have been more surprised if he'd told me he had decided to become a priest. "You turned down sex?"

"Hey. Haven't you been trying to teach us that we should treat women like people instead of like a convenient set of holes for us to stick our dicks into?"

"*Trying* to teach is exactly right. I had no idea you'd actually learned anything."

"What the hell..."

The flashing lights of what looked like every police car in Mississippi surrounded the frat house.

Russell hung a 'U' turn, ducked into a mall parking lot, and grabbed the notebooks. "Come on, missus. They're after us."

I followed him into the mall as he got on his phone and called the house for news.

"Cops picked up the phone," he reported. On a Saturday morning, everyone would be there. I'm going to call Brandon."

"We can't keep running to—"

"Look, missus. Maybe you've got problems with him or maybe you don't. But Brandon's my friend. If he needed anything, I hope he'd call me. Now I need something and I'm not too proud to call him."

About three minutes later, Brandon met us at the other end of the mall. We headed straight out of town.

"Uh, Brandon. We can't run away from our problems."

"Until we figure out what our problems are, we'd better steer clear of them," he said.

He drove about forty minutes, finally pulling into an old and small, but freshly painted farmhouse.

"Where are—"

"Come on in, Nicole. I'd like you to meet—"

The man coming from the house gave me a good view of what Brandon would look like in about thirty years. In his fifties, he still had a powerful physique, dark skin, and a full head of graying hair. The woman wore a smile so big I feared she might break something.

"You brought me to your *parents'* house?"

"You know the saying. 'Home is where they have to take you when you have to go there.'"

I did know that saying. I also knew people well enough that I didn't think this was like that at all—including my own mother. I dropped my quirt on the Brandon's Buick's floorboards. All I needed was to field questions about my riding experience.

"You must be Nicole," Mrs. Tiel said. "Brandon has told us so much about you."

"And you must be Mrs. Tiel." I held out my hand. "I'm so happy to—"

"Peggy," she said. "And Brad." She ignored my hand and drew me into a tight hug. "You are just the prettiest thing I've ever seen."

"Thank you Mrs. Ti—"

"Peggy," she insisted. "Come on in. I've always said that boy of mine can smell cookies baking twenty miles away. When I woke up this morning, I had this idea I needed to bake and I've got the first batch of chocolate chip on the cooling rack right now."

She introduced herself to Russell although she looked puzzled at his limited wardrobe, told Brad to find him some clothes, and ushered us into the Tiel home.

For the next five minutes, she bustled around, making sure all of us got plates loaded with cookies, big jelly jars full of iced tea, and comfortable seats on their enclosed front porch.

Brad Tiel winked at me and bent low to whisper in my ear. "Want to guess who's the boss around here?"

"You?"

"Brandon told me you had a sense of humor. Nope. Peggy is the boss. I always figured Brandon would get himself a boss-lady of his own one day. I mean, he's a great catch. But he never brought any of his ladies home until now. So, we're real glad—"

"Look, Mr. T—Brad. My ex-husband has sicced the police on us. We're here because we had to run somewhere."

"I've been looking for an excuse to get you out to meet my parents," Brandon observed mildly. "This seemed like a good excuse."

"These sure are good cookies," Russell added.

"Brandon said your asshole of an ex is giving you all sorts of trouble." Peggy bustled back from the kitchen, a fresh plate of cookies in her hands. "Got the cops after you again, did he?"

"Do you tell your parents every single detail of your life?" I demanded.

"Only when I think they'll be interested."

I couldn't understand that. The day I'd turned eighteen, a couple of weeks before my freshman year at Cambridge State, my mother had sat me down, told me I was an official adult, and that she had no further legal responsibility for my upkeep. I'd lived with a girlfriend until school had started and gotten by on grants and scholarships—until James had parachuted into my life. I'd thought parents that would continue to care, would be interested in my dating life, were television fantasy.

"So," Peggy said. "What have you got in the notebooks?"

* * * *

James had been a busy man.

I didn't recognize all of the women, but I knew plenty—starting with the wives of every professor in the department, the University Chancellor's wife. Even the police chief's wife, Missy, was there— tied up and with her mouth full of dick.

"Jeez. Now here's a guy who had a problem with objectification," Russell said. "He had you and he still went out and nailed all of these."

"I guess that's a compliment." I was busy, though, trying to figure out what to do with these pictures.

"I'm sure I'm not the only one who notices the problem," Brandon said.

"That this jerk is nailing all these pretty women in nasty ways when I'm not getting any action at all?" Russell guessed. "That problem?"

"What I had in mind is that he was the one taking all of the pictures."

"I doubt you'd find many people capable of taking pictures while they're tied up like that." Russell tapped a particularly lurid picture of the head of the English department, an attractive if definitely forty-something woman.

"I think Brandon's point is," I said, "we can prove that a bunch of women got nailed in mostly unpleasant and humiliating ways, but we can't prove that James was the one doing it."

"Well shit," Russell observed. "We're still screwed."

* * * *

Peggy forced a huge lunch down all of our throats while we went through the rest of the photos. Brad's laptop had a card reader, and we quickly reviewed the pictures stored on memory cards. What we found was more of the same.

Unless we could get an FBI penis expert, we were shit out of luck.

"Think he took all those pictures for fun?" At least that's what I thought Russell was saying. His mouth was so full of Peggy's lemon upside-down cake that I had trouble interpreting the words.

"Maybe he started that way," Brandon answered. "From what Dr. Cotton said, and from the dozens of panties Nicole described, it sounds like he had something of a fetish for collecting reminders of his conquests. But we saw an even darker side after we freed Amber, remember? He threatened her with blackmail. I wonder what other women thought they were having a fling with the handsome math professor and ended up having to go along with whatever he suggested because the alternative was having their reputation destroyed."

Russell swallowed. "Speaking of which, where are the pictures he took of Amber? Did we miss those somehow?"

I shook my head. "Hate to say it, but he must still have that memory card in his camera. The blackmail is still on."

"The blackmail is still on for all of them," Russell reminded me. "Remember, he's got that encrypted file on his computer at home."

Brandon cleared his throat. "Not exactly."

"Huh?"

"I hacked into his computer and re-encrypted that file. We still can't open it, but now he can't either. I'm not sure how that helps us, though."

I was. "Seems straightforward enough to me. As far as faculty and staff go, most of the female members of the disciplinary committee are there and all of the male members' wives are. I don't think we'll have any problems with the student members unless the faculty and administration press them. As my grandmother used to say, sauce for the goose, sauce for the gander. Once these pictures hit the Internet, they're going to have one hell of a time keeping their jobs. They're going to be way to busy to worry about whether a fraternity party got out of hand. And as for James's theft charges, that safety deposit box was in my name."

I thought it was a pretty good plan. From their expressions, neither Brandon nor Russell agreed.

"What?" I demanded.

"You're talking about ruining innocent women's lives," Brandon reminded me.

"Innocent? What kind of innocent women mess with another man's husband?"

He sighed. "You already know James d'Angre is an abuser—the kind of man who'll back a woman into a corner, take advantage of her, then blackmail her into doing worse. We don't know what d'Angre might have done to put any of these women in the situations they found themselves in."

"You're right, we don't know. We don't even know that James was the aggressor. He isn't a complete dog, you know. A lot of women find him attractive, pursue him."

Brandon practically growled at me. "You're right about that. Because he is attractive, nobody's ever taken charges against him seriously. And from what I'm hearing, you're just as guilty as everyone else."

"I don't know what makes you such an expert on this. You're beautiful enough that you've always had the same benefits. Like that Lisa at the library. She'd lick your boots if you'd pay her any attention."

"That's not the point."

I understood his point. I also understood we were talking about the lives of a lot of students who'd never done anything worse than join a formerly unpopular fraternity. Compared to them, ruining the reputations of a few women who should have known better didn't seem that big a deal.

"I'm not going to argue with you, Brandon. Maybe these women were victims, too. But what choice do we have? When I took my job as adult supervisor for the fraternity, I promised I'd do whatever I could to keep the guys in school. That meant not letting them drink, not letting them party all night, not letting them waste all their time watching porno DVDs or on-line. But it's not just about stopping them from doing the stupid things twenty-year-old males will do. It's about actively taking steps to prevent bad things from happening to them. I feel horrible for all those women, but I'd feel worse if I let my guys get kicked out of school."

Brandon shook his head. "I really thought you were bigger than that, Nicole."

"Bigger than doing my job for the guys?"

"Bigger than thinking some people are more important than others. If the answer to a question is that you've got to destroy the lives of a bunch of people, maybe you're asking the wrong question."

"I don't live in Shangri-Lai, I live in Cambridge, Mississippi. And if you live in the real world, sometimes you have to make hard choices, sometimes you have to settle for less than perfect. Besides, think about this—we're really doing these women a favor. Sure, they'll have some explaining to do to their husbands. Sure some of them will have a rough time keeping their jobs considering the hypocritical bastards who fund the university. But at least they won't have this sword hanging over their heads any more. They'll be free from James's blackmail."

Brandon pushed his lunch plate away and tossed his keys at Russell. "Somehow I'm just not hungry any more. Take her back whenever you want. You can use the computer in my old bedroom if you want to go on line and check to see if the police still have the fraternity under lockdown or to post your dirty pictures. Frankly, I just don't want to see you again, Nicole. I really thought you were better than that."

"I didn't say I was married to the plan," I protested. "If you have any better ideas, let me—"

"My better idea is that we don't ruin the lives of a lot of people. I know most of these women, Nicole. You know some of them, too.

They're not all bad. They don't deserve what you're planning on doing to them.

He walked to the door and shut it gently behind him. I would have felt better if he'd at least slammed it, if he'd had enough emotion to show anger. Instead, he seemed just sad and disappointed—in me.

"Am I doing the right thing?" I asked Russell.

"I was wondering if I could blackmail any of them into sucking *my* dick and thinking I should have taken Lucy's offer. I mean, for an older woman, she wasn't too bad and that Winfield guy, man, he sure hasn't been taking your classes. Anyway, rigt now I'm not your highest moral authority."

I ran my fingers through my hair. "We'll only release the pictures that are directly connected to the hearing tonight. No point in ruining more lives than we have to."

"You can't be fairer than that." Russell's agreement was a bit too ecstatic, as if he were more interested in convincing himself than me.

"Damn it, Russell, we've got to do this. Otherwise the fraternity goes down."

"And we're all expelled," he agreed. "If my parents find out I got expelled from here, they'll cut me off. And there sure aren't any decent jobs in Birmingham that don't require a college degree."

"Get on the phone and see if you can find any of the brothers," I said. "I'll work on getting these together for uploading."

"You won't be able to post them on YouTube," he reminded me. "They kick off anything more explicit than underwear. These pictures are a lot more than that.

Well, yeah. I'd say that a bunch of women in bondage, with bottles and dildos sticking from all of their slots, and with semen and piss splashed over their faces, tits, pussies, and hair was a lot worse than the occasional chick in her Victoria's Secrets.

"James used to watch a lot of user-created pornography," I admitted. "I know where we can post these."

"What sites are those?"

I felt like crap because of the way Brandon had walked out on me, but I still couldn't help laughing. "I don't know how gullible you think I am, but I'm not *that* dumb. Do you have any idea how much time you can waste with pornography? And to think I was proud of you for not treating Lucy like an object."

"Doesn't mean I don't like *looking* at chicks."

"Call the guys and see if they're in jail or running free. If they're in jail, the police chief's wife is the first set of images we post. Pretty ironic sticking that nightstick up her ass, wasn't it. Ol' James always was a kidder."

"Yes, Mistress," he said.

I took the pictures into Brandon's childhood bedroom, fired up his scanner, and started putting together video slideshows of our town's best-looking and best-connected women.

James, I thought. *You really are a jerk.*

The guilt got to me, of course. I was sure Brandon had intended it would. Working in his room, surrounded by things that had once been important to him, made me even more aware of his feelings about what I had to do.

But then I thought about the guys in the fraternity. They'd taken me in when my alternative was turning tricks in the street. They'd let me boss them around when I so desperately needed something I could control. They'd stood up for me when James had tried to assault me. And not one of them had suggested firing me to get James off their case. Which they could have done, I realized. If he'd gotten me and Brandon fired, James would have moved on to his next victim. Mere students weren't enough for him to bother with.

Brandon had claimed that *all* these women were James's victims, that publishing their pictures made me exactly the kind of uncaring dominant James was. He had to be wrong.

I do care, I told myself. *But I care more about my own than I do about women who two-timed with my husband.*

My justifications were starting to feel repetitive.

"They hauled all the guys down to the police station," Russell said, breaking into my increasingly morbid thought pattern. "But Stretch's dad is a lawyer. He got on the phone to a couple of local politicians and the whole gang was cut loose within half an hour."

"Some good news for a change," I said.

"But the police are still looking for you," he said. "James claims you assaulted him with a horsewhip."

I guess a quirt could be called a horsewhip. Certainly jockeys whip their horses with them. Naturally, James wouldn't bother reporting that he'd pulled a gun on me before I'd hit him.

"Okay," I said. "That does it. Missy Biglow, AKA Mrs. Police Chief, goes on the Internet first."

"The Internet is real big," Russell reminded me. "Just because there are dirty pictures of her up there doesn't mean anyone will find them, especially not anyone who knows her."

"I've got a plan for that. How does www.CambridgeStateUniversitySkanks.com sound to you?"

"Cool. I'll write that do—"

"You are not going to waste your time looking at James's trophy shots."

"Everyone else is going to. Why shouldn't I?"

I hadn't thought about that angle. Still, there was already enough filth on the Internet that it could keep everyone busy forever. The little bit I added wouldn't make any appreciable difference.

I clicked the upload button and Missy Biglow went live.

The second I finished the upload, a surge of guilt even higher than any of the others hit me.

I did a search for Missy Biglow, of Cambridge, Mississippi, and learned that she'd been a cheerleader, had married at seventeen when she got pregnant during her senior year of high school, was active in her church, and worked as an administrative assistant in the French department at the University.

She also slept with your husband, I reminded myself. The French department was located in a building adjacent to the Math department. James had probably picked her up during a lunch break. Then he'd given her something bigger than the average hot dog to munch on.

Since I'd been a kid, I'd been given the lecture about not putting personal information on the net. Missy must have been sleeping that day because her address, phone number, the names, ages and schools her kids attended, and even her book club was listed. They were reading Betty Friedan.

I stared at that phone number, then realized I needed to call her, needed to let her know that I'd ended her misery, taken away any leverage James had over her, and ruined her marriage as a consequence.

I suspected she wouldn't care. That smile on her dick-filled mouth didn't look like she was hurting any.

I borrowed Russell's phone and called the number.

French department, Bonjour."

"Can you put me through to Missy Biglow, please?"

"Speaking."

"Missy, this is Nicole d'Angre."

"Oh."

"Don't hang up, Missy. I have something important I'd like you to see."

"If you're calling about James, don't bother. He dumped me a long time ago."

"He didn't completely dump you." I read her the URL and waited for her scream.

Which took all of two seconds. She must be a slow typer.

"Nicole, you can't do this. If my boss sees this, my husband will divorce me and the judge will never let me see my children again."

"And you and your husband will never be able to ruin innocents' lives without someone whispering the word 'hypocrite'."

"Tell me what you want. I don't have much money, but I can give you some. Maybe a hundred a month."

I wanted to laugh. Instead I felt sick. Missy reminded me of the way I'd sounded that day James had told me I'd gotten too old and that he wanted me out of the house.

"I don't want your money, Missy. I want you and your husband discredited, destroyed."

"What possible benefit could that give you? I told you I'm not with James any more so you can't warn me away from him. There's nothing I can do to help you get him back. And you definitely can't believe that you can keep James from screwing other women. That man is an amoral asshole."

"I don't want him back."

"Then why hurt me?"

"It's nothing personal, Missy. You're just the first. I'm going to destroy the reputations of so many people on campus and off that James's little complaints about the Pi Iota Sigma fraternity will seem like the trivia they are."

"You're ruining all of our lives to keep your job as a cleaning lady? I told you I'd pay you. I'll tell Harry I've hired you to clean our place. You won't even have to—"

"It's not about my job. It's about my boys. They're going to expel them all."

"Oh." She paused. "I'm afraid I can't do anything about that." Missy's snuffling gradually turned into deep, lung-sucking sobs.

I couldn't do it. I clicked the delete button. "Okay, Missy. I deleted the pictures."

"Maybe I can pay you more." She gave a pathetic hiccup. "I can get another job, I've heard—"

"I don't want your money, Missy."

"I'll tell Harry what a turd James is."

"Sure, Missy. You do that."

I hung up and glared at Russell.

"What?"

"I can't do it. Don't you hate me? I *could* keep you from getting expelled and a few tears from some woman I don't even know turn me into a sissy."

He nodded. "This reminds me a lot about one of those problems my Philosophy prof makes us think about."

"Except those all have right answers, right?"

"Oh, no. In philosophy, there aren't any absolutely right answers. My professor says if the answer is that easy, that means it was a bad question."

One by one, I called the other women, letting them know that I'd stolen the pictures and that I was destroying them. I was setting them free, but not in the way I'd planned. Rather than attacking their reputation, I was letting them hang on to the hypocrisy and deceit they'd nearly ruined their lives with.

A few cursed me. One thanked me. Most of the others sounded mystified, as if I'd offered them a free vacation and they were waiting for the time-share hard sell.

I finished making calls about four. Then I borrowed Brad's hammer and smashed the memory cards.

The negatives and contact sheets were a bit more trouble. I tried tearing them, but the negatives were tough plastic. Finally Peggy suggested her pinking shears and I had a good time cutting them up.

I wanted to beg Russell to tell me I was doing the right thing. I wanted to track Brandon down and tell him I'd seen the light, but I didn't want to put Russell on the spot and Brandon had already looked me in the eye and decided he didn't like what he saw.

Still, I liked myself a lot better when it was done.

I decided I'd like myself better still when I stood up in front of the University Greek Council and took all the blame for whatever James was accusing us of. I wasn't going to drag the guys down with me if I could help it.

Unfortunately, James seemed intent on spreading the destruction widely and I'd just chopped up the only weapon I had against him.

Chapter Seventeen

Brandon's parents lived less than thirty miles from the university. Under normal circumstances, we could have covered the distance in forty-five minutes. But nothing was normal about these circumstances. With every cop in northern Mississippi looking for me, simply driving into town was not in the program. Instead, we organized the fraternity, Amber's sorority, and, thanks to Harry's efforts, the entire football team to scout the location of every cop and watch every university security officer.

A dozen different students, varying from studious pencil-necks to no-neck football players chauffeured me from place to place, staying one jump ahead of the police and keeping to a timetable complicated enough to have served for D-Day.

At exactly eight that evening, Harry pulled me up behind the small science lecture hall, which was where the disciplinary hearings were held.

Russell and I piled out and rushed toward the always-locked back door.

A second before we smashed our noses into it, Stretch opened it from inside and then closed it behind us when we slipped in.

I tried to keep a low profile as Russell and I joined the other fraternity brothers on a wooden bench that looked suspiciously like a pew pulled out of the chapel.

The guys looked good and I was proud of them. They were all in black, and I couldn't remember ever seeing so many toned arms and chests in black t's.

James had been looking the other way, lobbying an assistant dean. I didn't know if he sensed movement, smelled me, or whether the dean said something, but he whirled, his arm out, pointing at me like he thought he was God about to smite Sodom. "There she is. Arrest her."

Chief Biglow cleared his throat. "Don't worry. We'll make sure she doesn't get away."

James shook his head. "Check her for weapons, for God's sake. She assaulted me with a horsewhip earlier."

"Do you have any weapons, Mrs. d'Angre?" Biglow asked.

"Just my body."

That got a few giggles from the crowd. I didn't see any of the administrators laughing and they were the real deciders. The Greek Council was supposedly half student and half faculty/administration, but the students got one vote for the entire group, compared to one vote each for the administrators and faculty members.

"You might check Professor d'Angre for a semi-automatic pistol, though," I said. "He threatened me with one earlier today."

Chief Biglow turned to my ex-husband. "Professor d'Angre. Do you have a—"

"You believe her?"

"She's leveled a serious accusation, professor."

"Fortunately we live in America where it's legal to carry a weapon. Ever since she and her gang of hoodlums assaulted me, I have carried a firearm, and I intend to keep doing so until she's under lock and key."

"The university rules state that this is a no gun facility."

"I'm sure that rule doesn't apply to me. I am a full professor here, after all. You're here to protect me from that bad influence. And so far, you haven't been doing much of a job."

Chief Biglow nodded. "Perhaps you'd allow me to hold your weapon for you, just until we've finished here. I assure you, I'll protect you from any vicious women."

The university Chancellor banged his gavel. "Gentlemen. Let's get this proceeding started. This is a disciplinary proceeding against the Pi Iota Sigma fraternity. Our task is to determine what punishment is appropriate for a fraternity which has stepped over the line, conducted acts of debauchery, promoted unnatural behavior between young boys and an older woman, and finally, during a drunken orgy, attacked a senior member of the facility."

"Quite right," James agreed.

"Those are conclusions," I protested. "We've been accused of—"

"You'll have your chance to argue for leniency," the chancellor interrupted. "For now—"

"For now, I think the lady has a point," the assistant chancellor said.

The chancellor turned a pale shade of purple. There was nothing pale at all about James's face. I'd seen grape juice that wasn't that dark.

"Have you gone completely insane," my ex-husband exploded. "They're having orgies on university-owned property. The state will cut us off without a dime if we don't demonstrate our willingness to stomp them down like the cockroaches they are."

"Very poetic," the assistant dean agreed.

My heart, which had jumped into my throat, sank into my gut. James was right—state funding for higher education is a tough sell in a state with one of the lowest percentages of college graduates in the country. If word got to the state legislators that we were running sex dens, they'd happily take the money and spend it on building monuments to themselves.

"If we can continue," the chancellor said, "Professor d'Angre--"

"Just a moment," the assistant chancellor said. "I said the professor was poetic, I didn't say I agreed with him."

"How can you not? You're responsible for our funding. You know we've already cut to the bone. If the state—`"

"Why should the state cut our funding?" Professor Ironer put in.

She was one of the women whose pictures I'd cut up earlier that afternoon. A youthful forty, Professor Ironer was from California and still looked like she should be on a surfboard rather than in front of a freshman composition class. Although she was way older than the age James preferred, she was an influential campus leader. It only made sense that James would use sex to control her.

"If you haven't heard, you're probably the only person on campus who hasn't." The chancellor sounded frustrated. Things weren't going as he'd anticipated and he didn't know why. Quite frankly, I didn't know why, either.

"Professor d'Angre," he explained patiently, "has discovered that his ex-wife, whom he divorced because of her unnatural desires and appetites, has turned an already substandard fraternity into an S and M den of sin. We owe him a huge debt for uncovering this before it spread, like a malignant cancer, through our entire campus. Can you imagine if our co-eds were subjected to that kind of cruel abuse, their tender breasts tied with silken ropes, their youthful—"

"Fortunately," James interrupted before the chancellor got too carried away, "we're in time to prevent all of that."

"Uh, yes."

A Zoology professor who, according to campus legend, slept through every single disciplinary meeting and then voted for the most severe punishment raised his hand.

His wife was a redheaded number who, at least according to James's pictures, enjoyed life on the definitely kinky side. She'd worn a big grin, an enormous strap-on dildo and nothing else in the pictures I'd seen of her. I wondered if she'd used that dildo on James, or if he'd brought in other women for her to penetrate. In either case, I'd had to think long and hard before I'd brought myself to destroy her pictures. She might just be on the same page as James when it came to sexual predation.

"This university," the professor nicknamed 'Hang-'em-high' Haverstone for his proclivity to throw the book at anyone accused of anything, intoned, "is second to none in protecting the morals of our young people. Our reputation is spotless and must be vigorously protected."

I gripped down on the pew in front of me so hard I almost expected to feel the wood shatter under my hands. I'd been surprised at the apparent support we'd gotten from the assistant dean and French professor. But Hang-'em-high Haverstone seemed intent on destroying our momentum. I wondered how he'd feel if I flashed a few of his wife's pictures. Maybe he wouldn't be quite so full of his morality proclamations if he had to justify that big strap-on.

"Sexual depravity is worst," Hang-'em-high continued, where it impinges on the young, the helpless. Our young women are still impressionable, still capable of being formed, or deformed, by the kind of abuse we're discussing here. No penalty can be too severe for the disgusting specimens who prey on our co-eds, who use pain and torture to distort them."

"Quite right," the chancellor agreed as James nodded seriously. "It sickens me," the chancellor continued, "to think of young girls, held naked, their youthful pubes shaved, their dainty asses spread and shattered by—"

"Which is why I believe that Professor d'Angre must be removed from this campus," Hang-'em-high concluded.

"You mean Mrs. d'Angre," the chancellor corrected.

"Poor Mrs. d'Angre is a victim of this monster quite as much as many others, my wife included. From my research I've learned that Professor d'Angre fraudulently received Mrs. d'Angre's consent to an unjust divorce, attempted to force her into prostitution, and attacked her new boyfriend before any number of witnesses."

"That is exactly the point I was making," the assistant chancellor said.

The meeting deteriorated from there. When one brave female professor gave her own account of James's intimidation and abuse, and two aging professors grabbed one another by their herringbone smoking jackets and wrestled to the ground, the chancellor called a halt and sent everyone but the senior faculty members home.

"We won," Russell said. "Destroying those pictures was brilliant. How did you figure they'd turn on Professor d'Angre?"

I hadn't figured anything of the kind, of course. We'd been saved by pure luck—and a professor with his own ax to grind.

Chapter Eighteen

The guys wanted to celebrate.

It was Saturday night, so I let them stay up until midnight, playing music not quite loud enough to disturb the neighbors, and hosting a variety of co-eds from Amber's sorority and from the various dorms around the campus.

Some of the co-eds were pushy, cutting guys from the herd and dragging them to secluded corners.

I didn't have a problem with the guys dating, of course, but I didn't want anyone to get carried away in the euphoria of the moment. Getting a girl pregnant on a pre-first date was not the way to build a strong relationship.

When the big grandfather clock in the ballroom clonked out midnight, I breathed a sign of relief, called the campus police to escort the co-eds back to their dorms and sorority houses, got the guys undressed and sent them to bed.

By half-past midnight, I was in my bathtub, my legs resting on the tiled wall, and the spigot pouring water over my clit.

Masturbation had helped me a lot during the weeks after James had dumped me. As I'd gradually re-created myself, learned that I was more than what James had shaped me into, I'd found it empowering to learn that I didn't need to rely on James to fill my sexual needs, that I could take responsibility for myself.

My body responded to the plunging water and I managed an orgasm, but I didn't get as much satisfaction out of it as I needed. I didn't need a Ph.D. in psychology to figure out why, either. The guys might think I was a genius, but I'd fucked up when it came to Brandon. And Brandon mattered.

Brandon had been right all along about me. I wasn't a sub: that was a role James had forced me into. Perhaps even James had known that, had dumped me not because of my age as he'd claimed, but because I just wasn't submissive enough. And Brandon needed a dom, but not a dom who would ride roughshod over others. He needed the kind of dom I'd mistakenly told James I wanted— someone who would care about her sub, someone who could make submission safe.

When I'd decided to blackmail those women, I'd proved myself to be another James—a dominant who'd use her power for personal benefit. In short, I was a dominant who couldn't be trusted. No wonder Brandon had rejected me.

I got out of my bathtub and stood, naked and dripping on the bath mat.

A part of me wanted to track Brandon down, tie him up to make him listen to me, and have my way with him before telling him I wasn't really James, that he could trust me, that I wasn't the kind of woman who would pursue her goals without concern for anyone else.

The rest of me, though, reminded me that I'd proved myself to be exactly that. I wasn't so different from James. The reason Brandon and I could never be together was *not* that we were two submissives: it was that Brandon could never be safe from me. I was a rogue dominant.

"You're beating yourself up again, aren't you?"

I covered my breasts with one hand and pussy with the other, then whirled to see Stretch and Russell at my bathroom door. Both were naked except for their dick straps. Both plainly liked what they saw.

"I don't know what you're talking about," I lied.

Russell sighed. "You're thinking you're a terrible person because you considered using James's pictures for blackmail."

"Uh, not a big logic leap if you think about it. There's a reason blackmail is illegal almost everywhere. It's an asshole thing to do."

"But you didn't," Stretch pointed out.

"I was all set to do it. I meant to do it. Don't you get it—I'm a loose cannon."

"You're still learning about yourself," Stretch said. "When you first saw us, you didn't decide we were losers and dump us. You stuck with us, helped us change."

I grabbed a towel from the rack and wrapped it around myself. Call me vain, but I wanted the guys to think of me as an unattainable but sexy woman, not as a thirty-year-old whose breasts weren't quite as perky as they had been and whose butt didn't stick out as straight as it once had.

Doing the towel wrap didn't help the guys with their hard-ons, though. "I'm not touching those things," I said. "So, go point them somewhere else."

"You see?" Russell said, as if I'd proven some obscure point. "You're a good person."

"Lots of people don't screw college kids. That doesn't mean they've got any special virtue."

Stretch sighed. "The point is, while you might sometimes have been tempted to be selfish, you've mostly made good decisions, helped others rather than hurting them. Even when you were thinking about blackmail, you weren't doing it to protect yourself, you were doing it to protect your honorary children."

"Meaning you?"

"Definitely meaning us. Just because you turn all of us on, that doesn't mean we don't recognize that your feelings toward us are maternal. Unlike, say, your feelings toward Brandon."

From the stiff dicks those guys pointed at me, I didn't think either of them was having motherly thoughts about me.

"So you're saying I should just pretend I didn't—"

"Who said anything about pretend." I'd trained the guys not to interrupt me, so Russell had to be really distressed. "Just tell Brandon what happened. Let him sort it out."

I laughed. "Brandon is a sub. He has a hard time sorting anything out."

"Seems to me he does pretty well," Stretch pointed out.

Okay, Stretch had a point. "Maybe I'll see him around."

"Good idea." Russell tossed me the keys to his truck. "Brad and Peggy drove my ride back into town. Why don't you borrow it and see Brandon around right now."

"University rules require that I stay here on Saturday night."

"Lucky for you," Russell said, "it's Sunday morning. No rules require you to stay in on Sunday morning."

Considering that the fraternity was still under investigation, I thought that was playing a little loosey-goosey with the rules.

Then I wondered how I'd feel if I went after Brandon and he shot me down—again. Hadn't I already put up with more of that than I could stand?

"You're letting James do the talking now," Russell said.

"Nobody's talking," I objected.

"That's the problem." Stretch tossed me my miniskirt and bustier. "You're not talking and you're not moving because you're afraid." He pitched his voice to a falsetto that bore absolutely no resemblance to my own tones. "What if someone doesn't like me? What if someone rejects me?" Lowering his voice to a more normal tone, he continued. "When the worst thing that can happen is that you'll go on as you are now, why not try for something better?"

"You don't trust me with your truck," I reminded Russell.

"Oh that's so true. Lucky my parents pay for the insurance."

That wasn't really the kind of recommendation I'd wanted. Still, Stretch had a point. If Brandon rejected me, would I be worse off than if I'd stayed in the frat house and wallowed in my misery?

Chapter Nineteen

Who knew driving a clutch could be so difficult.

I knew the basic principle: you push the clutch pedal in, shift the big stickshift into the slot marked on the knob on its top, let off the clutch, and drive.

I'd seen Russell do it a dozen times. If *he* could do it, an intelligent woman like me should have no problem.

But every time I let up the clutch pedal, I'd lurch forward a few feet and then the truck stalled.

I would have been faster jogging, except I didn't really feel like wandering around the campus in a miniskirt that left both my cheeks exposed to the air and a bustier the guys had insisted I lace so tightly I couldn't get any oxygen and my breasts threatened to explode right out of it.

An hour later, and less than half a mile down the road, Russell's truck lurched into a dumpster, setting off both car alarms and every dog within five miles of the campus, I dug for my phone to call Russell and demand that he chauffeur me.

A knock on the windshield jerked my attention from the phone.

"Officer, I can ex…"

I ground to a halt when I saw not one of the campus cops, but a sexy librarian.

"You weren't fair to me," I said. When it comes to submissives, the best defense is a strong offensive.

"You're right."

Well, go figure. I guess a submissive's best defense is capitulation. How could I get mad at him if he agreed with me?

"Just because I thought about blackmailing those people doesn't mean I actually did it."

"I know."

"And even if I had, it's not like I was doing it for me. I'm not James."

"I absolutely agree. You're about as far from James as a dominant can be."

"I might be a dominant," I admitted. "But that doesn't mean I have to be mean all the time."

"Excellent. I wouldn't want you to be mean all the time."

All through the hour I'd been trying to drive toward Brandon's home, I'd been planning this conversation. Then Brandon went and screwed with my plan—and with my mind. I decided to give it to him straight. "Here's the deal, Brandon. I'm not giving up the fraternity. These guys need my help. But they could use your help, too."

He nodded. "Okay. I'll move in with you there."

"The problem is, the University is going to be going through some serious finger-pointing once more dirt comes out on James—and from what I saw earlier tonight, there's going to be a lot of dirt coming out. I shredded the blackmail pictures and all of a sudden, people want to blab about it. How backwards is that? So, anyway, we just can't live together, no matter how much I'd like to."

"That isn't the most romantic proposal." Brandon smiled at me. "But I accept."

"What?"

He reached into his pocket and pulled out an old-fashioned but beautiful emerald ring. "It was my grandmothers. My mom said it should be yours. I agree with her but if you want something else—"

"I'd love your grandmother's ring."

"I'll wear your collar, of course," Brandon said.

I grinned at him. "You'll wear my collar, my dick-straps, and you'll wear a wedding band, too."

"There's only one thing—"

I jerked off my skirt, shoved it in his mouth, and looked around.

"There's a patch of grass over there," I told him. "How about you get on your back and I have my way with you. I'm going to be a lot better at talking once I have a couple of orgasms."

He tried to say something but he couldn't make words come out.

That, of course, wasn't the real disadvantage of the gag and I took it out just a couple of minutes later. After all, I had much more interesting things to put into Brandon's mouth than a hunk of fabric. My clit being number one, my tits being two and three. And then there was kissing.

Only later did I learn that the guys had stationed themselves all over the neighborhood, warning the cops to steer clear. Russell had guessed right about my driving technique. He'd called Brandon and told him to get his submissive butt out of bed and his submissive dick into my pussy.

It was an excellent plan—the fraternity brothers had come a long way in only a couple of months.

I planned on keeping that up, and on doing some serious coming, myself.

Books by Robyn Anders

The CEO's S.O.S.
Counterfeit Cowboy
Dynamiting Daddy's Dream House
Half a Ranch
Hometown Hero
The Truth About Cats
Whipped Fraternity

www.ingramcontent.com/pod-product-compliance
Lightning Source LLC
Chambersburg PA
CBHW070116260626
47160CB00004B/1489

* 9 7 8 1 6 0 2 1 5 2 5 5 7 *